ALWAYS FAITHFUL

OTHER BOOKS BY JOHN C. KERR

Cardigan Bay
A Rose in No Man's Land
Fell the Angels
Hurricane Hole
The Silent Shore of Memory
The Argyle of San Antonio

ALWAYS FAITHFUL

A NOVEL

JOHN C. KERR

FORT WORTH, TEXAS

Library of Congress Cataloging-in-Publication Data

Names: Kerr, John C., author.
Title: Always faithful : a novel / John C. Kerr.
Description: Fort Worth, Texas : TCU Press, [2022] | Summary: "As the story opens John
    Reynolds is recuperating in Auckland after being wounded on Guadalcanal. After recovering,
    he rejoins his battalion at the Marine encampment north of Wellington. Visiting the city on
    a pass, he meets Grace Lucas, a local girl. This is the beginning of a love affair that culminates
    in the couple's secret engagement weeks before the marines sail from for an amphibious assault
    on Tarawa. In one of the bloodiest battles of the Pacific war, Reynolds is severely wounded
    and evacuated to Honolulu, where he's left in a coma. Grace, having received no news, fears
    the worst. When she discovers she's pregnant, she's banished by her parents to a farm in the
    countryside. Amid the horrors of combat, Always Faithful delivers a heartwarming story of
    faithfulness and redemption"—Provided by publisher.
Identifiers: LCCN 2021048316 (print) | LCCN 2021048317 (ebook) | ISBN 9780875658032
    (paperback) | ISBN 9780875658094 (ebook)
Subjects: LCSH: World War, 1939-1945--Campaigns--Pacific Area--Fiction. | LCGFT: Romance
    fiction.
Classification: LCC PS3611.E7635 A79 2022 (print) | LCC PS3611.E7635 (ebook) | DDC
    813/.6--dc23/eng/20211013
LC record available at https://lccn.loc.gov/2021048316
LC ebook record available at https://lccn.loc.gov/2021048317

TCU Box 298300
Fort Worth, Texas 76129
To order books: 1.800.826.8911

Design by Preston Thomas

Cover image: "Bullets and Barbed Wire" by Kerr Eby. Credit Navy Art Collection, Naval History
and Heritage Command.

Semper Fidelis

MOTTO OF THE UNITED STATES MARINE CORPS

PROLOGUE

ST. ANDREW'S CHURCH
AUCKLAND, NEW ZEALAND
APRIL 22, 2007

THE PASTOR, IN THE PLAIN BLACK ROBE AND STIFF WHITE collar of a Scots Presbyterian, gazed out over his flock, a small assortment of middle-aged and elderly white men and women, a number of dark Maori faces, and a handful of Asian college students. Bright morning sunlight shone through the rose-tinted windows of the vaulted sanctuary. The pastor nodded to the ushers at the rear. Accompanied by the mournful skirl of a bagpipe from a kilted piper, the color guard, two men wearing the dress uniforms of the New Zealand army, and three young women in US Navy uniforms walked slowly down the center aisle, one of the men carrying the flag of New Zealand and the other the Stars and Stripes. After presenting the colors, the guard draped both flags over the altar, itself draped with the Cross of St. Andrew's. Next to the altar, an easel supported a plaque, shrouded in purple cloth.

As he observed the solemn ceremony the pastor reflected on the modest turnout for the annual commemoration to honor the fallen men of the Australian and New Zealand Army Corps in the two world wars. He thought back to his long-ago boyhood and the crowds overflowing the churches of New Zealand on Anzac Day; many had lost sons or brothers in the Second World War, or grandfathers or great-uncles in the First. His gaze fell on the tall young man seated alone in the first pew, with neatly

1

parted dark hair, wearing a blue blazer with yellow tie and a paper poppy pinned to the lapel.

After the color guard retired, the pastor said, "Would you please rise for God Defend New Zealand." Accompanied by the organ, the small congregation mumbled through the anthem, which was followed by the Star Spangled Banner. Following the two anthems, an army veteran wearing a dress uniform and white helmet came forward and delivered the traditional Anzac Day valediction, ending with the words:

> With the going down of the sun . . .
> And in the morning, we will remember them . . .
> We will remember them . . .

Ascending the steps to the pulpit, the pastor read several selections of scripture, offered a prayer, and then delivered a brief homily on the importance of remembrance of the great sacrifices "of those who perished in the two great world wars in the cause of peace and freedom that we may be tempted to take for granted." Gazing out at the congregation, he said, "And now it gives me great pleasure to welcome Mr. Tom Reynolds, who has traveled a great distance to unveil the plaque we dedicate today in memory of Malcolm and Bell McDonald, and to tell us about the splendid gift to our church from his grandfather, Mr. John Reynolds of Houston, Texas, in the United States."

As the pastor stepped down, the young man rose, straightened his jacket, and walked to the center of the nave, clutching a sheet of notes. "I would like to thank Dr. McKinsey," he began quietly, "for inviting me to participate in today's ceremony and for having me over to dinner last evening. I'm here representing my grandfather, John Reynolds," he continued in a stronger voice, "who would have liked to have traveled here himself, but at age eighty-seven is having a hard time getting around. Granddad came to St. Andrew's in 1943 when he was recovering in the navy hospital after being wounded on Guadalcanal and while the rest of his Marine Corps division was in New Zealand to refit after the battle. When my grandfather visited the church, he was befriended by a couple, Malcolm and Bell McDonald, who invited him home for Sunday dinners and showed him your beautiful country. And the McDonalds, along with many New Zealanders, shared their hospitality with the men of the

Marine Corps during the eight months they were stationed here before being sent back into battle against the Japanese.

"My grandfather never forgot the McDonalds' generosity while he was recuperating so far from home. And so, nearing the end of a long and successful life, he decided to honor them with a donation to this church." Tom walked over to the easel and unveiled a bronze plaque mounted on oak. He turned to the congregation and read the inscription: "In memory of Malcolm and Bell McDonald and the members of St. Andrew's Church for their kindness to the men of the Second Division, United States Marine Corps, during the Second World War."

Amid a smattering of applause, Tom returned to his pew for the closing hymn. At the conclusion of the service, he accepted the warm congratulations and thanks, handshakes and pats on the back, from members of the congregation. As he turned to go, he noticed a stooped, elderly lady standing by the first pew. When he walked up, she smiled and said, "Pardon me."

"Yes, ma'am?"

"My name's Helen Pitt. I met your grandfather," she said. "Here in the church."

"Really?" said Tom with a look of surprise.

"And when I read about your visit, I was sure of it. So I did some digging. And this is what I found." She opened her handbag and reached inside for a folded sheet of paper. "It's a copy," she explained, "of a page out of the church guest register." She held it open for both of them to see. "Here's where I signed my name, Helen Pitt, and the date, 14 March 1943. And on the very next line," she traced the ruled sheet with a bony finger, "is where your grandfather signed."

Tom stared at his grandfather's familiar cursive. "John Reynolds," he read aloud as he brushed away a tear. "I'll be darned."

CHAPTER ONE

A YOUNG MARINE IN AN OLIVE DRAB UNIFORM WITH THE single bar of a lieutenant sat near the back of the large church, his head slightly bowed and hands folded in his lap as he listened to the minister's prayer at the conclusion of a rather pedestrian sermon. A pair of crutches rested on the pew beside him. The lieutenant's spirits were nevertheless lifted by the worship service, with its familiar Presbyterian liturgy and hymns. The service was well attended, mainly by older couples, the ladies in hats and gloves, plus a good many young women, but virtually no young men. It was, the lieutenant considered as he lightly massaged his right thigh, the closest thing he had felt to home since the troopship pulled away from the San Diego harbor what seemed an eternity ago. In reality the lapse of a mere five months—October of 1942.

"Pardon me."

The lieutenant turned toward the young woman seated several places away from him.

"It's the guest book," she said with a half smile, revealing an uneven row of teeth. She handed him a small, black volume with a pencil attached on a string. "I'm visiting too," she added awkwardly.

"Thanks," said the lieutenant, momentarily studying her, her brown hair tied back with a ribbon and blue polka-dot dress with gathered sleeves. Apart from the navy nurses at the hospital, she was the first girl who'd spoken to him in the six weeks he'd spent in Auckland. He opened the guest book, glanced at her name—Helen Pitt—and then took the pencil, signed his name, *John L. Reynolds*, and filled in his address: 165 Milford, Houston, Texas USA. He handed the book back to her and said, "Here you are, Helen." She blushed slightly and stole a quick look at his entry in the register. The minister announced the closing hymn, No. 333, *The Church's One Foundation*, the organist played the introduction, and the congregation rose with their hymnals, all except Lieutenant John Reynolds, who self-consciously remained seated. He nevertheless sang out in his clear, if slightly off-key, baritone voice. Following the hymn and benediction, Reynolds painfully rose from the pew and reached for his crutches as the rest of the congregation made their way to the aisles.

"Are you, ah, an American soldier?" asked Helen, standing several feet from him.

"A Marine," said Reynolds.

"Oh," said Helen. "My brother's in the army. In North Africa. We've just moved to town from the farm."

Reynolds smiled pleasantly and said, "Well, it's nice to meet you, Helen." He shifted his weight to the crutches.

"Excuse me," said a man standing in the pew behind them.

Reynolds turned to face a pleasant-looking, middle-aged man wearing a gray three-piece suit.

"I saw you were visiting," said the man, moving closer, "and wanted to say hello and welcome you to St. Andrew's." He reached out to shake hands, which Reynolds did somewhat awkwardly with the crutch under his arm. "I'm Malcolm McDonald. We haven't seen many American boys in town."

"I'm John Reynolds. Pleased to meet you, sir. Most of our men are in camp down near Wellington."

"I see." McDonald briefly studied the red divisional patch on Reynolds's arm and the distinctive globe and anchor pin on his lapels. "If you're free for dinner, John, we'd be pleased to have you over. Nothing fancy, I assure you."

"That would be swell," replied Reynolds, brightening. "I haven't had a home-cooked meal in ages. As it's Sunday, I've got a pass from the hospital."

"Well, come along and meet the wife and then we'll take the car."

When Reynolds turned to say goodbye to Helen he realized she'd quietly gone on her way. Leaning on his crutches, he followed Malcolm McDonald into the crowded narthex. There they found Mrs. McDonald, a petite woman in her forties wearing a navy blue, veiled hat that matched her suit and kid gloves that almost reached her elbows.

"Bell," said Malcolm, "I want you to meet—it's lieutenant, eh?"

"Yes, sir."

"Lieutenant Reynolds. I've invited him over for dinner."

"Hullo, lieutenant," said Bell McDonald brightly. "It's just roast lamb and potatoes but I do hope you'll join us."

The McDonald home was in a leafy neighborhood not ten minutes from the center of Auckland, one of many one-story bungalows with a wide front porch built after the First World War. Reynolds made the trip in the back seat of the McDonalds' Morris sedan next to their sixteen-year-old son Tim, who seemed somewhat in awe of the young Marine officer. Once inside, Reynolds slipped off his hat and placed it on the top of a bookcase in the small but cozy parlor, with a sofa and two armchairs on a braided rug before the fireplace. A clock occupied the mantel beneath a lithograph of a pastoral scene—presumably the English countryside. "Have a seat," said Malcolm, gesturing to one of the armchairs, "and Tim will bring us some lemonade." Reynolds leaned his crutches against the wall and slumped into one of the chairs. After a moment Tim emerged from the kitchen carrying a tray with a frosted pitcher and four glasses, which he placed on a sideboard and then served the two men. Taking a sip, Reynolds was struck with a fleeting sensation of déjà vu, transported to the living room of his family's home in Texas on a midsummer Sunday after church. "Mmm," he said after taking a swallow. "Good lemonade."

Malcolm McDonald, who'd settled in the other armchair, rested his arms on his knees and said, "Where do you call home, John?"

"A city called Houston, in Texas," replied Reynolds.

"Texas," repeated McDonald, "with all the cowboys and cattle ranches."

"Yes, sir, though Houston's a pretty big city, mainly known for the oil and gas industry."

"Is that what your father works in?"

"No, sir, he was in banking, until he, ah, retired."

Malcolm McDonald nodded and said, "Your division was on Guadalcanal?" Every New Zealander was keenly aware of the fierce fighting on Guadalcanal, situated to the northeast of Australia across the Coral Sea, and the recent American victory that had very likely spared the defenseless British commonwealths from Japanese domination if not invasion.

"Yes, sir. We relieved the First Marine Division, near the end of the fighting."

"What's that braided cord looped around your shoulder?"

"It's the fourragère," said Reynolds. "Awarded to the Sixth Marines by the French government after the battle of Belleau Wood in the First World War."

"The Sixth Marines?"

"That's my regiment. Part of the Second Division."

"Dinner will be ready," said Mrs. McDonald, walking briskly into the room, "in about fifteen minutes."

"Bell," said Malcolm, "get a glass of lemonade and have a seat. So the Marines fight on land?"

"Yes, sir. But we're trained in amphibious warfare. Storming a defended beach."

"That's what it'll take, I suppose, to defeat the Japs."

"Yes, sir."

"Tim," said Bell, seated on the sofa. "Will you please set the table?" She looked Reynolds in the eye and said, "Would you mind telling us, John, how you were injured? And where you're being cared for?"

"Our navy built a hospital in Auckland, in the Domain," said Reynolds. "They've taken good care of me there."

"American doctors?" asked Bell.

"Yes, ma'am," said Reynolds. "Navy doctors and nurses. Anyway, I was shot in the leg."

Tim, who'd returned to the parlor, looked at Reynolds with even more intense curiosity. "How?" he asked quietly.

"By a Jap machine-gunner," said Reynolds in a matter-of-fact way. "Concealed in a coconut grove as I was directing my men on the beach."

"When you came ashore?" asked Malcolm.

"No, sir. The beach where we landed was undefended. About four weeks later we were fighting what was left of the Japanese right along the beach."

"What was it like?" asked Tim with the directness and innocence typical of a teenaged boy.

Reynolds responded with a gesture and facial expression as if to say "I'm not sure" or "there's not much to say." Instead, he said, "It wasn't too bad." That was about as far as he could go, unless, of course, you had been there, like the other men in the hospital, with whom he could swap stories or jokes or talk a little about the combat experiences of his rifle company. Able Company, First Battalion, Sixth Marines. The 1/6. Reynolds, a second lieutenant, was a rifle platoon leader. His regiment had sailed from San Diego in mid-October, three thousand men crammed on board the *Matsonia*, a converted ocean liner. At the time, they understood that their destination was Guadalcanal, where the battle that had been raging since August was nearing its climax. But by the time the *Matsonia* made its long ocean voyage, the Marines had decisively beaten the Japanese at Bloody Ridge, and Reynolds's regiment was diverted to New Zealand for an additional month of training at a camp overlooking Cook Strait at the bottom tip of the North Island. So this was his second visit to New Zealand.

Malcolm McDonald sat at his accustomed place at the head of the table with his head bowed and hands folded in his lap. "Heavenly Father," he said with eyes closed, "bless this food to our nourishment and us to thy service. And bless and protect our family and Lieutenant Reynolds and his Marine comrades who are defending our liberty. Amen."

"Amen," repeated Reynolds in unison with Bell and Tim.

"There you are," said Malcolm, passing Reynolds a plate with several slices of roast lamb shoulder—served pink with thick gravy as opposed to the well-done lamb with mint jelly he was accustomed to—and generous helpings of potatoes and green beans.

"Thanks," said Reynolds. He waited for Bell to lift her fork and knife and then sampled the lamb and potatoes. "Delicious," he commented, dabbing his chin with his napkin. "The first home-cooked meal I've tasted since leaving home. Seems like all they serve at the hospital are beans. Navy beans," he added with a smile.

"What will you do," asked Bell, "when you're well enough to leave hospital?"

"I'm returning to my outfit. The entire division's in training camp at Mackays Crossing, on the coast near Wellington."

"I should have thought," said Malcolm, "they would have sent you home, after being severely wounded."

"We need every fit Marine," said Reynolds, "and I wasn't hurt that badly." An image flashed in his mind of the two men who'd been shot when they were trying to get him off the beach. His runner, the scrawny kid nicknamed "Chicken," and R. C. Patrick, a former football star at the University of Texas, another platoon leader. Reynolds was sprawled on the sand clutching his bloody thigh, unable to stand, and the two men had grabbed him under the arms to drag him off the beach. What they were trained *not* to do when they came under enemy fire. And sure enough, both men were hit when the Jap gunner fired the next burst, Chicken through the small of his back and Patrick in both legs. By some miracle, the pattern of the bullets had missed Reynolds. He remembered the splotch of scarlet that blossomed on Chicken Bailey's green utility shirt. Somehow, both men had survived.

Reynolds looked pleasantly at Malcolm and then Bell. His terse explanation evidently satisfied their curiosity—though not Tim's, who seemed to hang on Reynolds's every word—since nothing more was asked about Reynolds's time on Guadalcanal during the following weeks as the McDonalds lavished their hospitality on him. Only later, after returning to the hospital, did it occur to Reynolds that it was just a matter of time before Tim would be going to war.

The conversation turned to the prosaic subjects of people separated by a vast ocean but united by a common heritage—Reynolds's family, Malcolm McDonald's duties at the "freezer-works," Reynolds's own aspirations when the war was over. Following dessert of home-baked cherry cobbler, he thanked the McDonalds profusely and accepted a ride back to the hospital with sixteen-year-old Tim at the wheel. Returning to his ward, the familiar feelings of loneliness and isolation displaced his light-hearted mood as abruptly as if a candle had been blown out. Reynolds stripped to his undershirt and skivvies, briefly examined his bandaged leg, and lay down on the iron bed, painted white, with its hard, thin mattress. Staring at the bare walls, he thought back to the day he arrived in Auckland on the hospital ship. Then he thought of the day his company landed on the beach at Guadalcanal. On an LVT, an amphibious tractor or "amtrac" as the men preferred, on a hot, sunny morning on December 31. What had most struck Reynolds were the pale blue mountains in the distance beyond the bright green fringe of coconut palms. Burdened by eighty-pound packs and gear, they came ashore at Red Beach, to the east of Lunga Point, and quickly moved inland through the coconut groves and dense jungle vegetation. For a week they remained in their primitive camp in a jungle clearing, sorting gear and weapons and sleeping on cots under canvas tarps stretched over tent poles, awakening in the morning to swarms of mosquitoes and an-kle-deep water from torrential overnight rains.

As Reynolds dozed on the hospital bed in the warm afternoon—it was late summer in the southern hemisphere—a kaleidoscope of vivid images filled his mind. The company moving up into the line to relieve the beleaguered First Marine Division, marching in single file up and down the steep ridges through knee-high, razor-edged kunai grass, crossing the wide, brown Matanikau River on a swaying suspension bridge with the tall blue mountains in the distance, cloaked with cloud, and the nearer blue water of Sealark Channel, rechristened Iron-Bottom Sound for the forty-odd American and Japanese warships that had been sunk there . . . passing through vast plantations of coconut palms under the broiling sun or billowing masses of charcoal arced with lightning . . . Reynolds opened his eyes with a yawn and angled his forearm over his face, thinking back to his first experience with bloodshed, when two of his men, making their way down the reverse slope of a ridge toward a dugout, had been hit by a Jap sniper; one shot through the throat and the other in the shoulder . . . how he and another man had scrambled down to drag them out, the man bleeding from the shoulder so profusely that he was as slippery as a greased pig; Reynolds's intense embarrassment when, after helping carry the man to the aid station, he got sick to his stomach from all the blood.

The company, about two hundred in all, halted in the late afternoons, always moving west in pursuit of the retreating Japanese, usually in a torrential downpour, to dig their holes, lay their barbed wire, and site the machine guns. The Japs counter-attacked almost every night, not the earlier massed banzai charges the Americans had repulsed at Alligator Creek and Bloody Ridge, but probing attacks by patrols, supported by mortar fire, the Japs chattering and yelling to try to spook the Marines into firing and revealing their positions in the darkness. And so they were forced to stay awake, sheltering from the rain under ponchos in their shallow foxholes, staring into the jungle blackness with its eerie night calls. In the morning, moving out again, there would be a handful of Jap corpses scattered within a hundred yards of their lines. The real shocker, Reynolds remembered as he rolled onto his side, was the morning they encountered a long column of Marines marching in the opposite direction, not merely gaunt but sick and emaciated, their eyeballs sunken and yellow from the atabrine tablets taken to combat the malaria virtually all had contracted over the months of jungle fighting.

That was near the end of January. No longer able to reinforce or resupply their troops, the Japanese were trying to evacuate the starving remnant of the once-invincible elite force from the western end of the island. The 1/6 Battalion had moved past Tassafaronga Point several miles west of Point Cruz, mopping up the remaining Japanese in what amounted to a postscript to a battle already won. One afternoon, after sending out the usual patrol, Reynolds heard the sound of heavy firing. Accompanied by Lieutenant Patrick and the runner, Chicken Bailey, he passed through a grove of coconut palms onto the beach, where a sergeant was talking with a squad of riflemen. Reynolds was standing beside the sergeant, discussing the disposition of the men, when a Japanese machine-gunner concealed in the trees fired a burst that struck the sergeant in the face and hit Reynolds with a terrific impact that knocked him to the ground. Stunned, he tried to get up and found he was unable to move his right leg. Dimly aware of the sounds of shouting and more firing, he reached for his burning, stinging thigh and felt the warm blood soaking the herringbone fabric, realizing with a groan that he'd been hit. That was the moment Patrick and Chicken Bailey had grabbed him under the arms and started dragging him toward safety. Within seconds they were down from the next burst.

Reynolds rolled over and, staring up at the ceiling, massaged his bandaged thigh. The next thing he remembered was the corpsman kneeling over him, tying on the field dressing, giving him a shot of brandy, and injecting the Syrette; the odd sensation, almost like floating, from the combination of brandy and morphine that instantly dulled the pain and made him feel . . . well, like he didn't give a damn. He vaguely recollected the trip through the jungle on the stretcher borne by four of his men with his head propped up on his helmet; even more dimly recalled the long, bumpy ride on the jeep ambulance to the aid station at Henderson Field.

By then it was getting late, the sun setting. They laid him on a hard table in a large tent, cut away the bloody bandage, poured powdered sulfa on the wound like salt from a shaker, and tied on a clean dressing. That was it. And, oh, someone confiscated his prized .45 revolver, the one his uncle Jamie had carried in World War I.

Reynolds decided to get up, slip on his robe, and walk down the long corridor without his crutches. His leg hurt but he could feel the strength returning. He passed a nurse in her thick white hose and clunky shoes who seemed not to notice him. While there was much he couldn't remember about the day he was shot, there was one thing he'd never forget: the night he and the other wounded men spent in the "bomb shelter" next to the aid station. It was nothing more than a shallow slit trench, accommodating about twenty men lying on their bloody stretchers, and covered over with plywood and palm fronds. The Japs bombed Henderson Field almost every night. Reynolds had lain awake all through the night, listening to the men's screams and groans and Chicken Bailey struggling to breathe as his lungs filled with fluid, the drone of the Japanese planes and concussion of the bombs, intermittent claps of thunder and the rain beating down on the plywood, filling the ditch with water, conscious of the rats scurrying around the stretchers. With daylight came sweltering heat in the fetid enclosure, the men in agony, craving fresh air and crying out for water. For a long time, hours it seemed, their cries were unheeded until, at last, a corpsman lifted up the palm fronds and plywood and peered down at the trembling, sweating men in their filthy, bloodied uniforms. "Good God," he muttered before turning to get help. One of the wounded Marines was dead when finally they came for them.

Wearing the same uniform he'd been shot in, and with only one change of bandage in twenty-four hours, Reynolds was loaded on a C-47 with a red cross painted on the fuselage, which lumbered down the bumpy, bomb-cratered runway and tipped up into the cumulus-filled sky, slowly gaining altitude just as a squad of Jap medium bombers flew past, clearly visible through the Plexiglas window. Their destination was the island of Espiritu Santo, six hundred miles to the southeast. The Navy had built a supply base and primitive hospital, where Reynolds and a few other wounded men spent several days in a wooden shack and finally received a change of clothes. Reynolds smiled at the recollection of the Navy corpsman, a man named Cox, whom they nicknamed "Foxhole Cox" after he dashed from the structure at the sound of the air raid siren and twisted his ankle diving into a foxhole. But the corpsman had managed to scrounge a couple of bottles of cheap red wine from the Padre, and the men had thrown a little party. Finally, they boarded the large hospital ship, painted white and with prominent red crosses on the funnels, and illuminated at night with floodlights, that made the round trip between Espiritu Santo and Auckland, New Zealand.

Reynolds paused at the entrance to his ward, patting his thigh through the cotton fabric of the robe. It wouldn't be long before he was discharged and returned to his battalion. But first he intended to take Malcolm McDonald up on his offer to show him around the North Island countryside.

CHAPTER TWO

WHEN THEY ARRIVED AT THE AUCKLAND DOCKS, THE WOUNDED Marines were loaded into ambulances and driven to the U.S. Naval Mobile Hospital, adjacent to the Domain, Auckland's principal public park. Reynolds was wheeled to one of two open wards for officers, accommodating thirty beds, with bare white walls, gray linoleum floor, and natural lighting from a row of high windows overlooking the tree-filled grounds. Only a third of the beds were occupied, as most of the Marines wounded on Guadalcanal were in the First Division, which had been sent to Australia to rest and refit. Reynolds was assigned a bed midway down the ward, with clean sheets and a thin cotton blanket, beneath which he lay naked with his bandaged leg, as the orderlies had taken away the green utility shirt and trousers issued to him at Espiritu Santo. He knew only one other man in his ward, R. C. Patrick, who'd been hit when trying to drag Reynolds from the beach. But Patrick was at the far end of the ward, and Reynolds was unable to communicate with him. On the first day, a nurse handed Reynolds a sheet of Red Cross stationery and pencil on a clipboard with instructions to write home. He chewed on the pencil, staring at the bare wall, rested the clipboard on his good thigh, and then wrote:

February 3, 1943

Dear Mom and Dad,

There's been quite a gap in my letters, which must have caused you considerable anxiety. I hesitate to write what I'm about to say for fear it may cause undue alarm but it's really something to be thankful for.

Reynolds paused, wondering if his parents had received the usual telegram from the Marine Commandant informing them that their son had been "wounded in action in the performance of his duty and in the service of his country." Surely they would be worried sick that he was mortally injured or worse. With a grimace, he wrote:

At any rate, I am now in a navy hospital at a place other than the one where I received my slight wound. This wound is a flesh one and a few inches above my right knee caused by a bullet from a small-bore Japanese machine gun. There are absolutely no complications or danger—no bone or artery was hit and there has been no infection whatsoever. I'm receiving the best medical care I could ask for and expect to make a full recovery in a matter of weeks.

I trust all is well with you both and all of the family. Give my love to everyone and write soon.

With much love,
John

A week passed with no mail from home and nothing to read and almost no one to talk to. The two officers in the beds opposite him quarreled incessantly, as both were from Boston, one a working class Irish Catholic and the other a Harvard man. Reynolds was sinking into despair, suffering not only from homesickness but from ennui he couldn't shake and the loneliness of separation from the men from his unit. One morning the navy doctor making his rounds, after asking Reynolds the usual questions about his wounded leg, casually inquired about Reynolds's plans once he recuperated. "Why, go back to my outfit," he answered without thinking, as more than anything he missed the company of his fellow officers. His unthinking answer to the doctor's question was more a reflection of his loneliness than a sense of duty. Several days later, however, returning from the mess hall after lunch, he was stunned to discover that his ward had been emptied of all of the other wounded men, including R. C. Patrick, who'd required two surgeries on his shattered femur. All of them had abruptly been put on a hospital ship bound for the States, though most were no more seriously wounded than Reynolds, leaving him feeling wretchedly sorry for himself. Alone in the ward for several days, lacking the books that had occupied his spare time on board ship and in camp, he had ample opportunity for reflection. The myth of the invincibility of the Japanese soldier, he considered, was just that; though they fought with a suicidal intensity, in the end they were no match for the Marines' firepower, especially when they brought artillery to bear. But it was clear the war was really just beginning, and more than anything Reynolds longed for home, for the quiet evenings with his mother, father, and sister, and the time spent in the summers in East Texas with his uncles and grandfather. And he was determined to get back to the university and resume his study of law.

One morning, following the usual powdered eggs, bacon, and dry toast, Reynolds discovered that a number of new patients occupied beds in his ward, men from the Third Division who had just arrived in Auckland on a troopship from the States, not wounded but suffering from accidental injuries or illnesses contracted on the long voyage from San Diego. Not having experienced combat, the young officers bantered about girls back home, sports, and petty quarrels, driving Reynolds even deeper into depression and self-pity. The next day a stocky Marine colonel appeared in the ward with a Third Division patch on his uniform jacket. He moved slowly from bed to bed of the newly arrived men, visiting with them and inquiring about their health and treatment. As he drew nearer, Reynolds, to his surprise, recognized the officer: Colonel Sam Puller, who had commanded Reynolds's Platoon Leader Class at Quantico in the summer of '41. Sam Puller was the older brother of the legendary Lieutenant Colonel Lewis "Chesty" Puller, CO of the First Battalion, Seventh Marines, that had decisively defeated the Japs at Bloody Ridge on Guadalcanal. When the colonel reached the foot of Reynolds's bed, he paused, and his face seemed to register recognition. "Reynolds," he said after a moment. "Third Basic School."

"Yes, sir."

"What the hell happened to you?" asked Sam Puller as he ran a hand over his close-cropped hair.

"I was shot on Guadalcanal, sir."

Puller briefly studied Reynolds and noticed the absence of a uniform or other personal belongings at his bedside. "Where's your footlocker, Reynolds?"

"They were supposed to send it up from Wellington, but it must have gotten lost." When they shipped out for Guadalcanal in December, the men in Reynolds's regiment had left behind footlockers containing their spare uniforms and other personal belongings.

"Hmm," said Puller with a frown before moving on.

The next morning, again sinking into despondency, Reynolds was surprised to see Colonel Puller again standing at the entrance to the ward with a parcel under his arm. Puller strode quickly toward him without stopping to visit with the men from his own division. "Hello, Reynolds," said the colonel with a grin. "Thought these might come in handy." He removed the top of the parcel and dumped its contents on the end of Reynolds's bed: an olive drab jacket, matching trousers, khaki shirt, and tie. "See if they fit," said Puller, "and then you can get some shoes, socks, and skivvies from the BX."

Reynolds stared up at Puller, momentarily fighting back tears. He swallowed the lump in his throat and said, "Thank you, sir. You shouldn't have gone to the trouble."

"Nonsense, Reynolds. They told me you asked to be sent back to your regiment, and by God, every Marine's got to have his olive drabs."

That was pretty much the end of John Reynolds feeling sorry for himself. Within a week he'd persuaded the doctor to allow him to dress in his new uniform and try out his crutches on a stroll around the hospital grounds and then on walks in the Domain and around central Auckland, culminating in his visit to St. Andrew's Church and Sunday dinner with the McDonalds. Several days later, Reynolds received a note from Malcolm McDonald, inviting him to go along on a buying trip to the countryside.

Wearing his uniform, Reynolds stood on the sidewalk in front of the hospital at 9:00 a.m. in bright sunshine, resting on his crutches, as McDonald turned into the drive in the familiar dark-green Morris sedan.

"Climb in," said McDonald through the half-open window. Reynolds, who stood over six feet, squeezed into the passenger seat and placed his crutches in the back.

Malcolm McDonald was a buyer for the freezer-works, the term New Zealanders used for the slaughterhouse and refrigeration plant in Auckland that produced frozen lamb and beef for shipment across the oceans to Great Britain. As such, he was entitled to a far greater petrol allowance than the ordinary citizen, enabling him to drive to farms all across the North Island to select sheep and cattle for slaughter. Fifteen minutes after leaving the hospital and the leafy environs of the Domain, McDonald steered the Morris onto a two-lane highway headed south, entering richly verdant countryside with neatly tended farmhouses and barns, the rolling hills dotted with black-faced sheep and dairy cattle resting in the shade of sturdy oaks. McDonald tipped back his fedora and glanced briefly at Reynolds. "So, John," he said, "what do you know about farming?"

"Hardly anything. I'm a city boy, though I've helped out on the cotton farm in the summers."

"Well, you'll have a opportunity to learn a little about raising sheep. This is the finest sheep farming country in the world."

As they breasted a low hill, Reynolds gazed out on the blue-green in the distance beyond a sweeping half-moon bay, filled with dozens if not hundreds of small islands. The water sparkled in the bright sunshine, and cottony clouds, rimmed with charcoal and lilac, cast transient shadows on the hills and valleys. "Mighty pretty," said Reynolds, continuing to stare out the half-open window. McDonald swung the sedan onto a rutted drive and bumped along past a pasture where a border collie was expertly herding a flock of forty or so sheep into a pen, nipping at their back legs. A man wearing a straw hat and bib overalls was perched on the fence. Parking the car nearby, McDonald climbed out and waved a greeting to the farmer. "Come along, John," he said through the window, "and meet Mr. Robertson." Reynolds reached for his crutches, got out and hobbled over where the two men were standing.

Robertson, a tall, trim man in his fifties, gave Reynolds an appraising look and said, "An American?"

"Yes, sir."

"A Marine," said Malcolm McDonald with a look of almost paternal pride. "Shot by the Japs on Guadalcanal. John Reynolds, meet Ian Robertson."

Robertson thrust out his arm and gave Reynolds a firm handshake. "Pleased to meet you, son," he said. "We owe you Yanks a lot for driving the Japs off that island. We had no means of defending ourselves with all our lads fighting Germans in North Africa."

Over the next half hour, Reynolds observed McDonald's technique for evaluating the sheep he selected for slaughter and the good-natured haggling of the men over the price. After Malcolm McDonald and Ian Robertson shook hands on their bargain, McDonald and John Reynolds continued on the day's business, driving countless miles along paved highways and country lanes, calling on at least six more sheep ranchers—Reynolds lost count—and enjoying a pleasant midday repast prepared by the wife of one of McDonald's regular suppliers. As they made the hour-long drive back to Auckland, Reynolds was conscious of a dull ache at the back of his head and neck and shivered with a chill, though the late summer day was sunny and warm. Having exhausted all of his small talk and the lore, such as it was, of raising sheep, McDonald switched on the car radio, which was tuned to an Auckland station playing popular songs, mostly from Britain and the US. Reynolds lightly dozed, waking when they entered the city traffic. He rubbed the back of his neck, certain that his headache had worsened and struck by another chill.

"You all right, son?" said McDonald, glancing over at his passenger.

"I must be catching a cold," said Reynolds. "Feeling kind of achy."

By the time McDonald parked the Morris in the hospital lot, Reynolds's head was splitting and he was certain he was running a fever. "Thanks for a wonderful day," he managed to say as he reached for his crutches, opened the door and climbed out. "You've got such a beautiful country." Leaning on his crutches, John gave McDonald a wave as he backed up and drove away. With an audible groan, Reynolds started up the walk to the hospital's entrance. Reaching the lobby, he made his way through the door but then felt suddenly, overwhelmingly exhausted, fearing he might black out. *What's wrong with me?* he wondered as he leaned against a column. A passing nurse took one look at him and said, "Oh, my. Stay right there." She returned after a few moments with a wheelchair, into which Reynolds obligingly slumped, letting his crutches clatter to the floor.

Half an hour later, helped by an orderly out of his uniform and shoes, Reynolds lay on his back in his bed, eyes closed, trembling uncontrollably though covered with two blankets. A nurse in white, from her peaked cap to her stockings and shoes, stood at his bedside, staring at the thermometer in her hand. Looking up at her patient, she said, "One hundred-five. You're a very sick man, Lieutenant."

Reynolds nodded and groaned at the same time. "What is it?" he managed to say. "Malaria?"

"In all likelihood," she replied. "I need to draw some blood. And then we'll see if we can get that fever down."

There was no getting the fever down. The nurse tried aspirin and cold compresses, but his temperature remained stubbornly at 104°, inducing a delirium that filled his mind with bizarre dreams and contorted his shuddering body with chills. A vivid image of the beach at Galveston filled his mind, row after row of low breakers, puffy white cumulus clouds in the summer sky, only it wasn't Galveston after all; it was the deep blue sky over the wide curve of the muddy Matanikau river on Guadalcanal, his view through the barbed wire blocked by the tall, bright green kunai grass, his ears splitting with the deafening *whump* of mortar rounds and the unrelenting chatter of the machine guns. Reynolds called out as he thrashed under the covers, finally waking, grateful for the realization it was only a dream.

After four hours, when darkness had fallen, the fever broke as suddenly as it had struck, drenching Reynolds's exhausted body with sweat that literally accumulated in a puddle under his bed. His complexion flushed, he threw off the damp covers, imploring the nurse standing over him for a glass of water. After a night of fitful sleep, Reynolds awoke with a dull, throbbing headache, no appetite, and a general enervation that made movement of any kind difficult. By mid-morning the fever returned, steadily rising from 101° to 104° as the nurse took his temperature at half-hour intervals. At 11:00 another nurse arrived and announced that she needed more blood. "Why?" asked Reynolds feebly.

"The lab says they need another smear," she replied as she rubbed the crook of his elbow with an alcohol-soaked cotton ball. "They couldn't make a diagnosis."

"I can help them," muttered Reynolds as he winced from the stick of the hypodermic needle. "It's malaria."

"Give him another two of the universal pills at noon," the nurse instructed the orderly before turning and briskly walking away with her vial of dark-red blood.

After two more hours of febrile delirium, an interval which seemed to Reynolds in his agony more like a day, the fever broke, again drenching Reynolds and his sheets in sweat. He awoke to cast a bleary eye at the doctor at the foot of his bed, a plump, balding man wearing horn-rimmed glasses and a white lab coat. He glanced up from the chart and said, "How are you feeling?"

"Terrible. Too weak to raise my head from the pillow."

"It's a peculiar disease," said the doctor in an accent Reynolds couldn't place. He walked around the bedside and placed his fingertips on the inside of Reynolds's wrist. "Comes and goes in these bouts of high fever."

"So it's malaria," said Reynolds.

"We don't have a definite diagnosis," said the doctor, jotting Reynolds's heart-rate on his chart. "Have to get a good smear."

"Can I have some quinine?" said Reynolds. "I hear that . . ."

"No," said the doctor curtly. "Not until we get a good smear."

After the nurse returned for another blood draw Reynolds managed to get down some beef broth and a bit of dry toast; and then the fever returned, but not as high as before, peaking at 103° after the lights in the ward had been doused, leaving Reynolds groaning and sweaty. When he awoke the following morning his temperature was normal, but he felt too weak to stand. The orderly helped him to his feet and into a robe and supported him as he walked slowly to the bathroom. Wearing fresh pajamas, Reynolds was lying under a thin blanket, his head propped up on pillows, when the doctor returned. Reynolds gave him an expectant look as the man walked slowly up to his bedside. He noticed the doctor's name—Elmendorf—stitched above the caduceus on the front of his white frock. "Better today?" said the doctor. Reynolds nodded. "Well, I've got some good news," said Dr. Elmendorf in almost a cheerful tone. "With that last smear we were able to confirm a diagnosis. It's malaria, all right. The malignant variety."

Reynolds thought, *that's good news?* He said, "What's that?"

"Plasmodium falciparum," said the doctor with his arms folded across his rounded belly. "The particular type of parasite that carries the virus. It's called malignant 'cause it's much more serious than the other variety, can even cause brain damage or death in some cases."

Great, thought Reynolds. He thought the man's manner pompous and still wondered about his accent.

"But it's the most common form of malaria in the South Pacific," continued the doctor. "The carrier's the anopheles mosquito, the type that bit all you Marines on the Canal."

Reynolds resented the doctor's tone and use of the expression "the Canal," which he considered appropriate shorthand for "Guadalcanal" only by those Marines and sailors who'd fought there. "Why am I just now getting sick?" he asked.

"The atabrine you are taking," said the doctor, "delays the onset of the disease after you are infected, sometimes for as long as six months." Reynolds nodded. "Well," concluded the doctor, "we can start you on some quinine now. Should keep you from having another attack."

"Thanks," said Reynolds. "I wish you'd started me on it yesterday," he added sourly.

"I needn't remind you, Lieutenant," said the doctor, "that you're talking to your superior officer, and I consider your tone insubordinate."

"Sorry . . . sir. I thought I was talking to my doctor."

"Nurse," snapped the doctor to a homely young woman perched on a stool on the other side of the ward. "Start this man on quinine. The usual dose."

"One other thing," said Reynolds as the doctor turned to go.

He stopped and said, "Yes?"

"I was wondering where you're from?"

"From? Why, Chicago. Seems like most of you Marines are from somewhere down south, like Texas."

Reynolds imagined that the big city doctor looked down on anyone who spoke with a Texas drawl, which he probably considered a sign of inferior intelligence. "Well, you're right," he said with a faint smile, "I'm from Houston."

Though the quinine succeeded in preventing a recurrence, the bout with malaria robbed Reynolds of his strength and energy, and the medicine had its unpleasant side effects, ringing in his ears and a dulling of his taste buds to the degree that he couldn't enjoy the strawberries and cream they were served one morning. But after a few days of bed rest and regular meals he felt his old self again and was anxious to dress and leave the dreary confines of the hospital. He was pleasantly surprised to discover that over the course of his week of illness, his wound had continued to heal, to the point that he could now walk without crutches, albeit with a pronounced limp. Dressed in the olive drab uniform Colonel Puller had thoughtfully provided, he happily departed from the hospital on a bright, cool Sunday morning, like an early autumn day, and made the short walk to St. Andrew's Church. After the service, with its comforting litany and music, he was treated to another of Bell McDonald's home-cooked dinners, including an apple pie with ice cream, which he found delicious, notwithstanding the effects of the quinine.

Looking back, the following week in Auckland was among the most pleasant of the war, as Reynolds, fully recovered from the malaria and from his wound, accompanied Malcolm McDonald on another buying trip in the beautiful North Island countryside and took full advantage of Bell McDonald's lavish hospitality and home cooking. Reynolds had also conceived of an ingenious way to circumvent the navy's strict censorship of his letters by providing Malcolm McDonald with details of his wound, recovery, and his expected future, along with his father's name and address, in order for McDonald to send the information to his father via an uncensored letter. Returning to the hospital on Sunday afternoon, which he calculated was his sixth after arriving on the hospital ship, he found two envelopes on his bedside table, one an airmail letter postmarked Houston, Texas, and the other a yellow cablegram. He sat on the bed, tore open the envelope and read the letter from home, several sheets of stationery in his father's strong cursive, expressing his parents' immense relief upon receiving his letter assuring them that his wound was "slight," praying that he might be sent back to the States while acknowledging that he was likely to be returned to duty, and asserting that "he must have the courage to face and accept the trials that lie ahead." The balance of the letter was filled with news of his family, his sister's engagement to a boy who'd just enlisted in the navy, the death of a beloved great aunt, and an outbreak of polio in neighboring Fort Bend County. He tossed the letter aside with a sigh, relieved that contact with his family had been restored but feeling the deep melancholy that thoughts of home usually evoked. He then slit open the smaller yellow envelope and unfolded the telegram, which read:

REPORT AT ONCE TO FIRST BATTALION HQ MACKAYS CROSSING, PAEKAKARIKI, NZ SIGNED COL. W. K. JONES CO

At last, thought Reynolds with a thump in his chest, he was leaving the hospital and returning to duty, to be reunited with his fellow officers and men for the first time since he was carried out of that jungle what seemed much longer ago than a mere eight weeks. He sprang up from the bed and hurried to the office of the hospital superintendent.

CHAPTER THREE

CARRYING ONLY A SMALL, CHEAP SUITCASE HE'D PURCHASED at a department store, John Reynolds arrived early at the massive beaux-arts Auckland Railway Station and bought a ticket on the Scenic Daylight passenger train to Wellington, a ten-hour journey. Reynolds enjoyed the trip, seated by the window in a second-class carriage, gazing out at the beautiful countryside he'd traversed with Malcolm McDonald, and reading the latest war news in the Auckland paper he'd bought at the station. His only regret about leaving the hospital was that his departure was so hasty he hadn't had time to tell the McDonalds goodbye, and he wondered if he'd ever see them again. Nearing the end of the long day, as the outskirts of Wellington came into view, Reynolds thought back to the five weeks his regiment had spent at Mackays Crossing, the camp the Marines had built on the Kapiti Coast at Paekakariki, a town north of Wellington situated at the southern tip of the North Island on Cook Strait. That was in November and December, after the troopship arrived from San Diego. At the time it was just the Sixth Marines, about three thousand men sleeping in crude tents and receiving a final month of training and conditioning before being sent into battle. Now, Reynolds considered, the entire Second Division, almost twenty thousand men, occupied the camp on the narrow plain between steep grassy ridges and the wide, curving beach on the Tasman Sea.

There were so many Marines at Paekakariki that the division kept a bus at the train station. Reynolds spotted several men in olive drab and followed them outside to a dun-colored bus with the words "US Marine Corps" stenciled on the side. The civilian driver worked the mechanism to open the door and called out: "Climb in, lads, and we'll be on our way." The men tossed their duffle bags into the baggage compartment and boarded, Reynolds choosing a seat by the window away from the others who, he surmised, were buddies from the same outfit. Once the bus had passed out of the light downtown Wellington traffic, the driver turned on the main coastal highway, a good macadam road, and within a half hour they reached the main entrance into the camp. Since Reynolds was last there, the Marines had erected a large sign like a billboard that read:

MACKAYS CROSSING
2nd Division
United States Marine Corps

The camp had been greatly expanded since his regiment departed at the end of December and was now a sprawling mass, some three hundred acres, of neat rows of tents and a large number of hastily erected wooden buildings: the commissary, sick bay, brig, several churches, mess halls, laundries, warehouses, and the administration building and divisional HQ. The driver came to a stop before the latter, a long, one-story building painted pale green where the American, Marine Corps, and Second Division flags were flapping on poles in the light onshore breeze.

Reynolds grabbed his suitcase from the overhead and followed the others up the walkway into the office, where a square-jawed sergeant sat behind a desk. When his turn came, Reynolds presented his ID and waited as the sergeant consulted his directory. "Okay," said the sergeant after a moment. "Here we go. Sixth Marines, First Battalion. Report to hut three in Camp Mackay, which is across the road and . . ."

"I can find my way, gunny," said Reynolds with a smile. "Remember, I was here in December. And there's one other thing."

"Yes, sir?"

"They never sent my footlocker up to the hospital in Auckland," said Reynolds. "Does it say where they're storing it?"

The sergeant consulted a three-ring binder. "Hmm," he said after a moment. "Looks like they shipped it back to the States."

"You're kidding."

"My guess is the quartermaster was told the Marines in the hospital were being sent stateside and just assumed that included you."

Reynolds nodded and said, "Thanks, gunny." When they shipped out from San Diego he'd brought along his three-volume set of *Lee's Lieutenants* and was halfway through the second volume of the Civil War classic when they departed Wellington for Guadalcanal. Ever since he'd been looking forward to resuming his reading, but now the books were somewhere back in the US along with the rest of his things. As he made his way along the dusty road that bisected the camp he marveled at the numbers of Marines, many drilling on the parade ground in their combat utilities and billed caps—the largest concentration of troops he'd ever seen outside of Quantico. Though almost all of them had been on Guadalcanal, he'd never seen more than two hundred or so in any one place on that island of high grassy ridges, coconut palm groves, and dense jungle. The sight of so many men and the familiar environs of the camp buoyed Reynolds's spirits, and he picked up his pace, without a trace of a limp. He shortly arrived at a small wooden structure with the words *6th Marines* painted on the door, presented his orders to the duty sergeant, and just as it was growing dark found his way to the tents occupied by his battalion. Probably too late for supper, he nevertheless headed for the mess hall. When he arrived, all the tables were filled, but the men on KP were still at their stations, and Reynolds was able to grab a tray and pass down the line for a serving of lamb stew with potatoes and a glass of cold milk. Quickly searching the large room, he spotted a familiar group of men.

As Reynolds walked up, a man seated at the end of the table, tall and lanky, glanced up and exclaimed, "Well, Lord have mercy, if it ain't Johnny Reynolds!" The others stared at Reynolds with incredulous expressions, their forks suspended in midair. A compact fellow jumped up and said, "Welcome back, John," as he gave him a firm handshake.

"Hello, Travis," said Reynolds as he pumped his hand, almost dropping his tray.

Within seconds Reynolds was surrounded by a group of grinning Marines, one of whom clapped him on the back and said, "We figured they'd sent you home."

"Hey, you guys," said the tall man, "let the poor s.o.b. sit down and have some chow."

Once they were all seated and Reynolds had managed a few bites, another officer with the double bars of a captain on his collar said, "So tell us what happened to you."

"Well," said Reynolds after taking a swallow of milk, "they flew us out to Espiritu Santo, where they put us on a hospital ship that took us to a navy hospital in Auckland. Been there ever since."

"What was it like?" said the compact man, a second lieutenant from Texas named Travis Henderson.

"Not too bad," said Reynolds, "but the doctors are a pain and the chow was lousy. But I met this real nice family who showed me all around the North Island."

"They told us you'd all been evacuated to the States," said the lanky lieutenant named "Spook" Beck.

"Well, everybody except me," said Reynolds after taking a generous forkful of stew. "I was too dumb to get a ticket home. I told 'em I wanted to go back to my unit when my leg healed. Plus the other guys were worse off."

"What happened to R. C. Patrick and your runner, that boy Chicken?" asked Joe Thompson, a burly former football star from Tennessee. "Did they make it?"

"They both made it," said Reynolds, "though that first night at Henderson Field I didn't think they would." Reynolds thought briefly about Chicken's terrible groans and wheezing all night in the so-called bomb shelter.

"Well, it's good to have you back, John," said Porter Davidson, the captain and Able Company CO. "We need veteran officers like you and not more of these replacements."

Following dinner and a couple of beers at the officers' club, Reynolds followed the others to the battalion bivouac and the large pyramidal tent they shared, with a raised wooden floor, a coal-fired pot-bellied stove at the center and four neat cots. "So where are your things?" said Porter Davidson, warming his hands before the stove.

"They shipped my footlocker back home," said Reynolds. "This uniform is all I've got, plus some skivvies and undershirts."

"Well, you'll need to get fixed up at the BX first thing in the morning. We've got a live fire exercise on the beach at 0900."

Equipped with new green combat utilities, helmet, and boots; khakis and cap and the new, lined jacket the Marines were issued due to the chilly New Zealand climate—and refreshed after several days of strenuous exercise and hearty meals—Reynolds felt as strong and fit as he'd been when the regiment left for Guadalcanal three months earlier. Their battalion, the 1/6, had been chosen to train for landing on the beach in inflatable rubber boats, an innovation, as all of the other battalions in the division would go ashore in the next amphibious assault in landing craft—either amtracs, tracked armored personnel carriers that floated ashore and then drove up onto the beach, or Higgins boats, designed to carry a single platoon of riflemen. No one knew, of course, where that would be, but all were certain it would be another island strongly defended by the Japanese somewhere in the Pacific. As a consequence, the training consisted of practice landings on Whareroa Beach, often accompanied by live fire from US Navy destroyers positioned a mile offshore, constant physical conditioning, mortar fire in the steep grassy hills adjacent to the camp, and constant practice on the rifle range. The relatively light casualties the Second Division had suffered on Guadalcanal had been made up by fresh replacements sent out from Hawaii or California and by men like Reynolds who'd recovered from their wounds or bouts of malaria.

On weekends they were issued passes, almost invariably to enjoy the attractions of Wellington, a city of some two hundred thousand souls and the country's capital, a thriving port with decent shopping, restaurants, movie houses, and, of course, bars and dance halls. On his first trip into the city Reynolds immediately noticed that, as in Auckland, there were few young men about as virtually every able-bodied man between the ages of eighteen and thirty-four was serving in the British Eighth Army in North Africa. With upwards of twenty thousand Marines streaming into town each weekend, a young New Zealand woman on the arm of an American was a common sight and one that often provoked a strong negative reaction among the middle-aged and older men. While the young Marines were generally well behaved, their experiences on Guadalcanal left many with hair-trigger emotions that could explode into violence on the slightest provocation.

By early April, autumn had set in in the southern hemisphere: bright, chilly days and cold nights alternating with intervals of rain. For the Marines at Mackays Crossing, cots were drawn closer to the coal-burning stove in the tent; reveille was at 5:30 in the dark, followed by a two-mile run either on the beach or in the foothills, a hearty breakfast of eggs, bacon, toast, and the occasional lamb chop; a full day of training and, for the officers, lectures on subjects ranging from tactics and logistics to the psychology of the Japanese enemy, widely believed to prefer death over capture and fanatical in their willingness to sacrifice themselves for the Emperor. After enduring the hardships, short rations, and tropical diseases of Guadalcanal, the men were extremely well-fed and physically fit, apart from those who suffered from malaria.

Following breakfast on an Indian-summer Saturday, with sunny skies and temperatures rising into the seventies, Reynolds returned to his tent to don his green winter service uniform, with khaki shirt and tie, green fourragère, and leather Sam Browne belt and shoulder strap. As he checked his appearance in the small mirror on the tent pole, he reflected that this was no ordinary Saturday with a pass into Wellington, but a very special day for many of the Marines: a parade ground assembly to award Purple Hearts to the men wounded on Guadalcanal. The sergeants yelled to the men of Able Company to fall in, and they marched with the remainder of the battalion, about eight hundred men, to a large grassy enclosure where a band was playing the Marine Hymn. The entire regiment stood at attention as a color guard presented arms and the flags of the Sixth Marines, the Corps, and the Stars and Stripes.

General Julian Smith rose from his seat and walked to the podium. "At ease," he said and then, following brief remarks on the gallantry of the Marines who'd fought on Guadalcanal, announced, "I shall now honor those wounded in action with Purple Hearts." Accompanied by a photographer and his adjutant, who held a typewritten list and a box of medals, the general passed along each row of the three thousand men assembled on the parade ground, naming each recipient of the medal and personally pinning it on his chest. Moving down the Able Company row, he stopped before Reynolds, looked him in the eye, and in a strong voice said, "Lieutenant John L. Reynolds of Houston, Texas." As he pinned the heart-shaped medal with its purple ribbon and likeness of George Washington on Reynolds's uniform, the photographer snapped a photo and the general quietly added, "Good job, son."

When the hour-long ceremony had ended, strolling back to their bivouac with Spook Beck and two other Able Company officers, Reynolds said, "Well, boys, I'd say this calls for a celebration. Let's take the first bus into town and treat ourselves to a steak dinner at that joint across from the dance hall."

"I might even spring for the beers," said Travis Henderson with a smile.

The "joint" was McDougal's, a highly popular restaurant in downtown Wellington known for its New Zealand black angus steaks, lamb chops, and fresh seafood. Generally out of reach of most Marines with their modest pay, the four young officers had a table at the back, surrounded by nicely dressed middle-aged couples treating themselves to a rare night out, as food was strictly rationed. This was the cause of considerable rancor among the populace, as the country produced far more beef and lamb than could be locally consumed in order to supply refrigerated meat to Great Britain. "They took all our boys to fight the Germans," was an oft-repeated complaint, "and most of our beef and lamb, so we can go without."

Wearing their drab green winter uniforms, the Marines sat with arms crossed as a waitress served each of them a frosted mug of beer. "Here's to the wounded warrior," said Joe Thompson, holding up his mug.

"Cheers," said Reynolds, taking the first sip. "Mm, that's good. Nice and cold." When the waitress returned, Reynolds said, "I'll have the ten-ounce T-bone, medium rare, with the baked potato." The others followed suit, eliciting disapproving looks from some of the men and women at nearby tables, who shared the common misconception that the Americans on their island lacked for nothing when it came to food and drink. And female companionship. After the Marines had polished off their steaks and several rounds of beer, Travis slipped a cigarette from the pack in his jacket and tapped it on the face of his watch. "I think I'll stroll over to that dance hall," he said, taking a nickel lighter from his pocket and holding the flame to the tip of his cigarette. "It's Saturday night," he added, exhaling a cloud of smoke, "and there's bound to be a decent band and lots of girls."

"I thought you were saving yourself for your girl back home?" said Spook.

"Well, there's no harm in looking," said Travis.

"Agreed," said Spook, "though I doubt Sally would approve." Spook was one of the few married officers in the battalion.

"So long as you keep your hands off the merchandise you should be okay," said Joe Thompson with a smile.

"Y'all go on without me," said Reynolds after finishing the last of his beer. "For some reason I'm feelin' bushed, and I think I'll head back to camp."

After settling the check and leaving a generous tip, they retrieved their hats and walked out onto the sidewalk. Across the street a crowd of Marines and sailors had gathered at the dance hall, which was garishly lighted with neon, in contrast to most of downtown Wellington, whose buildings were dark even though the blackout had ended with the expulsion of the Japanese from Guadalcanal. "See you fellas later," said Reynolds. "Don't get in trouble and miss the curfew." He straightened the front of his jacket and began walking toward the nearest stop for the streetcar that would take him to the bus station, where he'd catch the shuttle back to Mackays Crossing. He felt a little dizzy, which he attributed to the beer. There were few cars on the streets, as most New Zealanders preferred to walk or use public transportation to conserve their small allowance of gasoline. As a consequence, despite the fact that it was almost eight o'clock, a small crowd was waiting at the stop. When the streetcar arrived, Reynolds was not only able to get on but also to find an empty seat. By the next stop, however, more passengers boarded, and all the seats were taken, with a good many people hanging on to straps. At the third stop, even more people crowded the streetcar, and Reynolds looked up to make eye contact with a young woman about his age, wearing a light wool coat, a navy-blue beret, and a purse over her shoulder. He smiled, and she smiled back, a smile that lit up her pretty face. With his inbred courtesy, Reynolds rose, gestured, and said, "Have a seat."

"Oh, no," she said.

"Please," said Reynolds. "I insist."

"Well, thank you," she said, dropping into the vacated seat.

Overcoming his usual shyness around strangers, Reynolds smiled again and said, "I'm John Reynolds."

"I'm Grace. Grace Lucas. You're the first American I've met."

"My pleasure, Grace. On your way home?"

"Yes." She paused as the streetcar came to a stop with a clang of its bell and more passengers crowded on and off. During the interval Reynolds stole a closer look at Grace. She was trim, with a good figure, attractive legs, light brown hair, and an oval face with beautiful hazel eyes. At least they seemed beautiful to him. Averting her eyes as Reynolds was staring, Grace said, "I work weekends at Kirkcaldies department store," she added with a trace of a smile.

"I'd be happy to walk you home," said Reynolds as the streetcar lurched around a corner.

"That's very kind," said Grace, "but I'll be fine."

Peering out the window, Reynolds said, "Well, I think this is my stop. Nice to meet you Grace."

"Likewise."

As the streetcar came to a stop and Reynolds started for the door Grace unexpectedly reached out, handed him a slip of paper, and said, "Goodbye."

CHAPTER FOUR

WHEN REYNOLDS AWOKE, HE WAS NOT IN THE FAMILIAR surroundings of his tent but in bed in a long room with exposed rafters, in the company of some twenty other recumbent men. He was not only confused but felt dazed after a night filled with dreams that were more like hallucinations; his head was aching, his teeth chattered with a chill despite the thick Navy blanket that covered him, and an audible groan escaped his parched lips. At this a corpsman appeared at his bedside and said, "Care for a drink of water, sir?" As all Marines were fighting men, the Navy supplied the medical personnel, including the doctors, nurses, medics, and orderlies, who were known by Marines as "corpsmen."

"Sure," said Reynolds. "Where am I?"

"Officers' sick bay."

"How did I get here?" Reynolds rubbed his bleary eyes.

"They brought you in during the night," said the corpsman as he poured water from a pitcher into a Dixie cup. "You were pretty much out of it."

Reynolds reached for the cup, took a sip, and slumped back on the pillow. He vaguely remembered returning to camp on the bus, feeling like he was coming down with the flu. By the time he heard the others come in—it must have been late—he was burning up but fell back asleep . . . It was the last thing he could remember.

The corpsman looked down at him and then took a thermometer from his pocket, removed it from the case, and gave it a couple of shakes. "I need to take your temperature," he said. "The doc will be around shortly." Reynolds opened his mouth for the corpsman to stick the glass tube under his tongue. "Then we can give you something for the fever." The corpsman studied his wristwatch, removed the thermometer and commented, "one-oh-three-point eight." With another groan, Reynolds closed his eyes and tried to go back to sleep.

When he awoke from a light doze, the doctor, a tall thin man in a white coat with a stethoscope around his neck, was at his bedside studying Reynolds's chart. Aware that Reynolds was awake, he looked at him and said, "Another attack of malaria. And you've got the malignant variety."

Reynolds nodded and said, "Can I get some quinine?"

"In a while," said the doctor. "We're running low, with so damn many cases in the division. For now we'll give you some aspirin and see if we can get that fever down."

It was only after the doctor left that Reynolds remembered the slip of paper in the pocket of his jacket. Even though he felt awful by the time he arrived at his tent, he had the presence of mind to hang his uniform in the locker he shared with the others, so the scrap of paper ought to be safe. The suggestion of a smile curled his mouth when he thought about the numbers printed on the paper—Grace's phone number, he assumed—and how pretty she looked when she gave him that shy smile. He fell back asleep but was soon tossing with delirium that robbed him of any rest. Finally, by early afternoon, the fever broke with the typical sweats. Reynolds kicked off the blanket, got the corpsman's attention and asked for a change of sheets. "And," he said, "can I have that quinine now?"

"I'll check." After a few minutes the young man returned, holding a stack of fresh sheets under one arm and a paper cup with two pills in it. "Here you go," he said, pouring the quinine tablets into Reynolds's outstretched palm.

By the next morning the attack had run its course after a decent night's rest, and his temperature returned to normal. As before in the hospital in Auckland, it left him exhausted, and the quinine took away his appetite.

Reynolds was propped up in bed, reading a long article in a day-old copy of the *Wellington Evening Post* about the New Zealand troops in the fighting that raged in Tunisia. Almost all the newspaper accounts and newsreels shown in the movie theaters were about the battles with the Germans and Italians in North Africa, which was understandable, considering that the New Zealand troops were in the thick of it. And yet it was depressing to the Marines, adding to the sense they were languishing in a faraway place that no one at home would know or care about. Reynolds glanced up from his paper to observe the doctor slowly making his rounds. When he appeared at Reynolds's bedside and gave him a cursory examination, the doctor said, "You can go back to your unit now. But no strenuous exercise for three days. And try to put on some weight."

Reynolds nodded and said, "Thanks. How long is this likely to go on?"

"Impossible to say," said the doctor as he rubbed his chin. "This could prove to be your last attack. But for most people the attacks come and go for months and for some, years. But if you have another attack, we may have to send you to Silverstream."

"What's that?"

"A new hospital we've built to handle the more serious malaria cases." Reynolds nodded, slowly rose from his bed, and reached for the blue cotton robe the corpsman was holding. "Can you make it back to the camp?" asked the doctor.

"Yes, sir."

By evening Reynolds felt well enough to join the others in the chow hall. He donned his lined jacket, as the nights were chilly, and as he walked along the well-worn path he felt for the folded slip of paper in his pocket. Passing down the line with his metal tray, he accepted everything the cooks had to offer—baked ham, string beans, mashed potatoes, a roll, and even a slice of pie—but after fifteen minutes of listless effort, most of the food was still on the plate, as it was tasteless, and he had little appetite.

"You were in a helluva state when you woke us up the other night," said Travis Henderson. "Moanin' and groanin' and out of your head."

"That's what a hundred and five fever will do to you," said Reynolds. "Thank your lucky stars you haven't come down with it."

"Not yet, anyway," said Joe Thompson, another Able Company platoon leader. "I hear the atabrine holds it off for a while."

"Say, Travis," said Reynolds. "Is there a pay phone in the officers' club?"

"Not in it, but in a booth outside. How come, you need to make a call?"

With an inscrutable smile, Reynolds pushed back from the table and said, "Maybe." He made his way to the officers' club while most of the men were still finishing their supper, jingling the coins in his pocket and whistling a tune. The phone booth was just outside the building in the darkness, but when he opened the bi-fold door a light came on. He took the scrap of paper and coins from his pocket, studied the instructions printed over the phone, and then dropped a shilling into the slot. He sat down, briefly listened to the dial tone, and then dialed her number. After several rings a woman answered. "Is this the Lucas residence?" asked Reynolds.

"Yes. May I help you?"

"Is Grace in?"

"May I tell her who's calling?"

"It's John Reynolds." He could hear background noise and the indistinct sound of voices, a man and woman. After a few moments Grace picked up the phone and said, "Hello? John?"

"Hi, Grace," said Reynolds. "I was hoping this was your number."

"When you didn't call, I thought perhaps you'd . . . or that you'd misplaced it."

"No, no. Sorry, but when I got back to camp the other night I was feeling lousy and woke up in the sickbay, so I couldn't call, but I would've . . ."

"The sickbay?"

"That's what we call the, ah, infirmary."

"Are you all right?"

"Sure, I'm fine now, just a little attack of malaria."

"Oh, my. I'm so sorry." Grace cupped her hand over the receiver and said, "It's an American I met the other night on my way home. I'll just be a minute." Returning to the phone, she said, "Sorry. So you have malaria?"

"Yep. Almost all of us got infected on Guadalcanal. The attacks come and go. Anyway, how are you?"

"I'm fine," she said quietly.

Sensing that she might have to get off the phone at any moment, and having rehearsed what he was going to say, Reynolds said, "Are you free for dinner this Saturday?"

"I'm working till six."

"I could meet you at the department store when you get off and we could have an early supper."

"Just a minute mother," Grace called out, and then in a low but excited voice said, "I'll look for you at the main entrance. Kirkcaldies & Stains, on Lambton Quay. Goodbye, John."

"Bye," said Reynolds, though he knew she'd already hung up. Well, he considered as he stood up and pushed open the door, mothers were all the same, no matter where you happened to be, and after all, he was a complete stranger, and an American to boot. As he started walking back to his tent, the thought of seeing Grace again, a girl he'd met entirely by chance on a streetcar, made him feel almost giddy with anticipation, though he couldn't possibly have explained it.

Reynolds stood before a fogged-up mirror over a washbasin, a damp towel wrapped around his waist, carefully parting and combing his hair. Joe Thompson emerged dripping wet from a shower stall and began toweling himself off. Thompson, who'd played left tackle at Tennessee and was six-one and powerfully built, glanced at Reynolds and said, "Somethin' special tonight?" Unlike most Saturdays, the three thousand-odd men in the regiment had spent the day on a strenuous ten-mile march through the foothills, burdened with sixty-pound packs, rifles, and assorted gear. It was Reynolds's first day of activity since the malaria attack, and though his stamina was not what it had been, he'd gotten through it.

"Yep," said Reynolds, turning his head to the side to study his profile and rubbing his just-shaved chin. "I've got a date."

Wrapping the towel around his waist, Thompson walked over to the next sink and took a comb from a jar filled with a blue antiseptic solution. "No kidding," he said as he started combing his hair. "Who with?"

"Girl I met last weekend."

"Last weekend? I seem to remember you headed back to camp after dinner . . ."

"Mm hmm," said Reynolds, turning to face Thompson. "I met her on the streetcar."

"That was fast work."

"Nothin' to it," said Reynolds with a grin. "She gave me her phone number, I called her up, and I'm takin' her out."

Winter uniform neatly pressed and shoes shined to a gloss, Reynolds took the first shuttle into Wellington, determined to arrive with time to spare. He walked from the depot to the center of downtown, where he discovered that Lambton Quay was in the heart of the shopping district. He had no difficulty finding his way to Kirkcaldies & Stains, the venerable department store in a large building that dated from the 1860s. Arriving at twenty before six, he stationed himself near the main entrance, periodically checking his watch. A few minutes after the hour Grace emerged from the revolving door, a smile lighting up her pretty face when she spotted him. Reynolds quickly walked up to her, returned the smile, and said, "Right on time."

"Hello, John," she said. "Shall we go? It's a bit early for supper."

"Whatever you like. We could have something to drink before dinner."

"I was thinking of a restaurant called Bolton's, though I've only been there once. I think they have a bar."

"Lead the way," said Reynolds, falling into step. Grace was tall and slender, with a long stride, and they made the walk to the restaurant, located in a fashionable block in the shopping district, in less than five minutes, just as the sun was setting over the harbor. Entering the foyer, he helped her out of her coat, which he checked along with his hat. Briefly surveying the dining room, with its dark paneling and crisp linen tablecloths, fresh flowers, and candlelight, he noticed the small, separate bar and said, "In the mood for a highball?" Grace cocked her head at the unfamiliar expression. "Cocktail," he said. "Something to drink?"

"Oh," she said. "Of course."

Reynolds chose a cozy table in the corner with two leather-upholstered club chairs. Within moments a waitress appeared, as they virtually had the place to themselves.

"I'll have a gin and tonic," said Grace with another of her easy smiles.

"That's what I ought to be drinking," said Reynolds, "but I'll have a beer instead."

"Why should you be drinking gin?" asked Grace.

"Not gin," said Reynolds, "but tonic. Quinine water. Maybe it would help with the malaria."

"Oh, I almost forgot. How are you feeling?"

"Just a little weak. It really lays you out for a few days."

The waitress returned with their drinks, and Reynolds raised his glass and said, "Cheers."

She repeated the toast, sipped her drink, and said, "So you're one of the Marines?"

"That's right. Our entire division is up at Mackays Crossing. At Paekakariki."

"The newspapers have been full of stories," said Grace. "Ever since the fighting on Guadalcanal. Nobody thought the Americans could beat the invincible Japs."

"Well, the Japs are tough but the Marines are tougher."

Grace gave him an admiring look and said, "Tell me about those badges on your lapels."

"The globe and anchor, you mean? The Marine Corps insignia, 'cause we fight on land and on the sea. We're sort of part of the navy but not really."

"My brother's in the New Zealand Corps," said Grace. "Like virtually all the boys from here. It's part of the British Eighth Army in North Africa."

"Older or younger brother?"

"Younger," said Grace. "Charlie's nineteen, and I'm twenty-two. There's just the two of us."

"Yeah, I've been reading about that big battle they just fought in Tunisia. Those, ah, native tribesmen sound plenty tough . . ."

"The Maoris," said Grace with a smile. "And what about you?"

"Well, I'm twenty-three," said Reynolds after taking a swallow of beer. "With one younger sister."

"Where does your family live?"

"A city in Texas called Houston."

"Texas," said Grace with a smile. "Are you a cowboy or an oilman?"

"Neither one. I've got one more year to go to finish law school. My dad works for a bank, or did."

"My dad's a lawyer," said Grace, rattling the ice in her glass. "Shall we go to our table?"

❖ ❖ ❖

Over the course of an excellent dinner—Grace had chosen the restaurant well—thick grilled lamb chops accompanied by sautéed potatoes and broccoli with hollandaise, Grace had discovered a surprising amount about John Reynolds; the quality of the cuisine doing nothing to diminish her inquisitiveness. She learned that he'd graduated from the University of Texas and enlisted in an officer candidate program two years before the attack on Pearl Harbor, so that when it came, during his second year of law school, he was almost immediately placed on active duty and sent overseas after a brief period of training in California. She was fascinated by his modest account of how, as a second lieutenant commanding a rifle platoon on Guadalcanal, he'd been wounded, his evacuation to Auckland, stay in the hospital, and driving trips around the North Island with Malcolm McDonald.

"And what about you, Grace? How long have you worked at the department store?"

"I left the university when the war started and went to work as a part-time sales clerk."

"What university?"

"Victoria. It's in Kelburn. I'd finished my second year there."

"Why did you leave?"

"My father thought it best. He doesn't believe in women having careers."

"Well, I disagree," said John. "What were you studying?"

"History."

"That's what I studied in college, mainly American history."

"I was research assistant," said Grace, "to a wonderful professor named Beaglehole, an expert on Captain Cook."

"For whom the strait's named," said John.

"Yes. I intended to teach."

"Well, maybe you'll go back to college and finish."

"And is there a girl back home?" asked Grace as dessert was being served.

"No," said Reynolds. "Not really." She looked at him skeptically. "Not what you'd call a steady girlfriend." He thought back to all the sorority girls he gone out with at the university. "How about you, Grace?"

"I had a boyfriend," she said with a surprisingly fragile expression. "We met at university. But he was killed last year, in North Africa."

"I'm very sorry."

She brushed away a tear and raised her eyes to his. "You're the first man I've been on a date with," she said, "since I got word that Tom had been killed."

Reynolds thought back to how she'd given him her phone number on the streetcar and wondered if that was true. After paying the bill— Reynolds felt like he could splurge, as his modest officer's pay had accumulated during the six months he'd been deployed and the exchange rate favored the US dollar—he accompanied Grace home on the streetcar, exiting at a stop two blocks from her house, a modest bungalow in a quiet neighborhood that reminded him of the McDonalds' home in Auckland. Along the way he'd had a chance to learn a little more about Grace, that her father's law practice had something to do with the fact that Wellington was the national capital and that her mother was consumed with worry about her brother fighting in North Africa. Standing by the door on her front porch in a pool of lamplight, Reynolds reached for both her hands, smiled, and said, "Tonight was swell." She nodded. "When will I see you again?"

"Will you have another pass, if that's what they call it, next weekend?"

"Yes," said Reynolds. "We could go to dinner and a movie."

"Perfect," said Grace. "Meet me at the store." Perhaps sensing that her mother or father might appear at any moment, she squeezed John's hands, gave him a quick peck on the cheek, and hurried inside.

Dinner with Grace Lucas at Bolton's was the first of many Saturday evenings they would spend together; out to dinner, a movie, or just strolling the streets and parks, bundled up in warm coats. Occasionally, they'd spend an afternoon or evening at her home, talking about the war or their common interest in history, or Grace, who was an excellent pianist, would play selections from Chopin for him. John had prevaricated when he told her he'd never had a serious girlfriend, as he'd dated a girl from San Antonio all through his first year of law school, though they'd broken up. But the way he felt around Grace was unlike anything he'd experienced with another girl. While Grace seemed to feel the same way about him, Reynolds sensed there was something different in her feelings or attitude, something like caution or reserve. The more time they spent together, the more they enjoyed each other's company. Grace wasn't like any of the girls he'd dated in college or law school. She had a sense of humor combined with a seriousness and an intellectual depth that he found very appealing. Though neither would mention it, they both knew it was only a matter of time before he'd be leaving to go back into combat. Nor did it help that her parents clearly disapproved of the budding relationship; when Reynolds was finally asked over for dinner on one of his rare Sundays off, her father had alternated between interrogating him about his family and background and staring at him across the dinner table with a kind of frosty disapproval.

The following Saturday, the sixth in a row they'd been together, after taking in a light-hearted Hollywood romance with Bing Crosby and Dorothy Lamour, Reynolds suggested a milkshake at the corner drugstore. Waiting to be served, he turned to Grace on the stool next to him and said, "You know I'm crazy about you." She responded with a faint smile, looking into his eyes. "I like those hazel eyes," he added. "That's the first thing I noticed when we met on the streetcar."

"Really?"

"Sure was. I wondered why you gave me your phone number when I was getting off."

"That's simple," said Grace. "Because you were such a gentleman, and so good looking. I wanted to see you again."

"To be honest, Gracie, I'm a little worried about where things are headed."

"How so?"

"Well, it's just that you sometimes seem kind of, well, I'm not sure how to say it. Kind of like you're scared." He paused as the soda jerk walked up and placed their shakes on the counter.

"Well, maybe I am. A little," she said in a soft voice. He gave her an encouraging look. "Though we never talk about it, I'm sure it's just a matter of time before the Marines are sent back in to fight."

"Yes," said Reynolds. "That's for sure, though I don't know where or when."

"It scares me that I could fall for you and then . . ."

"That something could happen to me," said Reynolds. He decided not to mention her previous boyfriend, though obviously he was on her mind.

Grace nodded and sipped her milkshake through a straw. "That's delicious," she said. "We've got such good milk from our New Zealand Jerseys." After a few moments of silence, she said, "And that's not the only thing, John." Sipping his shake, he gave her another expectant look. "My parents are worried sick about me."

"Yeah. I can tell."

"You can't blame them," said Grace. "My mother's so frightened she'll never see Charlie again. And Dad is terrified I could run off with a Yank, and then . . ."

"Tell you what," said Reynolds. "Let's not worry about it. It's what the war is doing to moms and dads and people like you and me all over the place."

"That's true."

"Let's make the most of the time we have," said Reynolds in a reassuring tone. "And let things take care of themselves."

She smiled, leaned over, and kissed him lightly on the lips.

CHAPTER FIVE

JOHN REYNOLDS DUCKED UNDER THE FLAP OF THE LARGE tent and took a seat in one of the folding chairs among several of his fellow officers. Standing in front was Major William K. Jones, the battalion CO, known to his fellow officers as "Willie K" or simply "Bill." Jones, who was wearing his zip-up khaki jacket and smoking a corncob pipe, was Reynolds's idea of a Marine's Marine, tall, lean, with close-cropped hair and a soft-spoken, easy-going manner that belied his steady confidence in command and remarkable coolness under fire. "Say," said Travis Henderson, who was seated next to Reynolds, "did you hear about Yamamoto?"

"What about him?"

"We killed the sonofabitch," whispered Travis. "I just heard it on the radio. Our guys shot down his plane over New Guinea."

"Really?" said Reynolds, sitting up straight. "Sort of gets us even for Pearl Harbor."

After a few moments, when the rest of the officers, some fifteen men in all, were in their seats, Major Jones said, "Listen up, gentlemen." He reached for a box of matches and relit his pipe. "General Smith has dreamed up a screwball exercise." He took a folded sheet of paper from his pocket and puffed on his pipe. "He's ordered the whole damned division to make a forced march to some little town north of here called Foxton. And I don't just mean infantry, but cooks, corpsmen, clerks, and staff officers, with every man carrying a weapon and full transport pack. And once we get there, we turn around and march back."

"Jesus, sir," said Porter Davidson, leaning forward in his chair. "How far?"

"I looked it up on the map," said Jones. "About forty miles to Foxton. And here's the thing. We march all the way, over some pretty steep terrain, with just one five minute break an hour, and only the water and rations we've got with us."

"C'mon, major," said another captain. "A forty mile march without a break? A lot of these guys won't make it."

Jones nodded and took another contemplative puff on his pipe. "This sonofabitch obviously means to find out just how tough we are. And I want every damn man in this battalion to show him."

"Yes, *sir*," said Lieutenant Spook Beck, the executive officer of the battalion's weapons company and a well-known joker. "These raggedy-ass Marines may not be much to look at, but by God they can march."

Reynolds tugged on the shoulder straps of his pack and studied the men milling around, all wearing their steel helmets and combat boots, burdened with upper and lower packs filled with rations, extra clothing, a blanket and poncho, cartridge belt, entrenching tool, canteen, Ka-Bar battle knife, and M-1 Garand rifle and bayonet, some eighty pounds in all. That was a heavy enough load for a rifleman, but the men in the weapons company had it worse. Reynolds glanced at a BAR man, carrying a heavy Browning Automatic Rifle, and one of the mortar squads, one man carrying the 81-millimeter tube, another the heavy steel base plate, and a third with eight mortar rounds in an apron in front and another nine rounds on his back. With his promotion to first lieutenant, Reynolds was now the executive officer, or second in command, of Able Company, at full strength with two hundred men. A battalion consisted of three rifle companies and a weapons company, and there were three battalions to the regiment, three regiments to the brigade, and three brigades to the division, some twenty thousand men in all. At the shouts of the master sergeants, the men of Able Company formed up in platoons, joining a column of men, four abreast, that stretched for miles. Thankfully, Reynolds considered from his position at the head of the company, the June morning was cold and bright, with temperatures expected to rise into the fifties.

The pace set by the battalion in front was not brisk but steady, and while the fit young infantrymen had no difficulty keeping up, a number of the battalion's other Marines—cooks, typists, staff officers—began to straggle when they reached a steep hill several miles after setting out from Mackays Crossing. Though there was a chill in the air, Reynolds mopped the sweat from his brow and could feel a damp stain forming on his shirt under the heavy pack, whose straps dug into his shoulders. For the first half hour most of the men engaged in lively banter, but after the column had covered about three miles they lapsed into silence, breathing rhythmically and concentrating on keeping up with the men in front of them. Precisely fifty-five minutes after they set out, a shrill whistle sounded, and the sergeants called out: "Five minutes' rest!" The men immediately slumped to the ground, leaning back on their packs, and taking long draughts of water from their canteens. After five minutes they were helping one another back on their feet, tugging on their packs, and reforming the column.

And so it went, mile after mile as the winter sun climbed higher; they followed a winding paved road up and down the steep hills, with occasional glimpses of the deep blue water of the nearby Tasman Sea, conserving their water and their strength with the five minutes of rest each hour. At one such break, Reynolds consulted his watch: twelve minutes past noon, over four hours since they set out. As he unscrewed the lid of his canteen he noticed several of the men starting to pull off their boots. "Don't take off those boondockers!" he called out to them, "or you'll never get 'em on again." They had halted in a road cut, and the company waterman, with a large container of water strapped to his front, was standing with his back against the limestone side of the cut as the men queued up to refill their canteens. Word passed down the line that the men were to eat part of their ration—most selected the chocolate bar—and then they were on the way again.

Seven hours into the march, having covered perhaps twenty miles by Reynolds's reckoning, many were straggling and some falling out, sitting or even lying on the roadside as the column marched slowly past them. Periodically an ambulance would drive slowly past, stopping to pick up those too exhausted to continue. But all of the men in Able Company, Reynolds considered proudly, were still marching in evident good spirits, though their shoulders burned, backs ached, and heels were rubbed raw. As the sun moved into the western sky the terrain thankfully flattened out, but now, after marching for over ten hours, there were many gaps in the column and more men sitting exhausted on the roadside. Every few miles the Marines would encounter a farmhouse, and the farmers' wives would invariably appear with a tray of cookies or scones, glasses of milk or a basket of strawberries. But the men were strictly enjoined by their officers from accepting the bounty, drinking only the water from their canteens and the meager rations in their packs.

Finally, after the sun had sunk into the wine-dark sea, word passed down the column that the CO had ordered a halt for the men to get some sleep. Having marched for twelve hours, using their packs or helmets as pillows, they were out the minute they closed their eyes. Two hours later they were awakened by the shrill blasts of whistles and back on their feet, trudging slowly along in the darkness the final six miles to Foxton. As Reynolds marched he studied the glittering stars in the unfamiliar constellations and occasionally dozed, waking when he stumbled, and found himself thinking of Grace, of her eyes and pretty smile, the sound of her soft laughter, certain that he was in love with her. At last the dim lights of the small village twinkled on the horizon. By then Reynolds, like all the others, had reached or surpassed the limits of his endurance and was able to keep going, to put one foot in front of the other, by sheer force of will and adherence to the iron discipline at the heart of Marine Corps training. Sinking again to the cold ground when the column halted, Reynolds called out to his men: "Remember, don't take off your boots or you'll never get 'em back on!" and then immediately fell asleep.

The men awoke with the sun and stumbled to their feet, every muscle and bone aching, especially their poor feet. During the night a convoy of trucks had arrived, and as the sky grew light the men could smell the aromas of bacon and fresh brewed coffee and see the cooks standing over their field stoves. Almost all of the men in Reynolds's company had complied with his admonition to keep on their boots, but a large number had not, pulling them off to attend to their blisters. And now, as predicted, none could get them back on and thus faced a humiliating ride back to camp in the back of a deuce and a half. But they all enjoyed a hot, restorative breakfast of scrambled eggs, bacon, toast, coffee, and milk, and those who had footwear were ready to begin the long march back, with spirits running high, before the hour of eight. Compared to the grueling march of the previous day, the return trip seemed, to Reynolds at least, somehow less arduous, perhaps because the hourly rests were extended by a few minutes or simply because of the men's greater confidence in themselves. Arriving at Mackays Crossing at midnight, the men who'd made it all the way collapsed on their cots with the vague awareness that they'd passed one of the greatest tests, apart from cheating death at the hands of the enemy, the Second Division would face in the Pacific war.

The following day, which was cold and windy, Reynolds, wearing his lined jacket, sat in his sock feet next to the coal-burning stove in his tent with a pencil in his teeth and several sheets of Red Cross stationery resting on a book in his lap. After a moment he wrote:

June 26, 1943

Dear Mom and Dad,

> While you're enduring the hot Texas weather, we're in early winter here, which is chilly but not really cold yet on the North Island.

Reynolds reached down to massage his swollen and tender feet and inched closer to the stove, considering that the censors no longer objected to the mention of New Zealand, as the Marines' presence there had been widely reported in the press. "We train hard all week," he continued,

> . . . but usually have a day off on weekends, and most of the men get a pass to go into town. The food's pretty decent and there's shopping and the movies and a couple of places to go dancing. In fact there are lots of cute girls as almost all of the young men have been sent off to fight in North Africa in the British army. I've actually met a wonderful girl named Grace, whom I'm sure y'all would like very much.

Last week they put us through a pretty interesting exercise. We marched 40 miles to a little town, with every man carrying a rifle and full pack, with only a five minute rest an hour, and then marched back. It was tough but I'm proud to say that every man in my company made it.

I had a nice letter from cousin Patsy who said the wedding was swell but that she's lonely living by herself in Norfolk with Ernie away on convoy duty in the Atlantic. And how's Betsy? I haven't gotten a word from her since leaving San Diego.

Please write with news from home as your letters do wonders for my morale as far away as I am and give my love to everyone.

Love,
John

p.s. my wound has healed nicely and I've gotten over the malaria

Reynolds folded the pages into an airmail envelope, which he quickly addressed. He briefly smiled at the thought of how they'd react, especially his mom, to his casual mention of Grace. Shivering in the cold, he leaned even closer to the stove, thinking he had just enough time to drop off the letter at the camp post office before heading to the mess hall for lunch.

Standing in line with his metal tray, Reynolds felt oddly fatigued; not sleepy but enervated. Maybe a hot meal would perk him up.

"Heading into town tonight?" said Spook Beck, who'd appeared in line behind him.

"You bet," said Reynolds as they shuffled toward the chow line.

"Hot date?"

"Yep. I'm meetin' Grace for dinner and a movie."

"Some guys have all the luck," said Spook. "Wish I could go out with one of those cute Kiwi gals, but the wife back in Portland wouldn't stand for it."

When his turn in line came, Reynolds accepted his plateful of roast lamb with gravy, peas, and mashed potatoes, picked up a glass of milk, and made his way to an empty space at the table occupied by several of the battalion's other officers. "Leave room for Spook," he said as he squeezed onto the bench. "He's right behind me." Taking his silverware from his napkin, Reynolds looked at his plate, unable to summon any appetite while the men all around him tucked into the meal with gusto. He tried a slice of lamb and bite of potatoes, which triggered a mild wave of nausea. After pushing the food around on his plate and forcing himself to take another bite and a swallow of milk, Reynolds looked up at Spook, who was seated across from him.

"What's the matter with you, Johnny?" said Spook. "Hardly touched your food."

"Must be comin' down with a bug or somethin'," replied Reynolds. "Think I'll head back and lie down for a while."

By the time he made his way to the tent Reynolds's head was splitting and he was certain he was running a fever. "Dang it," he muttered as he slumped on his cot, too weak to take off his boots. The amazing thing about malaria was how suddenly the attacks came on. He closed his eyes and tried to sleep but after a quarter hour he surrendered to the inevitable, forced himself to get up and shrugged on his jacket. When he arrived at the officers' sickbay he was wracked with chills and so wobbly a young corpsman took one look at him and quickly guided him into a wheelchair. Within five minutes he was out of his uniform and lying in one of the beds in the long open ward under two blankets, with a thermometer under his tongue. The corpsman at his bedside consulted his wristwatch, slipped the glass tube from Reynolds's mouth, noted the temperature, and jotted it down on a chart. At that moment a Navy doctor appeared at the end of the room and walked briskly to Reynolds's bed. The corpsman wordlessly handed him Reynolds's chart. After a brief glance at Reynolds the doctor turned to the chart. "One hundred four temperature," he said with a frown. "And the malignant strain of malaria. I'm afraid it's Silverstream for you, Lieutenant."

"When do I go?" said Reynolds, generally familiar with the special malaria hospital the Navy had constructed in the Hutt Valley about forty miles from Paekakariki.

"This afternoon," said the doctor, tapping a pencil on Reynolds's chart. "I'm sending a couple of other cases up there." *Jeez*, thought Reynolds, how could he get word to Grace? She'd figure he'd stood her up. "Give him the universal pill," the doctor instructed the corpsman, "and start him on quinine. The usual dose."

"Aye, aye, sir."

The doctor dropped the chart on the end of the bed and turned to go. When the corpsman returned with a handful of pills in a Dixie cup and glass of water, Reynolds said, "Say, I wonder if you could do me a favor?"

"What's that?" said the corpsman as he tipped one of the pills into Reynolds's palm and handed him the paper cup.

Reynolds gulped down the pill and then said, "I need to get a note to a buddy of mine. Could you deliver it?"

"Sure," said the corpsman cheerfully. "I get off at three."

"Great," said Reynolds as the corpsman gave him the other two tablets. "I'm with the 1/6. We're in Area 9 of Camp Mackay." The corpsman found him a sheet of Red Cross stationery and a pencil, and he hastily scribbled a note to Spook explaining he was being transferred to Silverstream and asking if Spook could meet Grace at the department store in Wellington at 6:00 and explain. After handing the corpsman the note, Reynolds collapsed on the bed, wrapping himself in the blankets.

Within an hour, in pajamas and a robe and bundled in a blanket, Reynolds was loaded in the back of a drab green ambulance with another malaria-stricken Marine and they were on their way, with a second ambulance following them, on the highway that wound up into the hills of the North Island interior. Within an hour they crossed the bridge over the Hutt River, turned north, and in another ten minutes arrived at the Silverstream hospital, a long, two-story wooden building painted white, situated on a hillside in the river valley. Reynolds slept the entire way, semi-delirious with a temperature over 104°. Navy corpsmen pulled the sick Marines from the ambulances and carried them on litters to one of the wards reserved for officers and into waiting beds separated from the others by cloth partitions. For the next three days, Reynolds endured bouts of extreme high fever followed by drenching sweats that left him utterly exhausted. Tossing with violent chills and delirium, he dreamed he was in a foxhole on Guadalcanal in a nighttime downpour under shelling by the Japanese and then he was with Grace in Wellington, but then it wasn't Grace but . . . the heavy-set Navy nurse peering down at him. Finally, on a regimen of quinine, with cold compresses for the spikes in fever, his condition gradually improved and, as suddenly as it arrived, the malaria disappeared altogether.

Exhausted from the fever and lack of nourishment, Reynolds was dozing when he heard the sound of men's voices and opened his bleary eyes to gaze at one of the Navy doctors, accompanied by an unfamiliar man in a white coat with embroidered caduceus. The doctors stood at the bedside of the man next to Reynolds, obscured by the cloth screen. "Feeling any better today, captain?" asked the Navy doctor. "This is Dr. Martinelli, the specialist from Milan I was telling you about." Reynolds propped himself up on an elbow to get a better look at the Italian doctor, who was tall, with wavy black hair.

"They have malaria in Italy?" said the captain, who'd arrived the day before suffering from an especially virulent attack.

"Oh, yes," said Dr. Martinelli, "all up and down the Po valley. The word malaria, after all, comes from the Italian. Mal . . . aria—bad air," he explained.

"They're experimenting with a novel way to treat the disease," said the Navy doctor.

"We administer the quinine with adrenaline," said Dr. Martinelli in his heavily accented English.

What the hell is an Italian doctor doing in a Navy hospital in New Zealand? wondered Reynolds.

"We're going to try it on you, Captain," said the Navy doctor. "In theory, the adrenaline amplifies the antiviral effect of the quinine."

"Okay," mumbled the captain.

Shortly after the doctors had gone the heavy-set nurse appeared, holding a large syringe. "Okay, Captain," she said. "Roll over on your side." After injecting the stoic officer in the buttocks she too disappeared from the ward, and for the next ten or fifteen minutes the captain appeared to be resting peacefully, allowing Reynolds to go back to sleep. But he was startled awake by a loud groan and the sounds of the captain thrashing uncontrollably, knocking over the cloth screen separating their beds. A corpsman dashed from the far end of the ward and tried to subdue the man. "Jesus!" he called to another corpsman. "He's havin' a seizure or something. Get the doctor!"

Within less than a minute the two doctors strode rapidly into the ward, followed by the nurse. "He's convulsing," said the Navy doctor, looking down on the captain, who was still violently shaking and loudly groaning.

"The last time I took his temperature," said the nurse with a worried expression, "it was almost a hundred five."

"Get ice-cold compresses on him," the doctor instructed the nurse. "And try to hold him down," he added to the corpsman. "Pray he pulls through it."

By the following morning the captain's fever had broken, and he was resting at last, though Reynolds had overheard the doctor explaining to the nurse that the man's disease had "gone cerebral." As it was Reynolds's fifth day at Silverstream, and his second without fever, he was allowed to dress in a robe and slippers and walk under his own power, albeit unsteadily, to the mess hall for breakfast. Though the quinine had robbed him of his appetite, he was determined to choke down a breakfast of eggs, toast, and sausage to start to rebuild his strength. When the doctor appeared at his bedside during his afternoon rounds, Reynolds looked up expectantly and said, "I feel fine. When can I get out of here?"

The doctor removed his wire-rimmed glasses and began polishing the lens with a handkerchief. "We probably ought to keep you under observation another couple of days," he said. "But the truth is, we need the bed. So I'll let you go in the morning."

Unlike his previous stay in the hospital, the Marine Corps had sent along a box containing his green utility uniform, underwear, socks, and boots. And the box also contained a letter, postmarked Houston. Seated on his bed, Reynolds studied the feminine handwriting, certain it was not his mother's. Tearing it open, he unfolded several sheets of inexpensive stationery and began reading the letter from his little sister Betsy. After relating the commonplace news from home and describing her job as a secretary in an accounting firm, she got to the point: "I'm really concerned about Mom."

Ever since she got word that you'd been wounded on Guadalcanal she's been frantic with worry. Dad tries to calm her down and says there's nothing they can do but pray for the best, but Mom won't listen. The latest is that her Aunt Julia knows Congressman Albert Thomas, who grew up in Nacogdoches and is real close to FDR. Mom's pressuring Dad to make an appointment to go see Thomas and see if he can fix things to bring you home.

Reynolds put the letter aside and looked up at the rafters. *My God*, he thought, *Dad wouldn't do that would he?* Turning back to the letter, he read:

> But Dad won't do it and he won't budge. It really made Mom mad, and I can tell you life in this house has been pretty miserable lately. I'm sorry, big brother, for bothering you with this, but maybe you could write Mom a letter making it clear that you're doing OK and wouldn't accept a ticket home even if they offered it to you.

Tossing the letter on his bed, Reynolds stood up and stretched. In a way he resented his mother's attitude, but he couldn't really blame her. He had been shot after all, and it was virtually certain they were headed back into combat. But he knew he could count on his father to do the right thing. Feeling weak but remarkably better the next morning, Reynolds showered, shaved, and donned his uniform to report after another hearty breakfast to the hospital's lobby. "You Lieutenant Reynolds?" asked a burly sergeant, who was wearing a fleece-lined coat and hat with earflaps.

"That's right," said Reynolds.

"I'm your driver. Ready to shove off?"

As all the ambulances were reserved for men too ill to walk, Marines returning to Mackays Crossing were driven by jeep, thankfully with the canvas top up, as the temperature in the foothills was in the thirties, with a sharp breeze. "You'll need this," said the driver, handing Reynolds a heavy coat. After shrugging on the warm coat, Reynolds climbed in, and they were off, speeding down the highway into a small village and across the bridge over the river, the sound of the rushing wind making conversation impossible. By midmorning the driver turned into the main entrance at Mackays Crossing and came to a stop outside the divisional HQ, where the flags were flapping in the steady breeze. Reynolds climbed out, leaned down to the window, and said, "Thanks for the lift, Sarge." He started to unbutton his coat.

"Keep it, Lieutenant," said the sergeant with a smile. "It may come in handy."

CHAPTER SIX

JOHN REYNOLDS RETURNED TO MACKAYS CROSSING EXACTLY a week after he'd fallen ill, on a Saturday when the training regimen typically ended following the midday meal, and most of the men had passes to venture into town for an evening of relaxation and girl chasing. As he made his way to the battalion's bivouac, Reynolds was anxious to find Spook and see if he'd made contact with Grace. Approaching the tents assigned to Able Company he spotted Spook, wearing his khakis and garrison cap, chatting with several enlisted men. When Reynolds walked up, Spook broke into a wide smile, said, "Welcome back, John!" and gave Reynolds a firm handshake. "Damn it's good to see you," he added, avoiding his usual flippant tone.

"Gee, Spook," said Reynolds, "did y'all really miss me?"

"To be honest, we were worried about you. Another guy, Charlie Aycock in Baker Company, has such a bad case they had to replace him with a new man."

"That's a shame," said Reynolds. "Aycock's a good officer."

"But here's the worse part," said Spook, lowering his voice. "The new guy's a mustang, a noncom in the regular Marines before the war who got commissioned. And all he can talk about is killin' Japs."

"Listen, Spook," said Reynolds as they started walking in the direction of the officers' club, "I need to ask you about Grace."

"Yeah, I got your note," said Spook, "from that nice kid who works in the sickbay."

"Did you meet up with her?"

"Yep. It's a good thing I recognized her, 'cause she sure didn't know who I was. You've got a real sweetie, John."

"Yeah, I know. Was she OK?"

"Well, she was awful worried about you. I'd tried tellin' her you'd be fine in a couple of days, but I'm not sure she was buyin' it."

"Well, thanks," said Reynolds, putting an arm around Spook's shoulder. "I knew I could depend on you."

The two men walked up to the bar in the plywood structure that served as the OC. An unfamiliar lieutenant was seated on a barstool with a glass of beer, lighting a cigarette and gazing at the posters of several Hollywood starlets tacked on the wall. "Say, Arnold," said Spook, "say hello to John Reynolds, Able Company's XO."

Arnold Schulz stood up and reached out to shake Reynolds's hand. "Where you been?" he asked.

"Up at Silverstream," said Reynolds. "Gettin' over an attack of malaria." He quickly sized up the new man, noting his somewhat rough features and that he was years older than the other officers.

"Another Southern boy," said Schulz as he exhaled smoke from his nostrils.

"That's right," said Reynolds. "Where're you from, Arnold?"

"Scranton, Pennsylvania. Coal mining country."

"Well, we ain't all dumb Southern crackers," said Spook with a smile. "I'm from Oregon. Why don't we head over to the mess hall?"

Reynolds took a bite of chicken and rice and said, "So where were you, Arnold, before they sent you here?"

"Hawaii," said Schulz, pronouncing it as if the word ended in "ya." "With the old Fourth Marines. I joined up in '36 and got sent to Shanghai."

"Were you in Shanghai when the Japs arrived?" asked Spook.

"Damn straight. Saw with my own eyes what the goddam Japs did to them Chinks. Killin' babies and pregnant women with bayonets."

"Jeez," said another young officer with a surprised expression.

"I'm just glad as hell," said Schulz, "they assigned me to a rifle company. Can't wait to get my hands on some Japs and cut their goddam throats the way they did them poor damn Chinks."

"Bloodthirsty bastard," Spook whispered to Reynolds.

"So what year was your PLC class?" asked another officer. "'36?"

"Naw, I was an NCO," said Schulz with a hostile glare. "A master sergeant when the Japs hit Pearl Harbor, and then got my commission and made second louie. So you college boys have got a tough sarge from the Old Breed lookin' over your shoulders."

"Great," said Reynolds in an aside to Spook. Pushing back from the table, Reynolds announced, "I'll see you fellows later. Got a phone call to make."

Reynolds zipped up his jacket as he waited in line outside the phone booth. It was obvious that they should expect nothing but trouble from a mustang like Arnold Schulz, commissioned to help fill the desperate shortage of officers as the ranks of the Marines swelled in the aftermath of Pearl Harbor. Well, ironically, Schulz seemed to feel both superior to the "college boys," as he derisively referred to the other officers, and simultaneously *inferior* to them. The result was a big chip on his shoulder he was daring them to knock off. A young corporal emerged from the booth, and Reynolds stepped inside, dropped a coin in the slot, and dialed the familiar number. Grace's mother answered on the third ring. "Hi, Mrs. Lucas," said Reynolds cheerfully. "It's John. Is Grace in?"

"Hello, John," said Mrs. Lucas in a wary tone. "You haven't called in a while."

"No, ma'am. I've been, well, sick."

"I'll get her." After a moment Reynolds could hear voices in the background and then Grace picked up. "John?" she said in a trembling voice.

"Hi, Grace, gosh it's good . . ."

"Oh, John," said Grace. "I've been so worried. When you didn't call, I was afraid that . . ." Her words dissolved into muffled sobs.

"Hey," said Reynolds. "It's okay. It's just that they sent me up to this place called Silverstream where . . ."

"Yes, I know," said Grace, trying to compose herself. "Spook explained it to me. But still . . ."

"Listen, honey, I'm fine and dying to see you. I've got a pass."

"Let's go to dinner," said Grace. "I don't care to see a film or go dancing."

"Great," said Reynolds. "I've got an idea. "Why don't we go back to that restaurant where we went on our first date?"

"Bolton's," said Grace. "That would be lovely. Can you come for me at the house?"

"Sure. But don't you have to work?"

"No. I called in sick. Which, in a way, I was. Sick with worry."

"I'll be there at half past six. Can't wait to see you. Bye."

"Bye, John."

Wearing his sharply creased uniform and billed hat, Reynolds strolled the final two blocks with a spring in his step and lightness in his heart. The vestigial effects of the quinine had finally worn off and he couldn't think of anything more appealing than a good dinner alone with Grace. After a quick peck on the cheek at the front door, avoiding an encounter with her parents, he whisked her away to the streetcar stop for the short trip downtown. Seated in a quiet corner of the restaurant's intimate paneled dining room after the waiter had cleared the table, Reynolds took a swallow of beer and reached across the table to take Grace's hands. "You sure look sweet," he said quietly, gazing into her eyes in the flickering candlelight.

"And you look so handsome in your uniform," she said. "You know, John, I feel so close to you and yet in a way I hardly know you. Tell me about your family back home."

"All right. I've got a younger sister named Betsy, who lives at home with my folks."

"And what sort of place is Houston?"

"Well, it's a big city, over four hundred thousand, just a little inland from the Gulf of Mexico, with a big port. And Houston's the center for the American oil and gas industry."

"You said your father's a banker?"

"Well, he worked for a bank, that is, he did until he got laid off in the early part of the Depression."

"I'm sorry."

"To be honest, he hasn't really held a job since. It's really been hard on him, especially since his big brother, my uncle Henry, married money.

You know how it is, they're all together with my grandparents for Sunday lunch after church, that sort of thing. My mom never really lets Dad forget he's let her down."

Grace nodded and said, "It sounds like your father's a sensitive man."

"Yes," said John, "and a good man."

"The Depression has been devastating for a lot of good men," said Grace, reaching across the table to give John's hand a squeeze. "Tell me about that medal on your chest. In the shape of a heart."

"Well, it's called a purple heart," said Reynolds. "With a likeness of George Washington. It's given to every man wounded in action."

"I see," said Grace with a troubled look. "I just can't understand why they didn't send you home after you were shot. And now . . ."

"If they'd sent me home," said Reynolds, "I'd never have met you. But let's not talk about . . ."

"We've got to," said Grace with a gentle squeeze of John's hands. "We can't just pretend you're not going back into combat. When they sent you to that other hospital, I couldn't help thinking, what if something happened to you? And I just couldn't bear it. Not after what happened to Tom," she added in almost a whisper.

Reynolds stared into her eyes, pressing his lips together. "I don't know any other way to say this," he said after a moment. "I love you so much, Gracie," he said quietly. "I want to spend our lives together. Do you understand?" She nodded, fighting back tears. "But we came here to do a job. To defeat the Japs," he said in a stronger voice. "So you're right, there's no use pretending I'm not going back into action, and anything can happen . . ."

"Oh, John, I hate this war! Here we are in our beautiful little country, so far away from everything, and all of a sudden these terrible people are threatening to attack us, and you have to come all the way from America to fight them. And poor Charlie, sent half way round the world to fight those dreadful Germans in the desert." Grace stared into her lap, brushing away her tears.

"All I can say, Grace, is I love you. I don't know when we're shipping out, but I've got to think it won't be long." She looked up at him and nodded. "But if I make it," he added, "I promise I'm coming back for you. If you'll wait for me."

"Oh, John," she murmured. "I promise I'll be here for you."

❖ ❖ ❖

After paying the bill and getting Grace's coat, Reynolds stood with her outside on the sidewalk, debating whether to take her home. Anticipating the question, she said, "I don't want to go home, John. Not now, at least."

"Where would you like to go?"

"It's not too cold. Could we walk to the park?"

"Okay." Reynolds took her hand and they strolled down the empty sidewalk, passing from one circle of yellow lamplight to the next. After a while he put his arm around her waist and held her close. The small city park was illuminated with streetlamps, as all fears of an air raid had long since passed. They strolled by a middle-aged couple walking their dog and then stopped at a wooden bench in the shadows, obscured by a hedge from any passerby. Reynolds folded Grace in his arms, and when she raised her lips to his and closed her eyes, he kissed her, lightly at first and then with growing passion. "Oh, John," she murmured at last. "I love you so much." She sank onto the bench, and he sat beside her, his arm around her shoulders, holding her tight, kissing her with even more passion. She draped her leg over his knee and ran her fingers through his hair, while he gently unbuttoned her coat and let his hands roam over the soft fabric of her blouse. "Mmm," she moaned, her breath warm on his face. "I wish you'd take me someplace . . ." He kissed the soft skin of her neck, breathing her perfume. "And make love to me."

After a while he pulled away and looked in her eyes. "Do you?" he said. Grace nodded. "So do I," he said. "God, if only you knew how much." He put both arms around her and held her tight.

"I know it's wrong," she murmured, "but with this crazy war, and you going away again, it makes me not care what happens."

He reached under her legs and lifted her onto his lap like a child. With her arms around his neck she smiled and said, "You make me happier than I've ever felt in my whole life."

Reynolds nodded and said, "You make me feel the same way, sweetheart." He extricated his arm and glanced at his watch. "Uh, oh," he said. "I better get you home or I'm gonna miss the last bus back."

Standing under the porch light at Grace's front door, Reynolds put his arms around her waist and said, "I love you so much."

"And I love you."

"I was serious about wanting to spend the rest of my life with you." She looked imploringly in his eyes and then leaned her face on his chest and murmured, "Oh, John. Nothing would make me happier."

He lifted her chin, kissed her and then said, "Good night, sweetheart. I'll see you next Saturday."

Reynolds stared at his cards, debating whether to discard a seven and a three and draw. "C'mon, Johnny," said Travis Henderson. "What's it gonna be?" Reynolds tossed two cards on the discard pile and drew from the deck on the rickety card table the men had set up in their tent for their regular Sunday afternoon poker game. All four men were wearing their heavy coats on the late winter day. His face a blank mask, Reynolds inserted the cards in his hand.

"You still going out with that gal you met on the streetcar?" asked Porter Davidson.

"Yep," said Reynolds without taking his eyes off his hand.

"Man," said Spook, "just about every guy in this outfit has a New Zealand girlfriend, except for the old married men like me."

"Not me," said Travis. "I promised Bonnie back home I'd stay true to her." Henderson was from the small town of Brady in central Texas, the son of a cattle rancher, and a proud "Aggie" graduate of Texas A&M University.

"Yeah, well, not all the married guys are staying away from the local girls," said Porter Davidson as he drew two cards.

"Are you serious?" said Reynolds with a surprised expression. He tossed two red chips onto the pot.

"I fold," said Spook, tossing his cards on the pile.

"Damned right I'm serious," said Davidson. "Including at least one officer in this battalion. I'm out too."

"See you and raise you a quarter," said Travis, adding three chips to the pot. "Those guys are real s.o.b.s. Pretending to be single with those poor Wellington gals."

The four men looked up as a young private stepped through the flap and said, "Sorry to interrupt, Captain."

"What is it?" said Davidson.

"Major Jones called a meeting of all the officers, sir, at 0400."

"Ten minutes," said Spook.

"I call," said Reynolds, tossing another chip in the pot and overturning his cards. "Three jacks and a queen."

"Damn," said Travis, tossing his cards on the table. "Let's go."

By the time the four arrived at the HQ, most of the other battalion officers were milling around, discussing the usual scuttlebutt and wondering if the hastily called meeting meant that the big moment had finally arrived: orders to ship out to a destination unknown. The next big clash with the Imperial Japanese Army. "All right, men," said their CO, Bill Jones, in a loud voice. "Sit down and listen up." Conversation abruptly ceased as the men sank into folding chairs. Jones sucked on his pipe and expelled a cloud of smoke. "Orders from General Smith," said Jones. "Sometime next week we'll take the battalion to Wellington, where we'll board transports and head for the South Island. A place called Milford Sound. To practice rubber-boat landings." A collective groan passed among the men.

"Sir," said a young lieutenant. "Milford Sound's way down the coast on the South Island. The water's bound to be freezing this time of year. Why not practice here on Whareroa beach?"

"Smith's staff thinks the surf's too rough," said Jones with another puff on his pipe. "They're worried about the boats swamping and men getting drowned."

"Does this mean we're going in on rubber boats in the next amphibious operation?" asked another officer.

"Without a doubt," said Jones. "The decision was made, at the very top, as the CNO, to disband the Raider forces and designate one battalion in each regiment as the inflatable boat unit. And that's us."

"Any idea when or where we're headed, Major, for the next big show?" asked another.

"Not a clue. That dope is restricted to a small group on Smith's staff. But judging from their demeanor at our last meeting, I'd say they're plenty worried about it, and it won't be long. Any other questions? Okay, dismissed."

Standing outside, Spook Beck turned to Reynolds and said, "Hell, I s'pose it's a good idea to get these guys out of here and practice a real live landing. They're getting bored with nothing to do but go into town, get drunk, and try to get laid."

"Or fight," said Reynolds. "Did you hear about that brawl last week-end with some sailors from a British ship that just made port?"

"Yeah," said Spook, "those Limey sailors had no idea what they were gettin' themselves into, and our boys used their belts and put a bunch of 'em in the hospital."

"Well," said Joe Thompson, "I don't know about this Milford Sound place."

"What, are you boys scared of flippin' over your little rubber boats?" said Arnold Schulz, who was standing nearby.

"Who the hell asked your opinion?" snapped Reynolds.

"College boys," muttered Schulz with a smirk.

In an instant Joe Thompson was standing within inches of Schulz, flexing his fists. "I've had it with your college boys crap," he snarled.

"Oh, yeah?" said Schulz. "What are you gonna do about it?"

"Are you nuts?" said Reynolds, quickly stepping between the two men and shoving Schulz backwards. "Joe will knock your block off." Reynolds noticed for the first time that Schulz was wearing a wedding band.

"Oh, forget it, Reynolds," said Schulz. "I was just kiddin' around," he added as he turned and walked off.

"Way to go," said Spook, giving Joe Thompson a shove on the shoulder. "You showed that sonofabitch."

"Well," said Reynolds with a shake of his head, "I just feel for those guys in Baker Company with that jerk as their XO."

Reynolds sat cross-legged by the coal-burning stove in his tent with a notebook in his lap. He thought for a moment, and then wrote: "Dearest Grace,"

The time we had together last night was about the happiest in my whole life, and I want you to know that I meant every word I said. I honestly don't know how much more time we've got here, and it's not just that I want to make the most of it. I want to decide about you and me. Please pray about it. I love you so much.

John

CHAPTER SEVEN

JOHN REYNOLDS STOOD ON THE SHIP'S FANTAIL WEARING the fleece-lined coat the jeep driver from Silverstream had given him, staring at the straight line of the wake that reached all the way to the distant horizon. The eight hundred men of the battalion had boarded two transports in Wellington harbor at 8:00 a.m., with all their gear and several Higgins boats, the low-draft landing craft favored by the Marines designed to carry a platoon of riflemen ashore. As he gazed out over the expanse of blue water Reynolds considered what it must be like to serve in the navy, stuck in the cramped quarters of a ship for weeks on end in the vast, empty ocean, vulnerable to sudden attack by unseen submarines or dive-bombers. No, he wanted solid ground under his feet. Taking a final sip of the dregs of his coffee, he thought about Grace, the feel of her soft skin against his face, her subtle, sweet fragrance when his kissed her neck . . . so this was what falling in love was all about. Why not simply get married? he asked himself for at least the hundredth time. Lots of Marines, both officers and enlisted men, already had New Zealand brides. If only he could talk with his father, a quiet, thoughtful man on whom he could always depend for sound advice.

Turning away from the railing, Reynolds began strolling the deck, which was crammed with equipment and supplies as well as hundreds of Marines avoiding the heat, noise, and stench of the lower decks. As he walked past them he reflected that, with the exception of the NCOs, they were really just boys, eighteen or nineteen for the most part and right out of high school. After the long months of training and hearty food, they were in excellent shape and highly accomplished in handling their weapons—M-1 Garand rifles, BAR automatic rifles, 81 and 60-millimeter mortars, machine guns, and the newest weapon: flame-throwers. It was a formidable fighting force Reynolds was confident could defeat the enemy, but many would die or be grievously wounded, as the Japanese would almost certainly put up a fanatical resistance.

Finally, as the sun sank low in the west, the two ships turned toward shore and entered a deep fjord, ringed on all sides by steep mountains. Unlike the heaving ocean swells, the surface of the water was flat like glass, reflecting a mirror image of the deep blue sky, lilac-tinged clouds, and surrounding snowcapped peaks. As the ships glided across the pond-like water the beauty of the place took Reynolds's breath away. "Holy cow," remarked a young private standing next to him. "Did you ever see anything so pretty?" Reynolds listened to the crackle of static from a nearby loudspeaker.

"Now hear this," came a voice from the bridge. "Prepare to anchor in fifteen minutes. Mess will be served at 1900 hours."

"Hey, Johnny." Reynolds turned to Spook Beck, who had his hands in the pockets of his zip-up khaki jacket for warmth. "Jones called a meeting of all officers in the wardroom. Help me to round 'em up."

Reynolds and Spook were seated at one of the small tables in the cramped wardroom with fresh mugs of black coffee. Major Jones was the only man standing, wearing his khakis and clenching his unlit corncob pipe in his teeth. Reynolds often wondered how he managed not to lose the pipe under the stresses of combat but couldn't remember ever seeing him without it on Guadalcanal. "Okay, gentlemen," said Jones, "here's the drill. The men rise and shine at 0500 and have a hot breakfast. We dress in full combat gear and report on deck at 0630. Meanwhile the Navy crewmen are inflating the boats. We load the boats at first light."

"What's the weather forecast, sir?" asked one of the company commanders.

"Clear and cold," said Jones. "They're predicting an overnight low of twenty-five. With light and variable winds."

After chow, complete with navy beans that reminded Reynolds of the hospital in Auckland, he returned to the ship's fantail and stood at the railing gazing at the dazzling display of stars in the black sky, the unfamiliar constellations of the southern hemisphere. To Reynolds's way of thinking, the beauty of Milford Sound and the spectacular celestial array represented the polar opposite of war, with all its ugliness and senseless destruction of life and property. Or was it senseless? It had certainly been senseless in the First World War, he reflected as he watched a shooting star streak across the sky. But not this war. As terrible as it was, Reynolds was absolutely certain it had to be done, even if it meant, he considered with a shiver, that the life he dreamed of with Grace might never be. Turning to go below, he noticed another dark form resting his arms on the railing.

As Reynolds walked up, Spook Beck turned to look at him and said, "Hello, Johnny. Care for a drink?" He was holding a flask that glinted in the moonlight.

"Sure." Reynolds took the flask and tipped back his head to take a sip of straight bourbon. Handing it back to Spook, he said, "Are you OK? You seemed kind of glum."

Spook took another sip and then said, "Yeah, well, I got some bad news. A letter from my folks before we sailed tellin' me my brother Ted got killed."

Reynolds stared at Spook in the darkness. "Jeez," he said. "That's terrible. What happened?"

"He was a paratrooper," said Spook. "All I know is he was killed in the landings on Sicily back in July. My big brother." He stifled a sob.

Reynolds took a step closer and put an arm around Spook's shoulder. "I'm sorry," he said quietly. "Real sorry."

Spook gazed out in the blackness and then took another sip from his flask. "Another thing, Johnny," he said after a moment. "You ought to ease off of Arnold Schulz."

"Me ease off?" said Reynolds with a surprised expression. "Why, he's the one who's always . . ."

"How would you feel?" said Spook, turning to look at Reynolds. "If you were the only guy without a college degree and never went through Quantico? Why don't you cut the guy some slack?"

"Okay," said Reynolds with a nod.

On the late winter day in the far southern latitudes, the sun was in no hurry to rise, peeking over the summit of a nearby mountain in blinding, prismatic rays at half past seven. Three-hundred-odd Marines were packed onto the transport's deck, wearing their combat utilities, helmets, and packs, plus a bulky life belt encircling their waists. Hours earlier the ship's crew had inflated the rubber boats with compressed air hoses, and now forty or so of the boats, strung together with ropes, were bobbing in the icy water off the side of the ship. The men were arranged by platoons, with A Company forward and B Company aft. As bright sunlight flooded the fjord, the order was passed along to commence loading, and the men clambered over the side, picking their way down to the water on cargo nets, eight men to a boat. The loading went forward without incident in the calm water, the boats scarcely moving in the gentlest of swells, and once completed, Higgins boats maneuvered into position, attaching towlines to three columns of rubber boats. On the orders of the Navy petty officers, the Higgins boats started for shore, approximately two miles in the distance, at a speed of no more than five knots. The Marines crouching in the boats held on tight, trying to keep warm and avoid the freezing spray. Finally, about eight hundred yards from the shoreline, the towlines and ropes were unfastened, and the men began to paddle. It seemed to Reynolds, on his knees in the back of a boat in the middle of the pack, a comparatively safe way to go ashore, as the little boats floated on the surface and thus avoided the risks of striking a mine or grounding on a reef. When the little flotilla was about three hundred yards from shore, shrill whistles signaled the order to stop and turn around, reattach the ropes, and wait for the Higgins boats to tow them back to the ship.

Over the course of the day the battalion repeated the exercise three times, and each time it went more smoothly, with fewer men tangled up on the cargo nets or the boats nearly capsizing. The Marines, Reynolds reflected, were uniquely trained for amphibious warfare, skilled infantry accustomed to traveling on ships and storming a defended beach on small landing craft. Someone high up on the Corps general staff in the

1930s must have envisioned exactly the sort of war they would ultimately have to fight with Japan, capturing island after island across the vast expanse of the Pacific with a Navy large enough to make the complex logistics feasible.

The next morning Reynolds awoke on his cot jammed into one of the ship's holds to the loud thrum of the engines and rocking of the hull. They were moving. He quickly dressed and made his way topside. Judging from the angle of the sun, now obscured by thick clouds, they were headed north, and the mountainous coastline was miles in the distance. He wrapped his arms around himself in the cold and walked quickly down to the wardroom. Though most of the men were still getting dressed, he found Travis Henderson at one of the tables, sipping black coffee and smoking a Lucky Strike. "Pull up a chair, boy," said Travis, "and one of these fellers will bring you some java." Within moments a Filipino messmate appeared and served Reynolds a steaming mug.

"Where're we headed?" said Reynolds before blowing on the surface of his coffee and taking a sip.

"I asked Jones," said Travis, "who was up early too, and he said some place called the Franz Josef Glacier." He took a drag on his cigarette and knocked off some ash on the side of an ashtray.

"Funny name for New Zealand," said Reynolds.

"Well, we're gonna practice some more rubber boat landings and then head for home."

By midmorning, standing at the railing, Reynolds noticed that the wind was rising off the port quarter and the ocean swells were deeper and cresting with white spray. At 1100 hours an announcement crackled over the loudspeakers: "Assemble on deck in platoons at 1300 hours in full battle dress." Reynolds watched as the Navy crew lowered the inflated boats over the side. The ship turned into another fjord surrounded by steep mountains like Milford Sound but with a massive, blue-white glacier at the far end that wound down the mountainside to the water's edge. When the ship ground to a halt, the bow was pitching in heavy swells, and some of the men were already seasick, retching over the side. *Maybe they'll call the damn thing off*, thought Reynolds. But precisely at 1300 hours the men were ordered over the side, clambering down the cargo nets into the bobbing rubber boats. Towlines were attached to the

Higgins boats, and the flotilla of some eighty rubber boats was moving toward the distant shoreline, the Marines clinging to the sides and trying to avoid the icy seawater that washed over the bows. Once the boats were cut loose, and the men began to paddle the final eight hundred yards, a twenty-knot wind was blowing, filling the fjord with whitecaps. The men paddled hard, struggling to keep the awkward boats moving toward shore and avoid capsizing. *C'mon*, thought Reynolds as water streamed from his helmet and stung his eyes, *let's turn these boats around.* Just then a powerful wind gust raked the little boats, instantly flipping one over, immediately to the right of Reynolds. Weighed down by their heavy gear, the eight men briefly disappeared below the surface and then shot back up again, fighting for breath. "Inflate your life belts!" yelled Reynolds and several sergeants, referring to the cords the men were instructed to yank to fill the belts with compressed CO_2. But they were too stunned by the frigid water to find the cords and in obvious peril of drowning. "Haul 'em out!" bellowed a master sergeant, reaching out to one of the thrashing men with his paddle.

Within minutes all of the men had been fished from the water and were back in their boat, dazed and coughing up seawater. The boats were quickly roped together and attached to the towlines for the ten-minute ride back to the ship. By the time they arrived, the men whose boat had capsized, in shock from hypothermia, were hoisted on deck in slings and immediately sent to the sickbay. The others hurried below to get out of the freezing wind, strip off their gear and waterlogged utilities, and change into dry clothing. When Reynolds finally made it to the wardroom and poured a mug of hot chocolate, he turned to Spook Beck, standing in line behind him, and said, "That was some dumbass idea. A whole bunch of guys could've drowned." Spook merely nodded and helped himself to hot chocolate. They made their way to a table occupied by several other officers.

"You're right, Johnny," said Spook as he sat in one of the vacant chairs. "I don't know what Jones was thinking."

"This is a glacier fjord," said Reynolds. "Like I've read about in Alaska. If we hadn't gotten those guys out of the water in under five minutes, they'd all be dead." The other officers at the table, who'd evidently been too far away to witness what had happened, gave Reynolds a curious look. "And the way that wind was blowin'," said Reynolds, "it's a wonder more boats didn't flip over."

"Yep," said Spook with a sardonic grin. "We gotta keep these boys alive long enough to go back and fight the goddam Japs."

The near-drowning incident must have chastened the CO and his staff, as without any further announcements the transports weighed anchors and began steaming north. Arriving at Wellington harbor after midnight, the Marines spent another night in the ships' cramped, fetid holds and then were up at dawn, packing their gear and eager to return to Mackays Crossing. When his bus turned in at the main entrance, Reynolds rubbed the stubble of beard on his chin and listened to the growl of his empty stomach, trying to decide whether it was Thursday or Friday. Thankfully, it was Friday, and after a shave, hot shower, and donning fresh khakis, the word was passed among the officers that the battalion had been granted an all-day pass, beginning at ten o'clock Saturday morning. As soon as he was able, Reynolds placed a call to Grace, leaving word with her mother, who responded with her usual lack of warmth, that he'd be calling on Grace by noon the following day.

On the bus ride into town, Reynolds gazed out the partially open window on the clear morning, the hillsides pale green after months of cold and rain and beginning to fill with wildflowers. It was October, he reflected, almost a year since they'd sailed from San Diego, all but two months of which he'd spent on the North Island of New Zealand or on board ship. How much longer would it last? Several more months, or possibly just weeks? Arriving at the depot, he bid his comrades goodbye, straightened the front of his olive drab tunic, and started on the familiar walk to the streetcar. When he arrived at the Lucas bungalow, Grace was sitting in the porch swing, wearing a bright floral dress and a hat worn on the back of her stylishly curled brown hair. She waited until he mounted the last step and then sprang up to embrace him, her slender arms encircling his waist and face pressed against his chest. "Oh, John," she said. "What a treat. The whole day together!"

He pulled away, looked in her eyes, and said, "Shouldn't we go inside?"

"No," said Grace with an emphatic shake of her head. "I had an awful row with Mother and don't want to go through it again."

"Over what?"

Grace hesitated and then said, "Over us." She reached for her purse, put her arm through his, and said, "Let's be on our way."

Exiting the streetcar in downtown Wellington, Grace took John's hand and said, "We've got all day. What should we do?"

"I want to go shopping," said John with a smile.

"Shopping? For what?"

"None of your beeswax. Now I suppose you can find your way to Kirkcaldies."

"That's the last place I want to go on my day off."

"Fine," said Reynolds. "You can sit in the park while I go shopping. I won't be long." Grace gave him a quizzical, sidelong glance and began walking. When they arrived at the massive department store, Reynolds looked at his watch and said, "Why don't you wait over there?" He motioned to the small park facing the harbor. "I should be back in twenty minutes."

"Should I come with you?"

"No, ma'am. You just wait for me in the park." Reynolds gave her hand a gentle squeeze and turned to walk to the revolving door. Once inside he quickly consulted the directory and took the escalator to the second level. After checking with a clerk, he found his way to the jewelry department and caught the attention of one of the ladies behind the glass counters.

"Another Marine," she remarked. "Let me guess. Shopping for an engagement ring?"

"That's right, ma'am. But I'm on a budget. A hundred American dollars."

She walked midway down the counter, unlocked the glass case, and removed a selection of gold bands with small diamond settings. Ten minutes later Reynolds was on the escalator down to the first floor, patting the small box in his tunic pocket. Exiting in the warm sunshine, he quickly found Grace on a park bench, gazing out on the forest of masts in the harbor. "Hi, sweetie," said Reynolds, walking up from behind and giving her a hug and kiss on the cheek.

"What did you buy?" asked Grace. "You should have asked my advice."

"Not today," said Reynolds with a grin. "I'm starved. Let's have lunch."

Seated in a booth by the front window in a nearby lunchroom, Reynolds sipped his milkshake through a straw and looked happily at Grace. She took a final bite of ham and cheese sandwich and then said, "Tell me about Milford Sound. I've never been."

"You should go. It's one of the most beautiful places I've ever seen. But I'd wait till summer."

"You were practicing in boats?"

Reynolds nodded as he finished his shake with a sucking sound. "Little rubber boats," he said. "They tow us most of the way in and then we paddle the last half mile to the beach."

"Why not simply ride in on the larger landing boats?"

"Good question. They're some places where it's too hard or dangerous for the landing craft—what we call Higgins boats—to go ashore. So one of our battalions goes in on inflatable boats, which can land just about anywhere."

Grace looked out the window, appearing to study the people walking past on the busy sidewalk. After a moment she turned back to John and said, "I hate the thought of you landing on some island, crawling with Japanese soldiers . . ."

Reynolds stared into her hazel eyes and nodded, conscious of the warmth of her hands. "What would you like to do, sweetie?" he said after a minute. "We could go to the movies."

"Do you remember Doris?" said Grace. "I introduced you at one of the dances."

"Sure, I think so."

"She's one of my oldest friends from school, and she's having a party tonight," said Grace. "At her parents' house overlooking the bay. We're invited."

"That would be swell," said Reynolds, relieved at the change of subject. "Are you finished with lunch? Where would you like to go?"

"Have you taken the cable car up to Kelburn?"

"No, but I've heard about it."

"It's such a lovely day and the view's beautiful. We could visit the Botanic Garden."

Rounding the corner, they walked past a small photography studio whose proprietor was standing in the doorway. "Say, Marine," he called out to Reynolds with a smile. "Get your picture taken with your girl?"

Exchanging a brief look with Grace, Reynolds said, "Why not?"

Standing behind a partition against a black backdrop, Reynolds slipped his arm around Grace's slender waist. The photographer bent over his camera, which was mounted on a tripod, and said, "Smile!" They both complied, and the photographer snapped the picture with the pop of a flashbulb. "Just fill out this card," he said, "and let me know where you want me to mail the photo. That'll be fifty shillings." Reynolds reached into his pocket, paid the photographer, and then walked with Grace out onto the sunny sidewalk. Within ten minutes, they were squeezed into the farthest back seat of a bright red cable car, which was packed with Marines, their girlfriends, and a number of older couples, making its steep ascent from the central shopping district to the heights of the Kelburn suburb. Arriving at the summit, Grace took John's hand and they strolled to the overlook with its panoramic view of the city, the harbor below, and the deep blue water of Cook Strait. They wandered the adjoining Botanic Garden, with its profusion of exotic flora and trees native to the island, saying little and savoring the sensation of holding hands or her arms around his waist, conscious of the preciousness of their little time together. As the shadows lengthened, they sat on a wooden bench next to the rose garden, with Reynolds's arm around Grace's shoulder, enjoying the roses' special perfume. "You know how much I love you," he said softly. She merely nodded and scrunched closer. "I want to marry you," he said. She pulled away, looked into his eyes, and then kissed him.

"Oh, John" she said after a moment. "That would make me so happy."

"Your folks would never approve."

"It's not their decision," said Grace. "It's our life, John."

"I wish you could meet my mom and dad. They'd be crazy about you."

"They must be wonderful, after all the things you've told me about them."

"Listen, sweetie," said John, giving Grace a serious look. "I've been doing a lot of thinking. We don't want to run off and get married without your parents' consent, right before I have to . . . before we ship out."

"No," she said with a forlorn expression. "I suppose not, though it would serve them right."

"So," said John with a small smile, "I've got something for you." He reached into his pocket for a small velvet box and handed it to her. She glanced from the box to John. "Go on," he said. "Open it."

"Oh, my gosh," said Grace, opening the box and staring at the ring.

"It's an engagement ring, sweetie. Nobody needs to know but you and me."

"Oh, John," exclaimed Grace, throwing her arms around him. "I love you more than you'll ever know."

Reynolds took the ring from the box and gently slid it on her finger. He squeezed her hand and said, "We'll get married just as soon as I come back. And we talk to your parents."

CHAPTER EIGHT

JOHN STOOD AT THE RAILING ON THE VERANDAH ADMIRING the view of downtown Wellington, whose lights were beginning to glimmer, with a band of mauve just above the hilltops beyond the city. Grace was inside with her friends, helping with dinner in the kitchen of the rambling, two-story cottage in the Lyall Bay suburb, a fifteen minute ride by streetcar from Lambton Quay. Hearing men's voices, he turned as three Marines appeared on the front steps and let themselves in. All three were lieutenants with a single silver bar on their shoulder straps, but unfamiliar to Reynolds. He took his half-finished bottle of beer and went inside. His entrance coincided with that of the party's hostess, Grace's friend Doris Campbell, and two of the other women.

"Hello, ladies," said one of the Marines, taking off his hat. "I'm Jim Wilson, and these are my buddies, Tom O'Hara and Fred Brown."

"I invited Jim," said one of the women as she walked up to him and put her arm through his, "and told him to bring along some friends."

"Welcome," said Doris, who was tall and athletic but not very pretty. "Help yourselves to something to drink while we're getting supper ready."

"I'll show you where to find the drinks," said Reynolds as he walked up. "John Reynolds, with the 1/6."

The men gave Reynolds friendly handshakes, explaining they were with the Second Battalion, Eighth Marines. "And we brought along another guy," said Wilson, "from your outfit, but he stopped to buy some smokes."

"Really?" said Reynolds. "Who's that?"

"Arnold Schulz," said the man named O'Hara, who looked older than the others. "Old buddy of mine with the Fourth Marines in China." Like Schulz, O'Hara spoke with a distinctly working class, Northern accent.

"Yeah, I know Arnold," said Reynolds. *Jeez*, he thought. *I can't believe they invited that jerk to the party.*

"So that thing you guys from the Sixth wear on your shoulder," said O'Hara.

"The fourragère?"

"Yeah," said O'Hara with a smirk. "I heard it means you got VD." The other men snickered.

At that moment Arnold Schulz appeared at the door. Quickly scanning the room, he said, "Hey, Reynolds. Whaddya doin' here?"

"Same as you, Arnold," said Reynolds with a thin smile. "Invited to the party. I'll show y'all where to find the drinks." The four officers followed Reynolds out onto the verandah, illuminated by a porch light, where there was a cooler with iced-down bottles of beer and soda pop and a punch bowl and glasses on a small table. The Marines reached for beers and opened them with a church key.

After taking a long swallow, Schulz tipped back his hat and said, "So, Reynolds. What'd you do to rate an invitation?"

"My girl's an old friend of Doris."

"Who's Doris?" said Schulz.

"This is her house and her party," said Reynolds irritably. At the sound of female laughter through the open window, the Marines returned to the living room, which was now filled with six young women. Reynolds walked up to Grace and said, "Hi, honey. Can I get you something to drink?"

"Punch would be lovely."

As he returned to the punch bowl, Reynolds considered that there were only five men to the six women. Just as he filled a glass and started for the living room, another officer appeared on the front steps wearing the uniform of an officer in the Royal Navy, with a single gold stripe on the sleeve.

"Good evening, Doris," called out the officer in a crisply enunciated British accent. "Ah, the men of the vaunted Unites States Marine Corps."

As Schulz and O'Hara exchanged slightly malevolent looks, Reynolds stepped forward, reached out his hand, and said, "I'm John Reynolds."

"Andrew Cadbury," said the officer with a warm handshake. "Lieutenant in His Majesty's Royal Navy." O'Hara chuckled quietly at the British pronunciation of "lieutenant."

"Andrew's ship recently made port," said Doris. "He's an old friend, and I thought he'd enjoy meeting some Yanks."

"You from that British destroyer that arrived the other day?" said O'Hara.

"That's right. HMS *Tenacious*."

O'Hara glared at Cadbury and then said, "Your crew beat up some of our guys." *Uh oh*, thought Reynolds.

"Actually," said Cadbury equably, "it was the other way round. Our sailors were on the losing end of that melee, as I understand it."

"Relax," said Reynolds. "It was just a friendly little barroom brawl." He stepped between the two men.

"John," said Doris tartly, "would you please show Andrew where he can find the drinks?"

Reynolds walked with Cadbury out on the verandah and reached for two bottles of beer. "Here you go," he said before popping off the caps. He noticed that Schulz had followed them and was standing in the shadows by the punch bowl.

"Your division was on Guadalcanal?" said Cadbury before taking a swallow.

"Just at the very end," said Reynolds. "We relieved the First Division. By then the Japs were pretty well licked, though they did manage to put a bullet through my thigh."

"I see," said Cadbury. "We've been on patrol off the north coast of Australia. Rather dull duty." Reynolds and Cadbury leaned against the railing, looking across the bay at the twinkling city lights. Unobserved, Schulz took a pint bottle from his breast pocket, unscrewed the cap and tipped its contents into the punch bowl before slipping back inside. Five minutes later, Doris appeared and announced: "Come along, everyone. Supper's on the table."

Grace walked out on the verandah and said, "John, could I have more punch?" Reynolds ladled punch into Grace's glass and then walked to the dining room, where the places were set with steaming bowls of soup at two tables of six. He handed Grace her glass and then sat beside her. Thankfully, he noted, both Schulz and O'Hara were at the other table, and Andrew Cadbury was at his, next to Doris. Soup was followed by pot roast, with the women clearing the tables and waiting on the men. As Reynolds helped himself to a hot dinner roll he could overhear Schulz telling an off-color joke in a too-loud voice and, to his Texas ears, offensive Pennsylvania coal country accent. He gave Grace a pained expression and noticed that her glass was empty. "More punch?" he asked. Grace responded with a nod and he excused himself. When he returned with another beer and Grace's punch he observed that Schulz, who was smoking a cigarette at the dinner table, had his arm around the waist of the rather plain young woman in the chair next to him. He also noticed that the wedding band was missing from Schulz's left hand.

"Mmm," said Grace after taking a sip. "That's got quite a kick."

"Really?" said Reynolds, assuming it was only fruit juice and seltzer. The laughter and conversation from the other table grew even louder amid the haze of cigarette smoke.

"I've got a pie to take from the oven," said Doris, rising from her chair.

"I'll see if I can be of service," said Lieutenant Cadbury. Two other women also rose and began clearing away the dinner plates.

"Let's get a breath of fresh air," Reynolds suggested to Grace. He helped her from her chair and accompanied her to the verandah.

"That's better," he said, standing at the railing and taking a deep breath of cold night air. "I can't stand that guy."

"The one called Schulz?" said Grace quietly, standing close. Reynolds nodded and said, "And his buddy."

Grace reached for John's hand and gave it a gentle squeeze. "Let's have some more punch. It's rather good." Reynolds ladled two glasses and returned with Grace to the table just as Doris was carrying in her pie on a serving plate, followed by Andrew Cadbury with two bottles of champagne.

"Champagne!" said one of the girls. "Lovely!"

"I'll stick with the beer," said Schulz, pushing back from the table. Once the others had been served lemon pie and a glass of champagne Andrew Cadbury raised his glass and said, "I propose a toast. To the fighting men of the Marine Corps and a swift victory over the Japanese."

CHAPTER EIGHT

"And to the men of the Royal Navy," added Reynolds.

"And maybe," said Schulz, who was standing in the doorway, in a voice just loud enough to be heard, "the limeys will finally get off their butts and help us whip the goddam Japs." The room immediately fell silent.

"How dare you," said Cadbury with barely controlled fury. "I should take you outside and teach you a lesson."

Schulz almost stumbled as he moved toward the table and said, "I'd like to see you try."

He's drunk and about four inches shorter than Cadbury, thought Reynolds. *And Cadbury has had, at most, half a beer.*

"Sit down, Arnold," said Jim Wilson, who was evidently responsible for inviting him. "And apologize to the lieutenant."

"I ain't apologizin' to nobody," said Schulz.

"Very well," said Cadbury as he too rose from his chair.

"Please, Andrew," said Doris, who also was standing. "Let's not have a fight."

"Do something, John," stage-whispered Grace.

Reynolds leaned over and quietly said, "This guy's a real low life. It's time someone taught him a lesson." Cadbury, who seemed to know his way around the house, walked into the kitchen, followed by a sullen Arnold Schulz and his friend O'Hara and, somewhat reluctantly, the other three Marines, while the women remained in the dining room, staring unhappily at their dessert. Cadbury descended a staircase at the back of the cottage, switched on a porch light and walked out into a small, enclosed yard. He wordlessly took off his jacket and tossed it on the stairs and rolled up his sleeves as he watched Schulz do the same.

Reynolds walked up to Schulz and said, "Listen, Arnold. You're way out of line. That's no way for a Marine officer to . . ."

"Oh, so I don't rank as an officer in your book, Reynolds?"

"I didn't say that . . ."

"Aw, fuck you, Reynolds."

"And there's another thing," said Reynolds hotly, taking a step closer. "I'm fed up with you married guys pretending to be single." Without warning Schulz lunged at Reynolds and threw an awkward punch, just grazing Reynolds's cheek.

"Hey, just a minute!" said Cadbury, moving toward Schulz. Before Cadbury could intervene, Reynolds stepped in and delivered a quick

81

combination, a left jab and strong right cross, both landing squarely and sending Schulz to the ground. Stunned, Schulz rested on one knee, blood streaming from his nose.

"C'mon, Arnold!" yelled O'Hara. "Get up!"

"No, I think that's enough," said Cadbury, stepping between the two men. Turning to O'Hara, he said, "What don't you get some ice for your friend's nose and then take him back to base." Satisfied the brief contest was over, the other Marines disappeared into the house while Reynolds rubbed his cheek. Schulz sat on the grass, holding a hand to his bloody nose, unwilling to look up.

"C'mon," said Reynolds to Cadbury. "Let's go inside."

"Are you all right?" said Cadbury.

"Sure," said Reynolds.

Ten minutes later, after the others had gone, Reynolds sat on the sofa with his arm around Grace holding glasses of champagne facing Cadbury, with a glass of brandy, and Doris, with coffee.

"You're sure you're all right?" Grace asked Reynolds.

"I'm fine," said Reynolds. "You were right about that punch, honey. It does have a kick."

"And so does yours," said Cadbury with a smile. "Punch, that is."

"Well, I boxed in college," said Reynolds. "And that jerk was drunk. Believe me, he's not your typical Marine." Grace snuggled close to him. "He's a mustang," Reynolds explained, as much to the women as to Cadbury. "Promoted up from the ranks, with a big chip on his shoulder."

"A chip that just got knocked off," said Doris, giving Reynolds an admiring look. Reynolds glanced at his watch, noting that it was early, not even nine o'clock. Thanks to Schulz's outlandish behavior, they now had the evening almost to themselves, and in the privacy of a waterfront cottage for a change.

"Let's take a walk on the beach," suggested Doris. "It's lovely in the moonlight."

"Y'all go on without us," said Reynolds. "Grace and I don't get too much time alone."

"I'm game," said Cadbury, rising from his chair.

After a few moments Doris and Andrew were out the door, and Reynolds stretched out on the sofa with Grace snuggling next to him. Placing his arm around her, he pulled her close and kissed her, lightly at first but with growing passion. "Mmm," she murmured. "Don't stop." He awkwardly leaned over and switched off the lamp. Reaching an arm around his neck, she kissed him, molding her body close to his. With her free hand she fumbled with the buttons of his jacket in the semi-darkness. "Oh, God," he whispered, "I love you so much." She reached a hand inside his jacket and massaged the hard muscles of his chest as he let his free hand roam over the soft fabric of her blouse. After a few minutes, he pulled away and said, "What if Doris comes in?"

"I've got an idea," said Grace with a tipsy giggle. "There's a little room downstairs where I used to stay when I'd come out for a summer weekend."

"Are you sure? I mean . . ." She stood up from the sofa, took him by the hand, and with a conspiratorial glance led him to the stairs. Descending, Reynolds could dimly make out a hallway, at the end of which was a small spare bedroom. Grace led John inside, switched on a lamp and carefully closed and locked the door. She kicked off her shoes and, standing on tiptoes, threw her arms around him and kissed him. "Mmm," she murmured again. "Take off your coat." Reynolds unbuckled his belt, shrugged off his jacket, and tossed it a chair. Taking both his hands, she fell back on the twin bed and pulled him down on her. Resting on his elbows, he kissed her with even more passion. He somehow managed to get off his shoes and rolled over on his side. He looked briefly in her eyes, which were flashing with desire, and fumbled with the buttons of her blouse while he kissed her. Vaguely aware that the alcohol had weakened his inhibitions, he ran his hands over her breasts while she pressed her thigh against him. *Oh, my God*, he thought, *we should stop before it's too late.* In the next instant her nimble fingers were untying his tie, unbuttoning his shirt, and undoing his pants, while he unzipped her skirt. "God, John," she whispered, "I love you so much. I don't care what happens." For a brief moment he hesitated, but then, overwhelmed with desire, he undressed her, and turning her on her back, made love to her for what seemed a long time. Both were novices but discovered to their delight how natural, how wonderful, was their lovemaking after so many months of restrained desire. At last, lying in each other's arms in contented exhaustion, they almost drifted asleep until they sat bolt upright at the sound of a door closing and voices from upstairs.

"Quick!" whispered John. "I'll get on my clothes and head 'em off." He sprang up and quickly dressed, buttoning up his jacket and smoothing his hair as he hurried down the hall and up the stairs.

"Where's Grace?" asked Doris, who was seated on the sofa.

"Oh, she'll be up in a minute," said Reynolds as he straightened the front of his jacket. "She was just showing me around the house." Reynolds was relieved when Andrew Cadbury entered the room until he realized that Cadbury was staring at his shoes, which in his haste he'd neglected to tie. He was about to say something when he heard Grace coming up the stairs.

"What's the matter?" said Grace with a smile when she appeared. "John and I have been downstairs necking in the spare room where I used to stay on sleepovers." Blushing in spite of himself, Reynolds sat in one of the armchairs and reached down to tie his shoes.

"Well, I don't blame you, Gracie," said Doris. "I know what I'd do if I had a great-looking beau like John."

Reynolds stole a glance at his watch. "Gee," he said, "we better run if I'm gonna make the last bus back to base."

Seated in the almost empty streetcar, Reynolds held Grace's hand in his lap and gazed into her eyes. "That was pretty wonderful, you know," he said after a moment.

She nodded and said, "It certainly was. And just think, once we're married we can make love whenever we like."

Standing in the shadows on the front porch of the Lucas's bungalow, Reynolds held Grace in his arms. "No matter what happens, John," she said, "I'll always remember tonight as one of the most special in my life."

Aware that if he lingered any longer he'd risk missing the last shuttle, Reynolds nodded and said, "Me too." He leaned down and kissed her.

She broke away and said, "You're leaving soon, aren't you?"

"Yes, but we won't know when until the day comes."

"I can't stand it," said Grace, her voice breaking. "How can I be sure that I'll see you before . . . before your ship leaves?"

"I'll get word to you somehow, I promise. You've got your ring?"

"Right here." She reached into her pocket and slipped it on.

"I love you, sweetheart, and I promise I'll be back for you."

Wiping away a tear, she said, "I love you, John. I'll be praying for you every day."

With a final kiss and squeeze of her hands, he said, "Goodbye."

Late the following day, a Sunday on which the entire battalion had taken a five mile run in the hills following church, Reynolds was enjoying a beer with Spook Beck in the Officers' Club. Spook took a drag on his cigarette and said, "I heard you beat up the Avenger."

"The Avenger?"

"The name the boys in Baker Company have given Arnold Schulz." Spook stubbed out his cigarette and took a swallow of beer. "Cause he's always talking about takin' revenge on the Japs."

"Well," said Reynolds, "Schulz is a big talker but I'm not sure how much fight he's got in him."

"I thought you were gonna cut him some slack, Johnny?"

"Hold on, Spook. It wasn't my fault. Schulz insulted this British naval officer and challenged him to a fight. And he showed up at this party without his wedding ring. It really pissed me off. Anyway, he threw a punch at me, so I let him have it."

"Right on the nose," said Spook with a frown. "It's the talk of the battalion. Which is bad for esprit de corps."

"Well, I'm sorry," said Reynolds. "But the guy's what we call poor white trash back in Texas." Both men turned as Travis Henderson hurried into the room, almost at a run. "Hey, Travis," said Spook. "What's up?"

"We're shipping out," said Travis breathlessly. "I just got word straight from the horse's mouth. The whole division's packing up and moving to Wellington first thing in the morning."

"Where to?" said Reynolds.

"Well," said Travis, lowering his voice, "officially, the destination's Hawke's Bay, for more landing exercises. But I'm sure we'll get the straight dope once we're aboard ship."

CHAPTER NINE

Up before dawn, the division's twenty-odd-thousand men donned their combat utilities and steel "hats," loaded their transport packs, and left their other uniforms and belongings behind in their footlockers. The First Battalion, Sixth Marines were wearing the newly issued camouflage uniform while most of the other units wore their standard green herringbone twills. By midmorning a long column of dull green buses pulled into the Wellington dockyards in a lightly falling rain, where the men were ordered to fall in and wait for the ships to be loaded for the short journey to their announced destination: Hawke's Bay, about fifty miles north of Wellington on the east coast of the North Island. By the time the buses arrived at Aotea Quay, the wharves were piled high with equipment and supplies, and none of it, so far as Reynolds could see, was going on board the ships, as there were no longshoremen in sight and the loading cranes were idle. Curious, he walked to the gate at the entrance to the nearest pier, where a burly Marine sergeant was engaged in a shouting match with a civilian official.

"Whaddya mean your men don't work in the rain?" said the sergeant.

"Those are the rules," said the official, his arms crossed over his chest.

"And you call this rain?" said the sergeant with a stamp of his boot. "It's just a light drizzle. Are your guys afraid of gettin' wet?"

"It's a safety regulation," said the official hotly.

Jeez, thought Reynolds, deciding to return to his company, *this looks like a real mess.* He walked up to Bill Jones, the battalion CO, who was consulting a loading chart, and said, "Sir, looks like there's a big snafu."

"What's that?" Jones puffed on his corncob pipe.

"The dockworkers are refusing to load the ships. Cause of the rain, if that's what you call this."

"I know," said Jones sourly. "Word came down from division that the union won't work in the rain."

"Can't the government make them?"

"Well, the general's trying. But he's not optimistic. It's a socialist government, and they probably won't stand up to the union."

"That's a heckuva note. We've come all the way down here to protect 'em from the Japs, and they won't even load our ships."

"We're gonna have to load the transports ourselves. I sent the order to Davis in Charlie Company. In the meantime, tell your men to sit tight."

"Yes, sir. But let me ask you this. Where are we really headed? I mean, we sure don't need all this stuff for another landing exercise."

"All I know, Reynolds," said Jones with another puff on his pipe, "is the destination's Hawke's Bay. I even saw the orders to transport the men back to Wellington on trains."

Despite the assurances that they were only boarding the large naval task force for more maneuvers, the rumor had spread like wildfire among countless young New Zealand brides and girlfriends that this was the long-awaited, and dreaded, event: the Marines' departure to assault another Japanese stronghold in the Pacific. Thousands of nearly hysterical women had forced their way into the dockyards, desperate for what might prove to be a final farewell; they were herded by the police and MPs into a block-long area cordoned off by wooden barricades. With the delay occasioned by the longshoremen's walkout, thousands of Marines, John Reynolds among them, crowded the barricades, searching the faces of the young women on the other side. As soon as he'd learned they were shipping out, Reynolds had waited in a long line to place a call to Grace to let her know. And now he stood at the barricade, gazing into the crowd. It was not so high to prevent a man, if he was lucky enough to find his wife or girl in the dense throng, from leaning across for a hug and kiss. In the midst of the chaotic scene, Reynolds could hear Grace's voice, calling his name, from somewhere in the back of the crowd. Gripping the wooden barrier, he scanned hundreds of faces until he saw her at last, pushing and shoving her way to the front. With tears streaking her face, she reached for his outstretched hands. "Oh, John," she said as he leaned over to embrace her. "I thought I'd never find you."

"It's okay, baby," he said, holding her tight.

"Everyone says this is the real thing," said Grace, pulling away and looking in his eyes. "That you're leaving to fight the Japs."

"That's just a rumor," said Reynolds as calmly as possible. "My CO swears we're just headed up to Hawke's Bay for maneuvers."

"John," said Grace, "if it's not, I promise I'll be waiting for you no matter how long it takes. And I'll be praying for you every day."

"And I promise I'll come back for you, Grace. I'll try to write, but you know how hard it can be to send mail." Hearing the shrill blasts of whistles, which he suspected was the order for the men to board the ships, Reynolds held Grace in a tight embrace. "Darling," he whispered, "I love you so much. And if something should happen to me . . ."

"Please, don't say it."

"I'll make sure someone gets word to you . . ."

"Just come back, John," she pleaded. "Please, just come back . . ."

"C'mon, you guys!" shouted a sergeant. "Get back to your units! Time to load up!"

Reynolds gave Grace a long kiss, holding her in his arms, and then said, "Goodbye, darling. I love you."

"And I love you too . . ."

He gave her a parting look before turning and starting to walk away with the mass of men, his ears filled with the sobs and wails of hundreds of women. With his heart in his throat he found his way to the area where his company was assembled. Thankfully, he spotted Spook Beck, sitting on wooden crate. "That our ship?" said Reynolds, gesturing to the vessel moored at a nearby pier.

"Yep, and she's a dandy," said Spook. "The USS *Feland*. One of the navy's rapid attack transports."

Reynolds studied the ship with its sleek lines, camouflage paint scheme, twin stacks aft of the mast, 40-millimeter gun turret in the bow, and brightly colored signal flags snapping on the halyards. A detail of

Marines was hauling supplies up the gangways. "She looks brand-new," he commented.

"Just commissioned in June," said Spook, "according to the skipper. And she's fast, cruises at twenty-five to thirty knots." The new transports were a key element of the Marines' plans for amphibious warfare, able to move entire divisions of heavily armed infantry, supported by aircraft, artillery, and tanks, swiftly across wide expanses of the ocean to strike the enemy almost at will.

Reynolds sat with his back resting against his pack and clasped his arms around his knees. As he stared at the ship he tried, unsuccessfully, to get the image of Grace from his mind, smiling in spite of her tears. With all the matériel going on board the *Feland* and numerous other ships in the harbor, he refused to believe they were merely sailing up the coast on maneuvers. No, this was no drill. The only question, whose answer was probably known to not more than a dozen staff officers, was where they would hit the Japs. Wake Island, to avenge the Japanese attack there, or maybe another stronghold in the Solomons? Finally, by midafternoon the ships were loaded and the men given the order to fall in and board by companies, with Able Company going last. When Reynolds, wearing his helmet and carrying a full pack, stepped off the gangway, Lieutenant Schulz was standing nearby, lounging against a bulkhead with a cigarette in his lips. He briefly made eye contact with Reynolds, an inscrutable look, and then turned away. In the days since the fistfight, Schulz had been careful to avoid Reynolds and had been shunned by almost all of the battalion's other officers, as Reynolds was one of the most popular. Reynolds turned to the deck to stand at the railing and gaze out on the docks and the Wellington skyline. The area where the women were cordoned off was out of view and, thankfully, out of earshot. He stayed at the railing until the last of the battalion's almost eight hundred men were on board and the crew began preparations to sail. Feeling the deck vibrating under his feet and the deep thrum of the engines, he turned toward the stern where the screw was churning the dark water. The order to cast off was shouted, and with almost the entire battalion crowding the deck, the *Feland* eased away from the pier and then gently turned toward the mole at the entrance to the half-moon harbor. As the ship gathered way, Reynolds spotted a small group of women at the end of a pier, clutching their hats and waving handkerchiefs. With a lump in his throat, he waved back, wondering if Grace might be among them. After a few minutes the women passed out of view as the ship glided from the harbor toward the swells of the open sea, in a convoy of sixteen transports. Reynolds tightly gripped the varnished teak railing, saying nothing to the men around him but paying close attention to the direction of the ship's bow in relation to the coastline. For a moment they were steering directly toward it but then slowly turned to port until the shore was on their starboard quarter.

With a frown Reynolds decided to go below. On his way down the companionway he encountered Travis Henderson, whose face was pale and drawn and who uncharacteristically merely grunted as he went past. Entering his cabin Reynolds found Joe Thompson, sorting the gear in his pack. "What's got into Travis?" asked Reynolds. "Looks like he's sick."

"It's just a bad hangover," said Thompson. "He managed to get drunk before they kicked him out of the OC last night."

"That's not like Travis."

"Evidently he got some bad news," said Thompson. "A letter from his girl back home."

Reynolds slumped on one of the lower bunks and said, "Well, you can forget about Hawke's Bay."

"How do you mean?" said Thompson, holding a rolled-up pair of socks.

"We're headed up the west coast of the island."

"So?"

"Hawke's Bay is on the east coast. We're sailing for parts unknown. I'm gonna go look for Trav."

Reynolds found him on deck leaning against the railing looking like he might throw up. Reynolds wordlessly stood next to him. After a few moments Travis turned to him and said, "You got any aspirin?"

"Yeah, I think so," said Reynolds. "In my Dopp kit."

"My head's killin' me," said Travis.

"I'll go down in a second," said Reynolds. As Travis extracted a cigarette and tamped it on the face of his watch, Reynolds said, "I heard you got a letter from Bonnie?"

Travis nodded as he lit the cigarette with his Zippo. He exhaled and said, "Yep. A regular dear John letter."

"Jeez, that's awful."

"And after I'd been savin' myself for her all these months. Christ, I've been goin' out with Bonnie since we were in high school."

"I thought y'all were more or less engaged?"

"Well, she didn't have a ring. And so this other guy comes along, and the next thing you know they're hitched. So it's goodbye to poor ol' Travis."

"Well, I'm really sorry," said Reynolds. "What a rotten break."

"And to make things worse," said Travis, "the guy's a goddam teasip."

"A Longhorn like me?"

Travis nodded and said, "Yep. A damned teasip like you, John."

"Well, she made a big mistake," said Reynolds as he patted Travis on the back. "I'll go below for those aspirin."

For the next two days they steamed north on the open sea under clear skies, and each day the temperature grew warmer and the transports were joined by naval escorts, destroyers and cruisers. Having been separated from his cherished books during his long convalescence in Auckland, Reynolds had made sure to pack three paperbacks, a history of the Battle of Gallipoli, Hemingway's *For Whom the Bell Tolls*, and a slender volume of Shakespeare's sonnets Grace had given him. When he wasn't reading in his bunk, he joined in endless games of bridge in the wardroom with Spook Beck, Travis Henderson, and Joe Thompson. The young enlisted men enjoyed the pleasant weather and calm seas sunning themselves on deck and playing poker or shooting dice. At last, on their third day, a voice over the loudspeaker announced that the ship would anchor at noon off the island of Éfaté in the New Hebrides archipelago, one hundred miles south of Espiratu Santo, where Reynolds had spent three days en route from Guadalcanal to Auckland. He stood on deck with the rest of the sun-drenched battalion as the *Feland* steamed into a tranquil, turquoise lagoon, admiring the sugar-sand beaches and a dark green volcanic peak fringed with wispy clouds. Spook appeared at Reynolds's side, his shirtsleeves rolled up above the elbows, and, as if reading Reynolds's mind, said, "Looks like a travel poster for the South Seas. Too bad there's a war to fight."

Reynolds turned to Spook, noticing his tanned face and forearms. "Yeah," he said. "I just wish to heck they'd tell us where we're goin' and let us go in and get it over with."

"I expect they will before long," said Spook. "That's the crazy thing about this war. We go for months and months with nothin' to do, then they put us on a ship, sail for a thousand miles, and expect us to storm a beach and whip a bunch of fanatical Japs."

"Yep," said Reynolds with a nod. "And I reckon we will."

That first night in anchorage the men were treated to a movie on deck under the starry skies, a romantic comedy called *Holy Matrimony* starring Gracie Fields with an all-British cast. Listening to the British accents, Reynolds felt a deep pang of nostalgia for New Zealand, thinking back to his many visits to the McDonald home, touring the North Island sheep farms, and his days and nights in Wellington with Grace. Someday, he vowed to himself, when the war was over and they were married, they'd get a car and spend weeks just driving from one end of the island to the other . . .

The following morning Major Jones ordered another practice landing in the rubber boats, though all of the other battalions in the division, which would go ashore either in Higgins boats or the new LVTs—amphibious tractors that could swim ashore and then drive up onto the beach—remained on their transports. As the men from the *Feland* went over the sides into the little inflatable boats there was jeering and heckling from the Marines on the other ships, as some wag had christened Major Jones the "Admiral of the Condom Fleet." The contrast to their last exercise in the frigid waters of the glacier bay could not have been more complete, as the rubber boats were towed across the clear, warm water of the lagoon rippling in a light breeze. Eight hundred yards from shore the towlines were cast off, and the men easily paddled through the gentle surf onto a sparkling white beach fringed by coconut palms. "That was a piece of cake," said Reynolds to Travis Henderson as the men dragged the boats off the beach.

"Just like a rubber ducky in the bathtub," said Travis. He reached for a cigarette and his lighter.

"I got a feeling," said Reynolds as he slumped down on the sand, resting his back on his pack, "it won't be so easy the next time."

That evening, after the men had finished their mess, Reynolds returned to his cabin, pulled off his boots, and lay on his bunk propped up on a pillow with a couple of sheets of writing paper on a book balanced on his knees. After thinking for a moment, he unscrewed the cap from his fountain pen and wrote:

November 4, 1943

My dearest, darling sweetheart,

This will probably be my last chance to write for a while as
we're in a port where we're told we have mail delivery. There's
darn little news of myself to report (that I can write about
anyway). I've been doing a lot of reading and playing a lot of
bridge, though not very well, and haven't really had a chance to
go ashore.

Reynolds paused, wondering if that line would get through the censors.
Well, it would be obvious from the postmark where the letter was mailed,
so why should they care if he mentioned going ashore? "What I want to
tell you, Gracie," he continued,

is that I'm madly in love with you. I could never, ever, love
anyone else even half as much as I love you. You're so sweet and
funny and perfect in every way. I long to hold you in my arms,
to kiss you, eat with you, laugh with you, and sleep with you. I
dream of you every night. As soon as I get through this I swear
I'm coming back for you, and we'll be married, have a big family,
and be happy for the rest of our lives. I promise I will.

With so much love,
John

Reynolds blew softly on the pages to dry the ink and then carefully folded
the letter in an envelope. Leaving it on the small shelf by his bunk, he
sat up and pulled on his boots, deciding to go topside for some fresh air
before turning in.

Despite the fact that the chances of a Japanese air raid were negligi-
ble, all of the ships observed a blackout, their silhouettes barely visible
in the pale light from a fingernail moon low in the sky. Observing a
few other shadows on deck and the orange glow of cigarettes, Reynolds
walked slowly to the railing. As he stared into the darkness toward the
island, a silvery web of lightning suddenly blossomed in the clouds atop

the mountain, followed after about five seconds by a deep rumble of thunder. Reynolds had always enjoyed the summer thunderstorms on Galveston Island, where his parents occasionally rented a beach house. As he watched another flash of lightning momentarily illuminate the island, he imagined he was home, watching a storm out over the Gulf from the screen porch of the beach house. The next lightning bolt was followed by a powerful thunderclap, like the sound of heavy guns firing, and the distinctive smell of ozone. It struck Reynolds as he watched the storm that the electricity in the atmosphere matched the mood of the twenty thousand men aboard the transports: tense, taut, fear mingled with eager anticipation for action after so many months of boredom. With a sudden gust of wind, heralding the arrival of the sharp, tropical rain, Reynolds turned and headed below.

The next morning the Marines awoke to discover that two new warships had anchored in the lagoon during the night: a dull, gray battleship with its enormous sixteen-inch guns and a boxy-shaped vessel with a flat deck aft of the superstructure that was unlike anything they'd seen before. The men aboard the *Feland* crowded the railing studying the ships. Before long the scuttlebutt made its way from the ship's skipper through the crew to the Marines; the battleship was the *Maryland*, which had survived Pearl Harbor and was Admiral Hill's flagship, and the strange-looking ship was the *Ashland*, one of the Navy's brand new LSDs. "Stands for 'landing ship docks,'" explained a young ensign who was standing beside Reynolds and Spook Beck.

"And what the hell is a dock landing ship?" asked Spook.

"They can carry a load of tanks," said the ensign. "And deliver 'em right onto the beach. Skipper says they'll load the tanks here at Éfaté and then the task force will be ready to sail."

Later that day, the sixteen transports, its escort of destroyers and cruisers, and the *Maryland* and *Ashland*—now designated the Southern Attack Force—weighed anchors, steamed from the lagoon, and set a course to the northeast. The next day they were joined by yet another battleship, the *Colorado*. At 1400 hours Major Jones was ordered to report to the flagship for a battalion commanders briefing with General Julian Smith, the Second Division CO, making the trip on the admiral's barge. By the time the sleek wooden boat returned to transfer Jones back to the *Feland* all fifteen junior officers were on deck, peering over the railing as the major made the hazardous leap from the bobbing boat onto a small steel platform. "Okay, men," said Jones when he appeared on deck. "Let's go below." Once the battalion's officers were seated in the wardroom, Jones motioned to two navy ensigns who placed a large map, draped with a piece of cloth, on an easel. Jones stood ramrod straight, his rolled-up khaki sleeves revealing tanned, muscular forearms, and his closed-cropped hair bleached from the sun. After lighting his pipe, he said, "I've just come from a briefing on Operation Galvanic, assaulting two Jap strongholds in the Gilberts archipelago, which is located about two degrees north of the equator, roughly two thousand miles southwest of Hawaii. Our division will land on the island of Betio in the Tarawa atoll, while the army's Twenty-Seventh Division will attack Makin Island a hundred miles farther north." Jones puffed on his pipe and then reached over to undrape the map. The men leaned forward to study the depiction of a slightly curved, narrow island. "This is Betio," said Jones, tapping his pipe on the map. "Code-named Helen." The Marines exchanged puzzled looks, as none had ever heard of the Gilberts or Tarawa.

Holding his pipe, Jones started to pace. "The Japanese," he said, "occupied the island a little over a year ago. According to the intel, they've built an airfield and revetments and reinforced concrete and coconut log bunkers for a garrison of almost five thousand men."

"How big is the island, sir?" asked Porter Davidson.

"It's tiny," said Jones. "About two miles long and a half mile wide. And flat as a pancake, no more than ten feet above sea level at the highest point." He walked back to the map and studied it for a moment. "But here's the problem," he said after turning to face his men. "On the north side of the island there's a coral reef about five hundred yards offshore enclosing a shallow lagoon." He traced the location of the reef with his pipe. "And at high tide there's maybe five feet of clearance."

"How much draft do the Higgins boats have?" asked another officer.

"About four feet. So the landings will have to coincide with high tide or the boats will get hung up on the reef."

"Why not come ashore on the south side of the island?" asked Travis Henderson.

"It's more heavily defended, including some eight-inch Vickers guns the Japanese captured from the Brits in Singapore. Can sink a ship fifteen miles offshore. The seas are much rougher than on the lagoon side, and the planners want this long pier to off-load supplies. So the landings will have to be the lagoon side."

"Looks like an awful tough nut to crack, sir," said Captain Davis, the CO of Charlie Company. "If we miss the tide and the Higgins boats get stuck on that reef we'll be sitting ducks."

"Well, the navy's got an answer for that," said Jones. "The plan calls for a massive bombardment with the big guns of the battlewagons and cruisers before the first wave goes in. The navy's confident they can knock out all resistance."

Spook leaned over to Reynolds and whispered, "It'll probably just stir 'em up and piss 'em off."

"And the first wave," Jones continued, "will transfer from Higgins boats to these new LVT Alligators and Water Buffaloes, which can climb over the reef." He reached down and flipped over the map, revealing another, more detailed, map underneath it. "Okay," he said, "here's the operational plan. Colonel Shoup worked it out at General Smith's HQ in Wellington. The first wave will hit these three beaches, designated Red 1, Red 2, and Red 3." He tapped his pipe on the three landing beaches. "The three-two will land on Red 1 on the far right, while the two-two will hit Red 2, and two-eight will hit Red 3, to the left of this long pier. Once the beach is secure, the assault teams will take out these heavy pillboxes"—Jones motioned to a number of black squares on the map—"and then advance to take the airfield. The one-two will be the reserve battalion. Colonel Shoup will be in overall operational command. Questions?"

"Well, sir," said a young second lieutenant, "where do we fit into the picture?"

"General Smith has decided to hold back the Sixth Regiment as the reserve for the entire Galvanic operation, including Makin." A collective groan passed among the men.

"Aw, hell, major," said Arnold Schulz from the back of the room. "You mean we're gonna miss out on the action?"

"I wouldn't be so sure, Schulz," said Jones with a grim expression. "Other questions?" He looked out at his officers, who stared back at him in stunned silence. "Okay," he said. "Dismissed."

Late that afternoon, Reynolds and Spook were relaxing on folding chairs by one of the *Feland's* antiaircraft batteries with their shirts off, soaking up the hot sun as they stared out on the vast empty ocean. Almost twenty-four hours had passed since the convoy sailed from Éfaté, and, cruising at over twenty knots, they'd covered more than five hundred miles, which placed them near the Santa Cruz Islands due east of Guadalcanal at a latitude of 10°. Turning to Spook, Reynolds said, "I just don't understand this plan. I mean, why wouldn't we want to hit this place with everything we've got? Nearly five thousand Japs dug in on an island only a half-mile wide, and we're gonna hold back an entire regiment?"

"I'll tell you why," said Spook. "So we can ride to the rescue of that army outfit at Makin when it gets up shit creek. Goddam third rate national guard division." Reynolds—who'd been raised in a household where the strongest language ever uttered was an occasional "hell" or "damn"—was surprised by Spook's angry tone and mildly offended by his swearing, though there was plenty of profanity among the men.

"What scares the hell out of me," said Spook, "is what happens if the Higgins boats get stuck on that reef and the men have to wade ashore, something like five hundred yards? They'd be cut to pieces before they ever hit the beach. And then they'll send *us* in on our dinky little rubber boats."

"Well," said Reynolds, "at least they'll have tanks and plenty of air power."

"Buddy of mine told me Shoup's plan called for another fifty of these amtracs that can climb over a reef, and a squadron of B-24s to bomb the hell out of the Jap pillboxes before the landings." Reynolds gave Spook an expectant look. "But the navy brass turned him down. They're so goddam sure their battleships will blast the Jap bunkers to smithereens."

"Well," said Reynolds, "I hope they're right."

"And if they're wrong it's these poor kids who'll pay the price. Hell," he concluded, "at least they don't have wives back home to worry about."

CHAPTER TEN

UNDER THE BROILING EQUATORIAL SUN, THE SOUTHERN
Attack Force steamed steadily northeast over the undulating ocean. Most
of the men on the *Feland* stayed below decks in their bunks, wearing only
their skivvies in the stifling heat, while the battalion's officers, other than
Arnold Schulz, whiled away the hours playing endless games of cards in
the wardroom: bridge, poker, and, in some cases, the fast-paced game of
pitch. Despite the fans mounted on the walls and open portholes, dark
stains formed on the backs of the men's khaki shirts. Schulz preferred to
spend his time with Baker Company's NCOs, kibitzing their games of
craps and poker. On the morning of their third day Schulz entered the
wardroom for a cup of coffee, pausing at the table where Spook Beck and
John Reynolds were playing bridge with two other officers. Spook looked
up over his shoulder and said, "Looking for something, Arnold?"

Avoiding eye contact with Reynolds, Schulz said, "Nope." He took
a sip of coffee, glanced at the card table, and said, "What's the game?"

"Bridge," said Joe Thompson without looking up.

"I thought bridge was a game for dames," said Schulz with a smile.

"Why don't you butt out," said Reynolds.

"No," said Spook. "It's OK. Pull up a chair, Arnold." He shot a disapproving look at Reynolds.

"Thanks but no thanks." Schulz moved on, and one of the others muttered, "the Avenger."

At a quarter to noon Porter Davidson, the Able Company commanding officer, walked up and said, "Let's grab a table in the mess hall. They're some things we need to go over."

Davidson sat down at a round table with his tray of hash, beans, and mashed potatoes. After a few moments he was joined by John Reynolds, the company's executive officer, and by Joe Thompson, Travis Henderson, and Bill Ford, all platoon leaders. After everyone had taken a few bites, Davidson's expression turned serious and he said, "I need to make sure everyone understands what's expected if they send us in." He looked at the faces around the table. "This won't be like the Canal. No reverse slopes to shelter from incoming fire, kunai grass to hide in or long slogs through the jungle. The Japs have fortified damn near every square yard of this island. And unless the shells from the battleships knock 'em out, our guys are gonna have to take these blockhouses and bunkers one at a time."

"Do you think the battleships can do the job?" asked Travis.

"There's a story going around," said Davidson, "that Admiral Turner bragged to General Smith that when the Navy gets done shelling the island a man could walk from one end to the other without getting a scratch. But I had a talk with Jones this morning after he'd come from a briefing. He said he'd never seen General Smith so worked up. Apparently, he demanded the Navy keep up the bombardment for three days, and Admiral Turner told him to forget it. You'll have a three-hour bombardment and then your men will go in."

"Jeez, Skipper," said Joe Thompson, "what does Jones think?"

"He doesn't believe the Navy's big guns will knock out the Jap fortifications," said Davidson in a low voice. "Something about the low trajectory compared to artillery. And he says Colonel Shoup's plenty worried about the tide and boats getting stuck on the reef."

"What do you reckon the odds are they'll send us in?" asked Reynolds.

"Only if the assault force runs into big trouble. And at that point the main concern is a Jap counterattack, probably at night. So you need to get with your platoon sergeants this afternoon and make sure they understand what to expect. My gut tells me this is gonna be one helluva fight."

✢ ✢ ✢

Later that afternoon, the news traveled quickly that an important message from the division's CO had been posted on the bulletin board. Accompanied by Spook and Travis, Reynolds headed below and joined a large group of young Marines crowding around the board. Spook, who at six foot three was taller than the others, strained to read it. "What's it say?" asked Travis. "They're sending us back to Wellington?"

Spook smiled and read aloud: "A great offensive to destroy the enemy in the Central Pacific has begun . . . The task assigned to us is to capture the atolls of Tarawa and Apamama. Our Navy screens our operation and will support our attack tomorrow with the greatest concentration of aerial bombardment and naval gunfire in the history of warfare."

"What's the rest?" said Reynolds as more men jammed in behind them.

"This division was especially chosen by the high command for the assault on Tarawa," Spook continued reading, "because of battle experience and combat efficiency. Their confidence will not be betrayed. We are the first American troops to attack a defended atoll."

"Go on," said Travis impatiently.

"I know you are well trained," read Spook, "and fit for the tasks assigned to you. You will quickly overrun the Japanese forces; you will decisively defeat and destroy the treacherous enemies of our country. Your success will add new laurels to the glorious traditions of our Corps. Signed," Spook concluded, "Julian C. Smith, Major General." He turned to Reynolds and Travis, smiled and said, "Semper Fi. Let's get some fresh air."

Despite being intellectually aware of their imminent assault on a heavily defended island, the message from the commanding general gave the reality of the invasion a stark certitude. Though most of the men had experienced their baptism under fire on Guadalcanal, and while it was reasonable to expect that, as the corps reserve, they would sit this one out, there was a noticeable change in the demeanor of the men, many of whom were writing final letters home or staring out on the ocean, lost in their ruminations. Maybe it was that line in the message, mused Reynolds as he slowly made his way around the ship on the open deck, about being the first American troops to attack a defended atoll that disquieted the men, or that bit of bravado about quickly overrunning and decisively defeating and destroying the Japanese.

After a hearty dinner, Reynolds went to his cramped cabin and sat on the side of his bunk to write a letter to Grace and another to his mom and dad. With the strict censorship there was very little he could say, and so he simply assured all of them that he was well, that the men were in good shape to face the challenges that lay ahead, saying how much he loved them and longed to see them again, and cautioning that he couldn't say when he'd be able to write again. He closed the letter to Grace with: "I dream of holding you in my arms and the day we're married." And in the letter home he carefully included a statement calculated to prepare his parents for his eventual betrothal to Grace, that "she's a wonderful girl whom you will come to love as much as I do" and "the perfect match for me." After carefully addressing the two letters and leaving them in the ship's mail drop he decided to take another turn on deck before lights out. He hoped to find Spook in the wardroom, but after a quick look he searched for him among the many dark forms standing at the blacked-out ship's railing. Encountering Travis Henderson with his usual cigarette, Reynolds said, "Hey, Travis, have you seen Spook?"

"Yeah, I saw him a minute ago over by that ack-ack gun."

"Thanks." Reynolds began walking toward the silhouette of an antiaircraft gun where he could dimly see two dark forms. "That you, Spook?" he said.

"Yep." Spook was resting his back against the steel plating of the superstructure. "Just havin' a little chat with the gunny."

Reynolds could make out the face of Sam Bellatti, the weapons company gunnery sergeant. "What do you think, Bellatti?" he asked quietly.

"Well, Lieutenant," he said, "I don't feel too good about this operation."

"Me neither," said Reynolds.

"Sounds to me," said the sergeant, "like they're countin' on the navy to knock out all the Jap pillboxes. But I doubt it."

"Listen, Bellatti," said Reynolds, "I need to have a private word with Lieutenant Beck."

"Right, sir." Bellatti drifted off into the darkness.

When they were alone, Reynolds said, "You still think they're holding the regiment in reserve to go to the rescue of that national guard division at Makin?"

"I can't think of any other reason," said Spook.

"I guess you're right," said Reynolds, "but here we are at Tarawa, and Makin's a hundred miles away. I gotta believe if things get tough . . ."

"Yep," said Spook with a nod. "They'll send us in."

"Listen, Spook," said Reynolds, "I need to ask you a favor."

"What's that?"

"Well, the truth is, Grace and I . . . Well, we're engaged."

"No kidding? How come you didn't say anything?"

"Well, it's a secret. Not even our parents know." Spook studied Reynolds's face in the faint starlight. "So if something happens to me, I need to make sure someone gets word to Grace."

Spook was silent for a moment and then said, "Listen, buddy, I'll make a deal with you." His tone was dead serious. "If you don't make it, I promise I'll get word to Grace, if you'll promise to write Sally if I buy the farm."

"Thanks," said Reynolds. "I really mean it. Here. I wrote down her address in Wellington." He handed Spook a folded slip of paper.

Spook briefly studied it in the darkness and then put it in his shirt pocket. "Hang on a sec," he said. He took a pencil and scrap of paper from his other pocket and quickly jotted something down. Handing it to Reynolds, he said, "It's my home address in Portland."

Reynolds slipped the note in his pocket and said, "If something happens, Spook, Sally will get the usual telegram, but I promise I'll write her. It's just that Grace, I mean there's no way she could get any information from the Corps . . ."

"Don't worry, pal. I'll get in touch with her. But I've got an even better idea. Let's get through this thing without a scratch."

Reynolds nodded and then glanced at the luminous dials of his watch. "We'd better go below and turn in," he said. "We're gonna need whatever sleep we can get."

Reynolds slept for two hours, though it seemed like less. Finally he decided to stop tossing and get up and dress in his camouflage utilities, thankful that he was in the lower bunk and able to get on his boots without waking the others. He stood up in the darkness and glanced at his watch: four-thirty. He wondered how early the Navy cooks made coffee. Though he could feel the vibrations of the engines, the ship didn't seem to be moving, only pitching on the swells. He made his way down the passageway, eerily illuminated by the blue ready lights, encountering only one other Marine, Arnold Schulz, who merely grunted, avoiding Reynolds's eyes as he walked past. A handful of other officers, however, were in the wardroom, including Bill Jones, drinking strong coffee. When Reynolds walked up Jones said, "Pull up a chair." Reynolds sat, and after a moment a Chamorro steward appeared and poured him a mug of coffee.

After taking a sip, Reynolds said, "Doesn't feel like we're moving, sir."

"We've taken up our station at the western end of the transport assembly area, about seventeen thousand yards northwest of Betio," said Jones. "The plan is to load the men in Higgins boats and then rendezvous with the LVTs outside the lagoon. Sun should be up in about a half hour, and we can go up and have a look."

"When is H-hour?" asked Reynolds.

"Eight-thirty," said Jones. "Smith wants the men to hit the beach by nine."

"So I guess that means the bombardment should start by . . ."

"Five-thirty," said Jones with a slight grimace. "The Navy will have exactly three hours to obliterate the Jap bunkers."

Reynolds considered asking Jones if he thought the bombardment would be successful but decided against it. "What are the chances, sir," he said instead, "that General Smith will send in the reserve?"

Jones pulled out his corncob pipe and a tobacco pouch. As he began to fill it and tamp down the tobacco he said, "Only as a last resort. If it looks like the assault on the beach could fail."

Reynolds took another sip of coffee, struck by the realization that what they were about to do had never been tried before, as the landings at Guadalcanal had been unopposed. Notwithstanding the Marines' years of preparation and training for amphibious warfare, this would be the first test. He nodded and said, "I see." He glanced at the portholes, looking for the first hint of dawn. "Well, sir," said Reynolds, putting aside his mug, "I think I'll go topside." Emerging on deck, Reynolds walked to the railing and studied the sky to the east, unable to make out even the faintest lightening. Stars shone brilliantly, and a quarter moon hung low in the southern sky. He could just discern the dark shapes of the other transports, in a row perhaps five hundred yards to port. The men on board should be finishing a breakfast of steak and eggs or checking their weapons and adjusting their packs in preparation for loading the Higgins boats. He scanned the southern horizon but was unable to see the chain of coral islands, and then checked the time again. Three minutes past five. As the ship gently rolled on the deep swells, scarcely making way, it seemed eerily tranquil. Reynolds almost had the deck to himself, apart from the Navy lookouts at their stations. Resting his arms on the teak railing, he stared into the darkness and then was aware that someone had appeared beside him. It was Billy Pollard, a young private in Reynolds's company and a fellow Texan. "Hello, Billy," said Reynolds.

"Hello, sir. Sure is dark and quiet."

"Well, it won't be for long."

"Are you scared, sir?" asked Billy quietly.

"Sure," said Reynolds, "but I try not to think about it."

"All I can think about is my girlfriend and my mom and dad," said Billy, "and how sad they're gonna be if I . . . if I don't make it."

"Well, don't worry," said Reynolds. "You'll be OK."

The young man drifted into the darkness. Reynolds tried to discern the horizon when all at once two bright flashes of orange flickered, followed seconds later by a dull *boom*. Within moments men were running up the companionway and crowding on deck. Another flash of orange appeared on the horizon.

"Jesus," said a young Marine. "What was that?"

"It's the Japs, you idiot," growled a sergeant. "Shootin' at us."

The words were drowned by a tremendous, ear-splitting concussion, a salvo of sixteen-inch guns fired by the battleship *Maryland*. Even at a distance of three thousand yards, the shock wave from the big guns almost knocked the men on the *Feland* to the deck. The muzzle flashes briefly illuminated the armada of over thirty ships. Within seconds fiery explosions appeared on the horizon, followed by thunderous crashes amid the cheering of thousands of Marines. As dawn began to glow in the eastern sky, a tremendous spectacle unfolded: the almost continuous fire of the *Maryland*'s and *Colorado*'s sixteen- and fourteen-inch guns joined by the smaller guns of the dozens of other warships arrayed in an arc outside the atoll's lagoon, raining fire on Betio, which was now engulfed with pillars of dense black smoke and clouds of dust.

For thirty minutes the massive bombardment was continuous, the bright muzzle flashes combining with the blinding rays of the rising sun, and the men cheering wildly with every hit and explosion. "There ain't no way," yelled a man standing close to Reynolds, "nobody could live through that!" Reynolds nodded in agreement. "Hell, this'll be a cakewalk!" yelled another Marine over the roar of the guns. *Thank God,* thought Reynolds, *it looked like that admiral's boast would prove accurate.* At about six o'clock the naval guns suddenly fell silent. Reynolds noticed that the Marines on the nearest transport were climbing down cargo nets into the waiting Higgins boats bobbing alongside. He turned to look back toward Betio, which was completely obscured by smoke and dust, with numerous fires raging. And then, to his surprise, he heard a succession of loud *cracks,* and tall geysers of seawater erupted within several hundred yards of the transports. The *Feland* almost immediately surged forward and turned sharply to starboard. "What is it, sir?" asked a young private standing next to Reynolds.

"It's the Japs," said Reynolds grimly. "They're shooting back at us." Another shell fell within a hundred yards, the geyser drenching the men on deck. Reynolds could see that the other transports were also underway, even with men hanging on the cargo nets, steaming to get out of range of the Japanese guns and scattering the little landing craft like a flushed covey of quail.

"Maybe it's our own guns," said the private, who was tightly gripping the railing.

"Well, our gunnery may be bad," said Reynolds, "but not that bad. No, it's the Japs." In their haste to get out of range a number of the transports narrowly avoided ramming the Higgins boats, which resembled a group of ducklings paddling alongside the far bigger ships. Feeling a knot of anxiety deep in his gut, Reynolds decided to look for the other Able Company officers.

He found Travis and Porter Davidson leaning against the bow railing. Travis was holding a pair of binoculars to his eyes. "Well," said Reynolds, "I guess Spook was right."

Lowering the binoculars, Travis looked over his shoulder and said, "About what?"

"About the naval bombardment just pissin' off the Japs. Looks like we've stirred up a hornets' nest."

"Jones says there's still a chance they'll send in a squadron of B-24s," said Davidson, "and bomb the beach with those five-hundred-pound daisy cutters." At that moment a squadron of Navy Hellcats banked low out of the east and executed a low-level strafing and bombing run on the Japanese fortifications. After a second pass, the planes disappeared into the sun.

Resting his arms on the railing, Travis lowered his eyes to the binoculars. "The guys in the Higgins boats," he said, "are going over where it looks like the amtracs are circling." The three men flinched at the crash of another salvo from the battleships' big guns. "I'm afraid those guys are headed into a shit storm."

Reynolds suddenly felt sick. He spit over the side, trying to rid his mouth of a bad taste, which he suspected was caused by fear. With a glance at his watch he said, "I think I'll go below. It's at least another hour before the amtracs start for the beaches." The skipper of the *Feland* had maneuvered the ship about a mile from its earlier location, presumably out of range of the Japanese guns. The ship's rolling motion worsened Reynolds's nausea. When he reached the companionway he encountered Sergeant Bill White, Able Company's Gunny.

"Mornin', Lieutenant," said the sergeant, whom the men called "Old White" as he was in his thirties with over a dozen years' service in the Corps. "Looks like the Japs have a lot of fight left in 'em."

"It sure does," said Reynolds. "They must be really dug in to survive that bombardment."

"If you look real close," said White, pointing in the direction of the smoking ruins of the island, "you can see some of the projectiles ricochet off the ground and splash in the ocean."

Narrowing his gaze, Reynolds was just able to discern a dark object that struck the island and then tumbled high into the air before exploding in a fountain of seawater. "Damn," he muttered. "No wonder the Japs are still firing."

"I seen a bunch of 'em just like that," said the sergeant. "I reckon they're gonna have to send us in before this thing's over," he added with a shrug.

"I wouldn't be surprised, Gunny." Reynolds made his way down the companionway and headed for the wardroom, thinking another cup of coffee might settle his nerves. He had the place to himself, apart from two

Chamorro stewards, as everyone else was up on deck watching the show. As he stared at the ripples on the surface of his coffee from each concussion of the guns he considered their good fortune at not being one of the battalions assigned to storm that fiery hellhole of an island. The table trembled, and so did his hand holding the coffee mug. Finally, he checked the time: twenty till nine. By now, he reflected, the first wave of amtracs should be starting their long run in to the beach. He reached into his back pocket for a handkerchief and wiped the sweat from his face. The heat below was almost unbearable, even at the early hour, and he reluctantly decided to go back up on deck for some semblance of a breeze. Just as he appeared at the top of the companionway the firing from the warships abruptly ceased. Reynolds studied the distant island, which seemed to be on fire from one end to the other, sending up towering columns of dense black smoke. He tried to imagine what it was like for the men on the amtracs, churning slowly toward the beaches and the inferno beyond. For the next hour he stood at the railing in the shade of the superstructure, staring at the smoke and dust rising high into the pale blue sky, listening to the distinctive bam-bam of the Japanese antiaircraft cannons and *crump* of their mortars, but unable to detect any sound of machine guns or small arms' fire.

Finally, at 1100 hours the ship's loudspeakers crackled with the announcement: "Now hear this. All officers report immediately to the wardroom." Reynolds joined the group of men hurrying below and took a seat at one of the tables. When Major Bill Jones entered, accompanied by the scowling battalion operations officer, the junior officers came to their feet and snapped to attention.

"Be seated, gentlemen," said Jones, and the men returned to their chairs. Looking out over their young, expectant faces, Jones said, "I've been in the C-I-C all morning, monitoring the radio traffic. And I can tell you our men are catching hell." Most of the officers leaned forward in their chairs. "The battalion on Beach Red 1 reports extremely heavy casualties. Major Crowe's men in two-eight got ashore on Red 3 in pretty good shape, but they're pinned down on the beach. I don't know about the battalion that was supposed to land on Beach Red 2. A lot of the boats got hung up on the reef and shot to hell by the Japs' seventy-five-millimeter guns, and the men had to wade in from five hundred yards under heavy machine-gun fire."

"But sir," said the CO of Charlie Company, "what about the tide? Can't they swim over?"

Jones shook his head. "Turns out it's what's called a dodge tide, somewhere between high and low tide. So the amtracs have to climb over the reef. But that's what they're designed for."

"What about the Higgins boats, sir?"

"They can't get over the reef, so all the reinforcements have to be ferried in on the remaining amtracs or just wade in."

"Are they sending in the Sixth Marines?" asked Porter Davidson.

"I don't know," said Jones. "But you need to get your men ready to go on a moment's notice. That's all." The officers all came to their feet and silently waited for the major and his number two to exit the wardroom.

CHAPTER ELEVEN

THEIR TRANSPORT PACKS LOADED, WEAPONS CLEANED AND oiled, Ka-Bar knives sharpened to a razor's edge, cartridge belts and canteens filled, the men waited on board the *Feland* all through D-day, November 20, 1943. The oven-heat below decks was unbearable, and so they gathered in what shade was available, straining to hear the sounds of the battle raging miles in the distance and staring for hours at the smoke and dust-enshrouded island. And yet no word came alerting the men to their orders, nor any news from the beachhead.

Unbeknownst to the three thousand men on the transports, the Second and Eighth Marines were locked in a desperate struggle with Tarawa's Japanese defenders, whose concrete and coconut-log blockhouses had proven to be virtually impervious to the tremendous naval and air bombardment. On Beach Red 1, to the right of the pier that reached some four hundred yards into the turquoise lagoon, the small number of Marines who'd made it ashore were scattered, disorganized, and demoralized, most of them sheltering behind a three-foot seawall yards from the water's edge. Many rifle companies had lost all their officers and most of their NCOs. To their left the two battalions under the command of Colonel David Shoup on Beach Red 2 were only slightly better off, continuing to take heavy casualties, pinned down behind the seawall or next to the pier, by Japanese firing from concrete pillboxes and gun mounts less than fifty yards from the water's edge. Only the battalions commanded by Major H. P. "Jim" Crowe on Beach Red 3, to the left of the pier, had partially achieved their objective: driving the Japanese defenders back from the beach and knocking out Japanese strongholds with explosives and flamethrowers. Most of the medium tanks that were ferried ashore from the *Ashland* lay in smoking ruins in the lagoon, along with the hulks of dozens of amtracs and the bloated bodies of hundreds of Marines in the bloody shallows. Since most of the radios had either been shot to pieces or submerged in seawater, communication between the forces tenuously holding the beaches or with their commanders offshore was haphazard or nonexistent. As darkness fell over the flaming, smoking, palm-tree-splintered square mile of sand and coral, it was obvious to every Marine still drawing breath that they were in imminent peril of a Japanese counterattack, a tactic they had repeatedly employed on Guadalcanal.

John Reynolds stood at the railing in the darkness with his friends Spook and Travis, watching the glare of the fires on the distant island and listening to the occasional cannon fire. The order to stand down had finally come, and the men were thankful to stow their heavy packs and gear. All afternoon Reynolds had tried, with almost no success, to take his mind off the desperate fighting, leaning against a bulkhead while thinking about Grace and reading the slender volume of poetry she'd given him. Travis Henderson slipped a Lucky Strike from his shirt pocket. "The order to send in our regiment has to come from the very top," he drawled as he snapped open his lighter. "As in Howlin' Mad Smith, the corps commander." He held the flame to the tip of his cigarette.

"And he's up at Makin on Admiral Turner's flagship," said Spook.

"Jeez," said Travis as he exhaled a cloud of smoke. "I gotta believe the big brass will release the Sixth Marines to division. Hell, we're all they've got left."

"If Admiral Turner gives the okay," said Reynolds. "What a dumbass decision not to throw everything we've got against the Japs."

"Well," said Travis, "I reckon we'll find out in the mornin'."

Morning came, miraculously, with no nighttime Japanese counterattack that in all likelihood would have driven the Marines back into the sea. Yet there were still no orders for the thousands of men waiting on the transports. Following breakfast, the eight hundred men of the 1/6 Battalion, Major Willie K. Jones's "Condom Fleet," were instructed, for the second time in as many days, to load their packs and gear in readiness to embark on the inflatable boats. Reynolds was in the wardroom, standing in front of the large map of Betio taped up on the bulkhead. The island was at its widest on the western end, tapering down to a narrow spit at the eastern end. A pointed projection of land on the northwest corner was identified on the map as the "Bird's Beak," from which the shoreline curved inland forming what was designated the "Pocket." The airfield was in the narrow interior on an east/west axis. The long pier was roughly at the island's center, facing north. All the Marines who'd stormed the beaches on D-day were scattered along the Bird's Beak, the Pocket, and on both sides of the pier. Reynolds studied the concave shoreline on the western end of Betio, designated Green Beach. Where the rubber boat battalion would probably land if the order to release the reserve was given.

The longer they waited the worse Reynolds felt about their odds. It wasn't a premonition of impending doom; in fact, with his deeply rooted Protestant beliefs, he rejected anything that smacked of superstition. It was just that in the absence of hard information, the mind started playing games. He'd be better off with a fatalistic view of their chances like most of the nineteen-year-olds. And praying. He decided to go to his cabin and start getting ready.

Standing in the cramped space by his bunk, Reynolds reached for the webbed belt with his canteen, Ka-Bar knife, and black leather holster with his .45 automatic. Marine officers carried only a sidearm, as they were expected to be too busy directing their men to fire a rifle. As he strapped on the belt, Porter Davidson appeared in the hatchway. "Hey, Johnny," he grinned, "guess what I just heard? They've released the regiment to division." Reynolds looked at Davidson but said nothing. He knew in an instant what it meant. They were going ashore. "When General Smith requested the reserve," said Davidson, "he sent the message, issue in doubt. Jones is on his way over to Colonel Holmes's ship for a conference with the other COs." Davidson disappeared down the passageway to spread the news.

Reynolds had never seen Davidson so keyed up. Things must be really bad, he reflected, if they'd sent the message "issue in doubt," which signaled the possibility of imminent defeat. The only other time it had been sent was during the Japs' final assault on Wake Island, where the Marines had held out against overwhelming odds for three weeks after Pearl Harbor before surrendering. At 1300 hours the officers assembled in the wardroom. "Okay," said Jones, who was calmly smoking his pipe, once everyone was seated. "General Smith and Red Mike Edson kicked around a lot of ideas, but here's the plan they decided on. Our battalion goes in first on Green Beach in the rubber boats. Major Mike Ryan has cobbled together a force of about two or three hundred men from the units that got all mixed up on Red 1. They've got a couple of tanks and supporting fire from the destroyers in the lagoon and cleared all the Japs from the western end of the island. So Green Beach is under Marine control. I've known Mike Ryan since Iceland, and he's a damned fine officer."

Jones relit his pipe and walked over to the map on the bulkhead. "Our orders," he said, "are to get ashore on the double, pass through Ryan's covering force in a column of companies, and attack along the south shore of the island toward the airfield." He traced the line of attack with his free hand. "We load the boats as soon as the ship gets into position and hit the beach by 1600 hours. The 3/6 will follow us in. Questions?" The room was silent, with all of the officers, notwithstanding the knot of fear in their guts, gazing admiringly at their leader. "Okay," said Jones. "Get your men ready. We don't have much time."

Reynolds returned to his cabin, shrugged on his pack, adjusted the straps, and then reached for his helmet. After a final look around, he headed down the passageway to the fo'c's'le, a cavernous room with bunks stacked four deep, jam-packed with young Marines. Feeling clumsy with his pack and gear, he began searching for his old platoon. Hearing a distinctive Brooklyn accent, he walked up to Gunnery Sergeant White, who was helping the men to adjust their equipment and dispensing advice to the replacements who'd joined the battalion in New Zealand.

"Hey, Lieutenant," said a corporal, a sandy-haired boy from Louisiana who was one of the stretcher bearers who'd carried Reynolds out of the jungle after he was shot. "I figured you'd gotten your million dollar wound."

"No such luck," said Reynolds with a smile.

"Afternoon, sir," said Sergeant White. He grimaced as he tightened the strap of one of his men's packs. "Ready to go?"

"Ready as I'll ever be." Reynolds looked at the boyish faces, some familiar, many not. *Which of them,* he wondered, *would survive the next several days, and which ones would never see their mothers and fathers again?* Pushing the thought from his mind, he patted Old White on the shoulder and said, "I just wanted to drop by and say good luck."

"Take care, Lieutenant," said the sergeant. "These guys are gonna make you proud."

Reynolds gave the sergeant a tight smile and, aware of an increase in the vibration beneath his boots and a slight rolling motion, turned to go. They were obviously underway and moving into position. He hurried up the companionway and out on deck. The sensation of the equatorial heat and humidity was like leaning your face into a hot oven, instantly beading his brow with sweat. To Reynolds's surprise, the ship was moving *away* from the island. He briefly glanced up and down the deck, which was crowded with sailors at various tasks and heavily laden Marines forming into assault teams. Reynolds moved toward the stern where after a few minutes he spotted several mortar men with their distinctive loads. "Say, Marine," said Reynolds to a young private carrying a mortar's base plate. "Have you seen Lieutenant Beck?"

"Yes, sir, he was right over yonder a minute ago." He pointed toward the fantail.

"Thanks." Reynolds could see a tall, lanky officer helping another Marine with his disassembled .30-caliber machine gun. Reynolds walked up from behind and said, "Hey, Spook."

Spook looked over his shoulder and said, "Be right with you." He finished strapping the tripod to the man's pack and then turned to Reynolds. "Jeeminy, criminy," he said, wiping his face with his hand, "it's hot as Hades out here."

"Yeah, and it's just gonna get hotter when we reach shore. Listen, Spook, I wanted to make sure you still had that note with Grace's phone number and address."

"Right here in my pocket," said Spook, patting the side of his utility trousers. "And you still have Sally's address?" Reynolds nodded. "Okay, pal," said Spook. "Let's just make sure neither one of us needs it." He turned to look toward the ship's bow. "Why in the hell are we moving *away* from the island?"

"I was just wondering the same thing," said Reynolds.

"Jap subs," said a nearby Navy lieutenant. "We got a report from one of the screening destroyers."

"Hell's bells," said Spook. "This is gonna screw up the timetable."

An hour passed before word was radioed that the report of enemy submarines was mistaken, a precious interval that delayed the Marines' embarkation on the rubber boats by a full two hours. At last, at 1600 hours the men were climbing down the cargo nets into the waiting boats, with Able Company loading first. Reynolds, as the company XO, chose to make the trip on the lead boat tethered to the landing craft that would tow them to within a thousand yards of the beach. After another half hour the rubber boat flotilla was finally underway, the men clinging tightly to the sides as the waves washed over the bows, chugging along at a speed no greater than five knots. Riding at the front of the lead boat, Reynolds kept his eyes on the island, which was completely obscured by dense black smoke. As they drew closer he could dimly see flames flickering through the smoke and dust and faintly hear the unmistakable rattle of machine guns and rifles and the thud of heavier weapons. It looked to him, and no doubt to every other man in the rubber boats, like they were sailing directly into the gates of hell.

The Navy petty officer in the cockpit of the Higgins boat thirty yards in front of them suddenly idled his engine. He turned around and yelled, "Time to cut you guys loose!"

Reynolds looked at the shoreline, certain they were well over mile out. "You gotta keep going!" he yelled back, "and take us to a thousand yards of the beach!"

"Sorry, sir," yelled the petty officer. "This is as far as I'm going."

Reynolds awkwardly got up on his knees and unholstered his .45 automatic. Aiming it directly at the petty officer, he yelled, "You take us closer in, sailor, or by God I'll get somebody else to drive that boat!" The petty officer took a quick look at the .45 and then turned around and engaged the engine. Reynolds looked to his left and observed that the Higgins boat towing the next string of boats had also come to a stop but, as he watched, started up again. Now, as they approached the drop-off zone, Reynolds could just make out a line of rollers and the white strip of beach. What vegetation was visible—a fringe of blasted coconut palms— was shrouded in dense swirling smoke, and his nostrils were assailed by the acrid smell of cordite and burning logs and the unmistakable stench of death. The entire island appeared to be on fire. The Navy helmsman abruptly cut his engine and, without looking back at Reynolds, quickly unfastened the tow line and turned the Higgins boat back out to sea. The men lifted their paddles and, burdened with packs and assorted gear, awkwardly began to stroke. Reynolds stared over the side; the water so shallow and clear he could see the bottom. Straining with each stroke, he noticed an odd-looking round object submerged on the other side of the boat two feet beneath the surface. A mine! Lifting up his paddle, he turned back to the other men and pointed down. The little rubber boat floated harmlessly over it.

One hundred yards out and the sound of small arms fire mingled with the roar of the surf. Fear overcame exhaustion, and the men paddled harder than ever, sweating profusely and drenched with seawater, desperate to get ashore. After one precarious spin atop a breaker, they coasted into the wash and the men stumbled out into foot-deep water. His heart pounding, Reynolds held onto his helmet and staggered to his feet, striding onto the beach as calmly as possible. In an instant he realized they weren't taking fire and uttered a silent prayer of gratitude. Up and down the beach hundreds of Marines were deploying under the shouted orders from their platoon sergeants. Here's where the training pays off, Reynolds reflected as he watched the rifle squads take their positions and mortar teams and machine gunners quickly assemble their weapons, as though on another exercise. After his momentary elation, Reynolds's heart sank. He turned and looked back out to sea. The bright red orb of the sun, magnified by the thick layer of dust, almost touched the horizon. The trip ashore had taken well over an hour, and now daylight was fading. He made his way to a shallow crater at the edge of the beach occupied by Porter Davidson and his radio operator. Crouching in the shell hole, Reynolds peered into the shattered palm trees in front of them, where he could see that about fifty Marines were dug in. Major Ryan's men; their welcoming party.

Davidson said something to the radio operator, who nodded, and then turned to Reynolds. "I managed to get Jones on the radio," said Davidson. "He's gone to look for Major Ryan and explain the plan. But by the time we get all our people into position it's gonna be dark. Aw, shit!" He ducked, holding onto his helmet at the distinctive successive *crumps* of enemy mortars. After an agonizing few seconds the shells exploded a hundred yards to their left, followed almost immediately by the shout: "Corpsman!"

"So what do we do?" said Reynolds.

"Go look for Henderson, Thompson, and Ford," said Davidson. "Tell them to set up our perimeter while there's still daylight. Have the men dig their fighting holes in support of Ryan's men." He partially stood up and swung his arm from left to right. "Over there."

"Aye, aye, skipper," said Reynolds.

Lying in their shallow holes, the Marines listened to the desultory exchange of rifle fire in the distance and tried to catch a few hours' sleep. Even at night the island was exceptionally hot, and it stank. Mostly of putrefying flesh, as by the end of the second day several thousand dead Americans and Japanese littered the tiny island. At about 11:00 p.m. the Marines heard a loud droning—an approaching squadron of Japanese Betty bombers, which dropped their loads blindly at high altitude. While the bombs did little damage, their screaming plunge to earth added to the night's terrors. At midnight a runner arrived in the area where Reynolds was dug in and said, "Is that you, Lieutenant?"

"Over here," said Reynolds.

The runner scurried over and said, "Major Jones needs the company COs and XOs at his command post."

"Thanks," said Reynolds as the runner disappeared in the darkness. Clutching his helmet, Reynolds made his way to the rear of the battalion's line where Bill Jones had set up his CP in a large tent on the beach. Through the open flap he could make out the faces of several men and the flicker of a flashlight. He ducked inside and dropped to one knee. He dimly recognized Porter Davidson and the CO of Charlie Company, his XO, and Spook Beck. After a few minutes the CO and XO of Baker Company crowded into the tent. Looking quickly at the men, Jones quietly said, "I was finally able to get the TBY set working, and we've got our orders." Reynolds glanced at the large, bulky radio that sat on an empty ammunition crate. "Red Mike Edson," Jones continued, "has taken over from Colonel Shoup, and he's ordered us to attack at 0800 along the south beach." He shone his flashlight on a finely detailed map of "Helen" and traced the location and direction of the attack with his finger.

"Here's the tricky part," said Jones. "We're attacking on a front only a hundred yards wide between the beach and the airfield. Meanwhile, Major Hays's battalion will be attacking in the opposite direction a couple of hundred yards, at most, to our left. And the Japs fortified the south shore even more heavily than the north. You think your men can handle it?"

The tent was silent until Captain Davidson spoke up. "With a front that narrow we'll have to make the attack in a column of companies. C will leapfrog B, B will leapfrog A, and so on. But I think we can do it."

"Will we have any supporting tanks?" asked Captain Krueger, the CO of Baker Company.

"Major Ryan's got a couple of Shermans," said Jones. "He's an old buddy of mine and I'm gonna ask him to loan 'em to us, provided I promise to give 'em back when we're done." Several of the men chuckled softly. "And I'm assigning mortar and machine-gun teams to each company. We've got all our people, all the ammo we can carry, and extra water for this infernal heat."

"Well, then, goddam, Major Jones, sir," said Spook with a big smile that was visible in the darkness. "We need to go kick some serious ass when the sun comes up."

"Yes we do, Mr. Beck," said Jones. "A helluva lot of fine Marines have already paid the ultimate price on this God-forsaken island while we were floating around on that damned transport. Now we've got a full battalion with all the firepower we can muster, and we need to avenge the honor of the Corps." Reynolds grit his teeth, for a split-second thinking about Grace and how badly he wanted to live, but then restraining the impulse to shout out "Semper Fi!"

CHAPTER TWELVE

EXHAUSTED, JOHN REYNOLDS SAT ON A LARGE CONCRETE SLAB, part of the remains of a Japanese pillbox that had taken a direct hit from a battleship's twelve-inch projectile. He unscrewed the cap of his canteen, took a long swallow, and surveyed the scene: concrete and coconut log blockhouses along the approaches to the airfield that had been filled with Japanese defenders, while others sheltered behind aircraft revetments, some manning lethal twin-mounted machine cannons. The blast from the naval and aerial bombardment had showered the bunkers with sand and debris. To the advancing Marines they resembled large mounds of sand littered with palm fronds on the flat-as-a-pancake landscape. With the temperature at least 100° and the sun at its zenith, the unrelenting heat was almost as much an enemy as the Japanese.

Attacking slowly along a hundred-yard front, so narrow that only a single platoon could be deployed, the Marines had destroyed the Japanese strong points with ruthless efficiency, pouring intense fire on each bunker while combat engineers tossed grenades or satchel charges down ventilation shafts or incinerated the hapless occupants with flamethrowers that fired a thirty-foot jet of burning gasoline. The two Sherman tanks Major Jones had "borrowed" from his friend Mike Ryan advanced in close proximity to the infantry, adding the firepower of their cannons to the destruction. Reynolds was appalled by ghastly images and smells of death and destruction that far exceeded anything Guadalcanal had prepared him for. Working his way along the beach, he'd stopped to inspect a concrete bunker where five smoldering Japanese corpses were sprawled, burnt black from head to toe. Overcome by the awful stench of burnt flesh, one young Marine had doubled over to vomit, while another, his face ashen, dropped to his knees and began sobbing uncontrollably. "Corpsman!" called Reynolds to a nearby Navy medic. "Get that man to the rear!" By noon the 1/6 Battalion's link-up with the remnant of the battalion that landed on Beach Red 2 two days earlier had been made. Their attack had achieved total success, securing the southern approach to the airfield and leaving behind some 250 dead Japanese at a cost of relatively light casualties. Reynolds cupped some water in his hand and mopped his face, wondering, what next?

After a few minutes a runner scurried up and said, "Hey, Lieutenant, the skipper wants to see you back at his CP."

"Where?"

"Follow me." The two men moved to the rear in a low crouch, threading their way past the Marines' rifle teams and bypassing piles of Japanese corpses, to Captain Davidson's command post, a large shell crater where two ponchos had been rigged to afford some shade from the brutal noonday sun. Davidson was squatting on an ammo crate next to his radioman. "Well, Skipper," said Reynolds as he dropped to one knee. "What are our orders?"

"I can't raise Jones on the phone," said Davidson. Reynolds noticed the expression of infinite tiredness on Davidson's sweaty face and wondered if he looked as bad. "The telephone wires we strung are all shot to hell. And the radio's only working in the clear. I'll have to send a runner."

"How about one of the code-talkers?" suggested Reynolds.

"Can you find one?" Reynolds ducked out of the shell hole, returning after a few minutes with a Marine whose face was deep brown with high cheekbones, a full-blooded Navajo.

"Listen, Chief," said Davidson, "I'm tryin' to get through to Major Jones, who took off in one of the tanks for Colonel Shoup's CP. Can you get one of your guys on the radio?" The dark-skinned Marine grunted. "Tell him the 1/6 has linked up with the Second Marines at the airfield. Ask him what are our orders." The radio operator turned a dial, toggled a switch, and gave the handset to the Navajo.

The others listened with intense curiosity as the Indian made contact with another Navajo at the division CP and communicated the message in their native tongue. After waiting a full five minutes, the code-talker grunted and gave the handset back to the radio operator. Turning to Davidson, he said, "Sir, orders are to advance through the Second Marines and resume attack at 1330 hours. Move one company to the left to link up with 2/8." He smiled unexpectedly. "Big Chief's on his way back."

"Good job," said Davidson. With a quick salute, the Navajo hurried from the command post. Davidson frowned and said, "If I shift Charlie Company to the left, we'll have to make the attack with just two companies."

Reynolds nodded and said, "And Spook's weapons company."

"Pass the word to the platoon leaders," said Davidson, "to move forward through the Second Marines. I'll wait here for Jones."

"Aye, aye, sir." Reynolds scrambled out of the crater and carefully made his way back. After locating Joe Thompson and Bill Ford, Reynolds found Travis Henderson reclining on his pack, with the thirty-odd men of his rifle platoon anchoring the far left of the company's position. Occasionally a Marine vehicle would venture onto the airstrip, immediately drawing fire from Japanese machine guns at the far end of the runway. Slumping down next to Travis, Reynolds took off his helmet, wiped his brow, and said, "Dang it's hot."

"I'm used to it," said Travis, "growin' up workin' cattle in the summertime." Reynolds slipped on his helmet and said, "I've just come from the skipper, and orders are for Able and Baker to resume the attack at 1330 after we pass through the Second Marines."

"What about Charlie?" said Travis.

"They're ordered to link up with the Eighth Marines near Red 3."

"Will we have any fire support?"

"The Tenth Marines' pack howitzers will lay down a barrage fifteen minutes before we jump off. And we'll have covering fire from the destroyers." Both men could distinguish two ships about a mile offshore.

"Where will you be, Johnny?"

"Right here with you."

"You oughta stay back with the skipper."

"Not unless I get a direct order."

"Have it your way." Travis hurried off to explain the plan to his squad leaders. After a few minutes the waterman arrived and the men topped off their canteens. Reynolds leaned against the blasted trunk of a palm tree and waited. The heat and stench made him feel faint. Closing his eyes, he bowed his head and silently prayed. When he opened his eyes, Travis Henderson was coming toward him in a low crouch. Reynolds had noticed a subtle change in Travis ever since he'd gotten the letter from his girl in Texas, not self-pity, but a devil-may-care attitude, which made Reynolds worry. With a glance at his watch, Reynolds said, "All set?"

Travis dropped to one knee and nodded. "This is a damn crazy maneuver," he said. "Advancing two companies on a front only a hundred yards wide."

"Any wider and we'd be firing at our own people, and they'd be shootin' back."

The same young runner scampered up and said, "Sorry, sir. The skipper says he needs you at his CP."

Reynolds looked briefly into his friend's eyes, put a hand on his shoulder, and said, "Good luck, Trav." He turned to follow the runner to the rear. Reaching the command post, Reynolds crawled into the shell hole, where Porter Davidson was conferring with Bill Jones.

With his corncob pipe clenched in his teeth, Jones turned to Reynolds and said, "Able Company will lead the attack, followed by Baker. Once we clear the end of the runway we can spread out and advance two companies abreast." Davidson and Reynolds nodded. "Good luck," said Jones before climbing out of the crater. At 1245 the order was given to advance through the decimated lines of the Second Marines. The veterans of three days of battle under the most appalling conditions stared vacantly at the fresh reinforcements. Once the 1/6 was in position, the pack howitzers opened up, concentrating their fire on the Japanese strong points two hundred yards in front of Able Company's line. A Navy destroyer joined the barrage with its five-inch guns. Able Company's Marines surged forward with a crackle of rifle fire and staccato bursts of machine guns, advancing about three hundred yards and destroying Japanese bunkers with acts of great individual heroism. Over two hours had passed, and some fifty Marines lay dead or wounded on the hot sand. While corpsmen attended to the most severely injured, the men sought shelter behind downed coconut trees and shot-up revetments as the Japanese continued to pound the narrow front.

Major Jones, whose command post was to the rear of Baker Company, listened to the dissipating sounds of the attack and the crash of the Japanese cannon with growing unease. It was almost five o'clock, and his men had been in action almost continuously since sunup. They were bound to be at the limit of their endurance and many suffering from heat exhaustion or dehydration. But they had to press the attack while there was still daylight. A runner, his face filthy and uniform drenched in sweat, stumbled into the CP. "Able Company's pinned down, sir, under fire from one of the big Jap guns." Jones thought for a moment and then turned to the operations officer and said, "Send a runner to Baker Company to shift their men across Able's position and continue the attack. And lay down new telephone wire. We've *got* to have communications."

"Aye, aye, sir."

John Reynolds tried to get comfortable in a shallow hole he'd dug with his entrenching tool, listening to the thud-thud of the heavy Japanese gun and watching the heat waves shimmering over the airstrip. His lips were cracked and tongue felt swollen, but he was determined to conserve the water left in his canteen. He wondered what had become of those two borrowed tanks. Looking to the rear, he watched clouds of dirty smoke and brown dust drifting across the blazing orb of the sun. Clutching his helmet, Reynolds crawled over to a blown-up Japanese coconut-log bunker where Davidson was sitting on a spool of telephone wire. "Do we have a phone hookup to Jones's CP?" asked Reynolds. Davidson nodded. "Then I think we should call in naval fire on that Jap gun."

"Hell, it's not even two hundred yards from our men," said Davidson.

"I think it's a chance we've got to take." As if to punctuate the point, a round from the six-inch Japanese gun slammed into their line, throwing up a cloud of sand and debris. Davidson briefly studied his map, which was divided into one hundred-by-one hundred-yard squares, and then telephoned the battalion command post and gave the operations officer the coordinates of the Japanese gun. He and Reynolds anxiously gazed out to sea and then ducked at the sight of the orange muzzle flashes of a destroyer's five-inch guns. One of the shells fell long, but the other, luckily, was a direct hit, sending pieces of the Japanese gun and turret high into the air in a fireball. The company's riflemen, who'd taken casualties from the gun for hours, cheered wildly. As Reynolds watched, several squads charged out of their holes and lobbed grenades at two light trucks mounted with 30-caliber machine guns, which were instantly set ablaze. The rest of the company surged forward, driving back the unseen Japanese defenders and advancing a hundred yards beyond the burning trucks.

Within an hour Baker Company successfully negotiated the complex and dangerous maneuver, passing through Able Company's lines and deploying to their immediate right, adjacent to the beach. But the sun was setting. Resting on one knee, Reynolds felt overwhelmingly exhausted. The division's eighty-mile march to Foxton and back flashed across his mind. No wonder the general had been so determined to toughen up the men. Several hundred yards to the rear the two Japanese trucks were still in flames. Reynolds surveyed the company in the gathering dusk: 150 or so men, digging shallow holes in the sand or sheltering behind wrecked Japanese fortifications. He struggled up and went to look for the captain.

He found Porter Davidson in a crater with the telephone handset pressed to his ear. With a quick glance at Reynolds, Davidson said, "Aye, aye, sir," and handed to phone to his radioman. "Krueger's been hit," he said. "Shot by a sniper. So that makes Schulz the acting CO of Baker."

"Schulz?" said Reynolds.

"Well, there's nothing we can do about it. Jones is convinced the Japs are gonna counterattack, and we need to get the men into position and set up our fields of fire."

"Listen, Skipper," said Reynolds, "I think we should pull the company back."

"Pull back? Are you nuts?"

"Those burning Jap trucks are directly behind us. Once it's dark our men will be silhouetted against the flames. We should pull back to the other side of the trucks."

Davidson considered, staring at the flaming wrecks. "I'm afraid you're right," he said after a minute. "But it won't be easy. I'll send a runner to Schulz telling him to keep his men right on our flank, and you need to find the platoon leaders and tell them what to do. And they better be goddamn sneaky about it." Reynolds nodded and disappeared into the twilight. Within a half hour the company had silently retreated, so that the flaming trucks were now between their lines and the enemy. Reynolds checked with the platoon leaders to make sure all their men were accounted for. "Everyone but Old White," said Travis Henderson.

"What about Old White?" said Reynolds.

"He's shot in the guts, and he won't budge."

"Oh, Jesus," said Reynolds. "Can't they get him on a stretcher?"

"He's in a shell hole up there with his BAR and lots of ammo and says if he's gonna die, he's takin' lots of Japs with him."

"But, dammit, Trav," said Reynolds, "that's right where we're siting our machine guns!"

"I know, but he refused to move. He's dying, John. He won't last the night."

Reynolds felt a lump in his throat and suppressed a sob. "Okay," he muttered. "Make sure your machine-gun teams have interlocking fields of fire. I'm pretty sure the Japs are gonna hit us with everything they've got." Returning to Davidson's improvised CP, he found the captain again on the telephone. "He's right here," said Davidson, handing Reynolds the handset.

"Yes, sir," said Reynolds.

"I want you to get over to Baker Company," said Bill Jones, "and find Lieutenant Schulz. I need to make damn sure he understands we've got to hold that position at all costs. If the Japs turn our flank, they'll get in our rear. Can you do that?"

"Yes, sir."

"Call me on the phone after you find him," said Jones. "I want your first-hand opinion. That's all."

Handing the phone back to Davidson, Reynolds thought, *opinion? Opinion about what?* "Jones ordered me to go find Schulz," he said.

"Why?" said Davidson. "You could get shot by our own people."

"Not sure. He wants to make sure Schulz understands his orders."

After a harrowing fifteen minutes, Reynolds finally succeeded in locating the Baker Company command post near a burned-out pillbox. "Where's Lieutenant Schulz?" he asked a young private who challenged him with his fixed bayonet.

"Over there, sir." The private jerked his head. Schulz was crouched behind a log-reinforced barricade. A racket was coming from the Japanese lines; someone banging pots and pans together, then a voice yelling: "Hey,

Mah-reen! You gonna die!" It was the same trick they'd used at night on Guadalcanal, trying to get a jumpy Marine to reveal their position by yelling back. "Hey, Arnold," said Reynolds, kneeling down besides Schulz. Schulz looked at him with eyes as wide as saucers.

"They took our reserve," said Schulz in a fierce whisper. The terror in his eyes was unmistakable, even in the darkness. The Japanese yelled more taunts, provoking a Marine to fire a short burst from his BAR. "Dammit!" said Reynolds. "You've got to order your men to hold their fire!"

"We gotta pull back," said Schulz with a quaver in his voice. "We can't hold 'em."

"Your orders are to stay put and hold this position at all costs." Both men ducked as a Japanese machine gunner fired a burst in the direction of the Marine BAR man.

Schulz merely shook his head, cowering behind the barricade. "No," he muttered. "Gotta pull back."

"Goddammit, Schulz!" said Reynolds. "That's disobeying orders!" He stared at Schulz, who refused to look at him. Realizing it was pointless, Reynolds crawled over to a nearby shell crater where he located the company radio operator. "Get me the battalion CP," he ordered. After a moment the man gave Reynolds the handset. "Lieutenant Reynolds for Major Jones, over," he said. As he waited, he kicked himself for losing his temper with Schulz.

"Okay, Reynolds," said Jones after a moment. "What's the situation?"

"Lieutenant Schulz is planning to pull Baker back, sir."

"What!" demanded Jones. "His orders are to hold in that position. Do you think he's capable of performing his duty?"

Reynolds hesitated. He swallowed hard and said, "No, sir."

"Put Schulz on the radio," instructed Jones. "Then get back to your company."

On his way back through the Marines' lines Reynolds almost collided with Spook Beck in the darkness. "Where are you going?" asked Reynolds.

"Jones relieved Schulz from command of Baker and ordered me to form a reserve with about thirty guys from the weapons company and a bunch of cooks and typists, armed with nothin' but these carbines—goddam popguns." Both men paused to listen to the sound of firing. "It's not the main attack," said Reynolds. "Not yet. The Japs are just probing, trying to find a gap between the two companies."

"Yeah, well, that's the gap my boys are gonna plug."

"Good luck, Spook." Reynolds disappeared into the darkness.

When it came, the Japanese counterattack, a succession of probing assaults over the course of the night culminating in a furious banzai charge by some four hundred Rikunsentai warriors, was a desperate, last gasp, a final paroxysm of violence in one of the war's bloodiest battles. The massed infantry came in waves, supported by artillery and light tanks equipped with powerful headlights that both exposed and momentarily blinded the Marines in their foxholes. But the Marines' water-cooled, 50-caliber machine guns had been carefully sited to trap the attacking troops in interlocking fields of fire. After the first wave was mowed down, the Japanese retreated, only to come charging back, the tanks raking the Marines at point-blank range. Reynolds watched the final massed attack unfold from the company command post until the private next to him was hit in the chest and instantly killed. "We've got to hold them off!" yelled Reynolds, grabbing the private's M-1 and charging out of the shell hole. Diving into another foxhole where a wounded Marine was writhing in agony, Reynolds raised the rifle to his shoulder and squeezed off eight quick rounds at the advancing Japanese. Fumbling with another clip, he winced at the concussion of two 81-millimeter mortars. Some thirty yards to his left a lone Marine climbed out of his hole and stood facing the oncoming Japanese. In the glare of the headlights from an advancing tank Reynolds could see it was Arnold Schulz. As Reynolds watched in astonishment, Schulz, firing his rifle from the hip, walked slowly toward the tank and was instantly cut down.

Spook Beck had deployed his ragtag reserve at an acute angle to the advancing Japanese, bolstered by two heavy machine-gun squads. He ordered the men to hold their fire until the attackers were almost in contact with Able Company, and then unleashed a murderous volley. The Marines surged out of their foxholes with savage shouts and dashed toward the advancing enemy. And then another wave of Japanese suddenly appeared out of the darkness, engaging Spook's men in brutal hand-to-hand combat with bayonets, grenades, Ka-Bar knives, and even the butts of their carbines.

Reynolds jammed clip after clip into his M-1, firing from the rim of his foxhole as the noise of battle—rifles and machine guns, the tanks' cannons, mortars, and screams—swelled to a crescendo. One of the last operable tanks pivoted and swung its cannon toward Reynolds's foxhole. A young Marine dashed from his hole and sprinted for the tank, climbing up to drop a grenade into the turret. Before it could explode, the cannon's muzzle flashed orange, scoring a direct hit on Reynolds's position.

Major Willie K. Jones surveyed a scene from hell as the lurid red orb of the rising sun flashed on the eastern horizon. Acrid black smoke drifted up from a hundred small fires, burning trucks, tanks, and destroyed fortifications. Even in the dim light Jones could make out hundreds of dead Japanese soldiers littering the battlefield, some piled in heaps. In fact, hardly a single Japanese attacker had survived the suicidal frontal assaults. Jones knew in an instant that the battle was won, but at a terrible cost. Porter Davidson and Travis Henderson, whose arm was in a bloody sling, wandered up as if in a daze. "Able Company did a superb job, Captain," said Jones. "I'm recommending you for a bronze star."

"All we can do, sir," said Davidson, "is put these boys into position. And then it's up to them and the NCOs."

Travis Henderson fumbled for a cigarette and lit it. "Has anybody seen John Reynolds?" he asked. "Or Spook?" The other two men shook their heads. "I gotta go look for 'em," said Travis. Details of Marines were already gathering up their dead comrades to remove for burial before rigor mortis set in. Travis began walking slowly along what had been the Marines' lines. About fifty yards out he spotted a dead Marine lying beside a burned-out Japanese tank. He walked up and rolled the man over. It was Arnold Schulz, his chest riddled with bullet wounds. Thirty yards to the right were the charred remains of the two trucks that had been on fire. Lying in a shell hole in front of the trucks, his BAR gun cradled in his arms, was the body of Gunnery Sergeant "Old White," surrounded by dead Japanese soldiers. As he walked back toward the Able Company lines Travis observed a burial detail lifting a body wrapped in a poncho. He hurried up, asked the men to stop, and carefully lifted the edge of the poncho. It was Spook Beck, shot dead by a bullet through his chest.

Wiping tears from his eyes, Travis continued his search. At approximately the center of what had been the company's line, he came upon a shallow foxhole where two men were sprawled. One, a young private, had been shot in the head, his body already rigid. The other man was lying on his side, his camouflage utility shirt caked with dried blood. Travis's heart leapt at the sight of lieutenant's bars on his collar. He knelt beside him and gently lifted up his helmet, revealing the pale white face of John Reynolds, eyes shut, lying as in peaceful repose.

CHAPTER THIRTEEN

Over a month had passed since Grace and John's tearful farewell at the Aotea Quay, and of course there was no word on the whereabouts or the fate of the Second Marine Division. Within days of their departure it had been evident to everyone in Wellington that the story about exercises at Hawke's Bay was just a ruse and that their real destination was some Japanese stronghold in the far reaches of the Pacific. As usual, Grace, dressed for work at the department store, took her place at the breakfast table at 8:00 a.m., where, as usual, her father was seated in his vest and shirtsleeves with his cup of tea and soft-boiled egg, reading the morning paper. "Have you seen this?" he said over his shoulder to his wife Vera, who was standing at the stove in the kitchen frying bacon.

"No, dear," replied Grace's mother.

"What is it, Father?" said Grace. Each morning for the past two weeks she'd been desperate for news of the Americans.

"The Marines have landed on some island called Tarawa," said Thomas Lucas. "In the Gilberts archipelago, wherever in blazes that might be."

"Is there a battle?" said Grace. "Does it say which Marines?"

"Oh, yes," said Grace's father. "It says the Marines met fierce Japanese resistance. Let's see, here it is. The Second Marine Division."

"Oh, no," moaned Grace. "That's John's division." She burst into tears, burying her face in her hands.

Grace's mother walked into the breakfast alcove and put her hand on Grace's shoulder. "But surely, dear," she said, "you knew they were going off to fight? That's why they were sent here." Unlike her daughter, who was tall and athletic, Mrs. Lucas was petite and favored old-fashioned dresses and a hairstyle that made her look mousy.

"I know, Mother," said Grace, wiping away her tears. "But that doesn't make it any easier, not knowing if he's all right." Mrs. Lucas studied her daughter, thinking *perhaps now she understands what I've been going through since Charlie's been in North Africa.*

The following days brought unremitting dread and nervous exhaustion to Grace and thousands of other young women in Wellington, as more news of the brutal battle for Tarawa appeared in each day's newspapers. At night she wept as she looked at the framed photograph on her dresser—John, so handsome in his uniform with his arm around her waist—and then knelt at her bedside and fervently prayed that the following day a letter or telegram would arrive with word that he was safe. Almost everyone in the city was sickened by the reports of the terrible casualties suffered by the Marines in a mere three days of fighting, over a thousand dead and 2,200 more wounded. And then, days before Christmas, the horrific photographs published in *Life* magazine of dead Marines floating in the shallows or partially buried in sand on the beach appeared in a local weekly, and footage of Marines storming the Japanese pillboxes was shown in the newsreels. Grace was almost physically ill from worry, scarcely able to eat or sleep. She took some consolation from the fact that two other girls at work had received no word from their Marine boyfriends, assuring one another that it was simply due to the great distances and interrupted communications. But with each passing day Grace fell deeper into despair.

She had another reason to be sick with worry. And simply to be sick. At first she attributed the morning attacks of nausea to her deep anxiety. But now it was late December, and over two months had passed since her last period. She reluctantly made up her mind it was time to face facts. Seated in the doctor's office, Grace nervously twisted her handkerchief into a knot. After a few minutes, the doctor, a balding, middle-aged man in a white coat, reappeared, accompanied by his nurse. Frowning, he said, "You're pregnant, Miss Lucas. But you're in good health, and I see no reason why you shouldn't be able to carry the baby to full term." Grace looked down, avoiding the nurse's expression of severe disapprobation. "A healthy diet is important," he continued. Grace took a deep breath, trying to calm her racing heart. The news was what she'd expected, but now she realized that some part of her had clung to the irrational belief that she wasn't pregnant after all. "Miss Lucas," said the doctor. She raised her eyes to look at him. "I trust you know who the father is?"

The impudence of his question was like a slap in the face. Reddening, she rose from her chair and said, "Indeed I do. In fact, we're engaged to be married. Except that he's away, fighting the Japanese, for the sake of preserving *your* liberty. And yours!" she added, turning to the nurse, who took a step back. Grabbing her coat and purse, Grace hurried from the small office, slamming the door behind her. Walking along the sidewalk in downtown Wellington on the warm summer day, she imagined she could simply go into the drugstore where she and John had often enjoyed a milkshake, and he would be sitting at the counter, smiling at her, so handsome in his uniform. *Will I ever see him again?* she wondered with an involuntary gasp.

As much as she dreaded it, she was determined to confront her mother and picked up her pace on her way to the streetcar stop. As she traveled the familiar route, she considered that there was the chance a letter or telegram would be waiting for her, letting her know that John was fine and would soon be coming back for her. To marry her and help her to raise their baby. A baby. She was having a baby. Returning to the bungalow, Grace was careful to avoid her mother, who was in her favorite chair in her sewing room. Grace gently closed the door and went to her dresser, where she'd concealed the small velvet box under her lingerie. Taking the ring from the box, she slipped it on her finger and held out her hand, admiring the tiny diamond in the sunlight shining in the window. With a quick look at herself in the mirror, straightening her hair, she squared her shoulders and let herself out.

"Hello, Mother," said Grace, standing in the entrance to the sewing room.

Glancing up from the needlepoint pattern in her lap, Vera Lucas said, "Hello, dear. Home early?"

"I didn't go to work today. I called in sick." She conspicuously held up her left hand to her face.

"But you're not ill. Grace . . . what's that ring?"

Grace walked into the room and sat on the arm of an upholstered chair. She held out her hand for her mother's inspection. "It's my engagement ring," she said. "John and I are going to be married."

"Oh, my Lord," said Mrs. Lucas with a sharp intake of breath. "Oh, Grace, how could you? Why, your father will be furious . . ."

"I can assure you," said Grace with a trace of asperity, "that John always intended to ask for Father's consent. But be that as it may, we *are* going to be married." After a few moments of stunned silence, Grace added, "It's important you understand that." Her mother responded with a puzzled expression. "Because of what I'm about to tell you."

"Oh, my dear me," said Mrs. Lucas, "I think I should have a spot of tea."

Once both women were seated at the table in the breakfast alcove with steaming cups of tea Grace looked her mother in the eye and said, "I've been to see the doctor today. The fact is, mother, I'm having a baby." An anguished look came over Mrs. Lucas's face and tears welled in her eyes. "John's baby."

"Oh, Grace," said Mrs. Lucas as tears trickled down her cheeks, "how could you? We'll be ruined."

"But Mother, I *want* the baby. I know John will be a wonderful father, and husband."

"But, Grace, you don't even know if John . . ." She let the thought die in mid-sentence.

Grace swallowed hard and said, "No. I don't."

"We've got to decide what's to be done with you," said Mrs. Lucas. "It won't do having you here at home, in your condition. And we'd better think of something before your father gets home."

"It sounds as though you're planning to send me away," said Grace. "I'm a grown woman and can make my own plans . . ."

"You've brought terrible shame on this family," said Mrs. Lucas, pushing away her tea, "and you'll do as your father and I believe is best."

Grace sat miserably in an armchair in the parlor as her father paced by the cold fireplace. Her mother hunched forward on the sofa, resting her arms on her knees, looking nervously from her daughter to her husband. "Yes, I suppose it will have to do," he said, stopping abruptly and glaring at Grace. "Goodness knows Uncle Dick owes me a favor after I helped him out of that trouble with the bank."

"But what will I possibly do, living in a shabby little farmhouse in the country?" said Grace.

"What you'll do," said Tom Lucas with his finger pointed at his daughter, "is keep well out of sight of our friends and acquaintances until you've had this, ah . . . this confounded baby!"

"It's absolutely medieval," said Grace. "But once I've heard from John, and am able to let him know what's happened, perhaps he can find a way, to take leave, that is, and . . ."

"You're talking rot," said Mr. Lucas. "In the first place, you don't know what's become of that damned American . . ."

"Tom," said Mrs. Lucas. "Please!"

"Well, you don't," he continued. "And even if he made it through that awful battle, it's impossible he could come back here, with the war on."

Grace held her head in her hands, staring down at the floral carpet. Raising her eyes to her father's, she said, "I know he's alive. Don't ask me how, but I'm certain of it. And he's coming back for me, and we're going to raise the baby . . ."

"Well, we'll find out soon enough what's happened to your American friend," said Mr. Lucas, stuffing his hands in his pockets. "But for now, you'll move out to live with Uncle Dick and Aunt Martha and you'll have this baby. And then we'll decide what's to be done with it."

Grace stood up, holding her father in her gaze. "No," she said coldly. "Then *I'll* decide what's to be done with my baby."

As her father steered his old Austin sedan off the macadam onto the dusty track the final hundred yards to the farmhouse, Grace gazed absently out the open window in the warmth of the afternoon. Thankfully, the trip from town had taken only forty minutes on Saturday, as hardly a word, apart from a comment on the pleasant weather, had been spoken between them. Over five weeks had passed since the Battle of Tarawa, with no word from John or of his fate, and no one whom Grace could possibly contact to make an inquiry. Blackness had settled over her soul, though it failed to extinguish the small inner voice that insisted he'd survived and someday would return for her. After several days of angry insistence that she'd remain in Wellington and continue in her job at the department store, she'd surrendered to the inevitable, submitting to her coerced confinement in the countryside for the duration of her pregnancy. Bumping along the rutted road, she gazed at the familiar green pasture, dotted with black-faced sheep, and the old hay barn. Almost every summer during her childhood and teens she and her brother Charlie had spent a week at the farm with her Uncle Dick Williams and his wife Martha, her mother's younger sister, learning the usual chores: milking the cows, churning butter, helping with the sheep, and gathering eggs from the chicken coop. In a way the thought of spending months with her aunt and uncle was welcome, as they, without children of their own, had always been fond of Grace, though less so of Charlie, whom they'd treated as a nuisance.

Her father pulled up in front of the modest, two-story house and set the parking brake. Uncle Dick appeared on the porch with a wave, followed a moment later by Aunt Martha, wearing an apron and a scarf over her graying curls. As Tom Lucas climbed out and walked around to the back to pop the trunk, Uncle Dick opened the car door and helped Grace out. "Hello, my dear," he said with a brief embrace. Aunt Martha walked up and gave Grace an appraising look.

"Here we are," said Mr. Lucas, lifting Grace's battered old suitcase and carrying it to the porch.

"That's everything?" said Dick.

"I'm afraid so," said Grace with a modest smile.

"Well, let's go inside and get you situated in the spare bedroom."

"I'd best be on my way," said Grace's father.

"You won't stay for supper, Tom?" said Aunt Martha.

"No, thanks," he said, pushing back his fedora and wiping his brow. "Take good care of yourself, Grace," he added, "and try not to be a bother. We'll be out for a visit before long."

"Goodbye, Father." She turned and walked into the house. Thankfully, the spare bedroom was at the back on the ground floor with its own bathroom, far removed from the two upstairs bedrooms. Grace followed Uncle Dick to the bedroom, where he laid her suitcase on one of the twin beds. "After you wash up and put your things away," he said, "why don't you join us for a cup of tea?"

"Thanks," said Grace as she reached down to open the clasps of her suitcase. The room was just as she remembered it, with two windows that looked out on the backyard and pasture, hand-sewn quilts on the twin beds, and an old-fashioned sampler on the wall. She folded her blouses, sweaters, nightgown, and underwear in the dresser drawers and hung her dresses, skirts, and coat in the closet, which smelled of mothballs. Lastly, she removed the framed photograph from the studio in Wellington, the two of them looking so young and happy, and placed it on the dresser. Pushing the empty suitcase underneath the bed, she went to the bathroom and turned the hot tap, after a moment washing her hands and then splashing her face. After toweling off, she brushed her hair and applied fresh lipstick, feeling she was ready to face them and the inevitable probing questions.

Her aunt and uncle were seated in matching easy chairs in the parlor, cradling cups of tea. "Pour yourself a cup, dear, and have a seat," said Mrs. Williams. "You're looking refreshed." Like Grace's mother, she was a small woman whose care-worn face and graying hair made her look older than her mid-forties.

"Yes, I'm feeling better," said Grace, "after that hot drive." She poured a cup from the teapot on a sideboard, stirred in milk and sugar, and sat on the sofa. Dick was a kindly if somewhat rustic-looking man in his late forties, but Grace was well aware how quickly his smile could turn to anger. And, Grace observed, he was much heavier than she remembered, wearing a cheap pair of elastic suspenders over his sizable girth. To her mother's annoyance, Grace had insisted on wearing her engagement ring, which now attracted Aunt Martha's notice.

"That's a lovely ring," she said. "And who is . . ."

"His name is John Reynolds," said Grace. "We're going to be married as soon as he has leave and can return to Wellington. And he's the father of the baby I'm expecting." The mention of the word "baby" appeared to startle Mr. Williams, as the fact that Grace was not yet showing had enabled him to indulge the fiction that she was not really pregnant. Grace took a sip of tea and gave him an expectant look.

"I see," he said after a moment. "And I gather that Mr. Reynolds is an American soldier?"

"He's an officer in the United States Marine Corps. I assume you've heard of them."

"Oh, yes," offered Aunt Martha. "Everyone's heard stories of these red-blooded American Marines. Frankly, Grace, I think it's a disgrace that so many of our New Zealand girls have allowed themselves . . ."

"A disgrace?" said Grace. "You make it sound as though there's something shameful about falling in love with an American."

"Perhaps not," countered Aunt Martha sharply, "though it *is* shameful, in my opinion, to be expecting a baby out of wedlock." Both Grace and Uncle Dick looked away. "There," said Aunt Martha with her chin uplifted. "I've said it."

"Well," said Grace, recovering her composure, "as much as I appreciate your hospitality, I assure you that coming here wasn't my idea."

"Well, dear," said Uncle Dick with an avuncular smile, "you *are* our family."

"And I also happen to know," said Grace in an even voice, "that in effect you're repaying a favor to my father by taking me in."

"Why, that's nonsense!" said Uncle Dick hotly.

"But you needn't worry," Grace concluded as she put aside her tea. "I'll live up to my end of the bargain, and earn my keep doing housework and helping with the chores. After all, you taught me and Charlie well all those summer holidays we spent here. And now I think I'll go to my room and rest."

Grace's initial interview with her aunt and uncle set the tone for her stay at the farm: superficially cordial, unvarying polite, but with mutual resentment and dislike lurking just beneath the surface. The New Year holiday had been a dismal affair, separated from her family and friends and accompanying the Williams to a "celebration" with pies, cakes, and lemonade at a neighboring farmhouse with a handful of other rustics. For the time being, Grace realized, she could be seen out in public, but that would soon change. And as each day passed with no news from John or one of his friends, a voice in her head cried out more insistently that he had been killed. Her daily routines—the chores in return for which her uncle had tacitly agreed to provide her food and lodging—were equally dreary. Up with the sun before six to milk the two cows and then lugging the pails of milk to the separator; sweeping out the barn, and gathering eggs from the henhouse; tasks which in her absence she knew would have been done by Uncle Dick or Aunt Martha, who now watched her perform them with something like grim satisfaction. After the first several weeks she increasingly hated her life on the farm and desperately missed her job at the department store and the simple pleasures of her old life in town. And more than anything, she missed John.

Most evenings after supper, which typically consisted of a grilled chop or piece of chicken or fish with potatoes and a canned vegetable, her aunt and uncle would retire to the parlor to listen to variety shows on the radio, and Grace would go to her room to read. She'd brought along several books but almost immediately wrote to her mother asking her to send more. She read novels, both cheap thrillers and serious literature; history and biography; and, for the first time in her adult life, she began reading the Bible. Reading the Bible, especially the Gospels and the Psalms, caused her to question the Williams's religious beliefs in a way she'd never really considered about herself or her parents. Uncle Dick and Aunt Martha were regular churchgoers and seemed to place great importance on strict adherence to Christian morals, but it struck Grace that there was nothing remotely spiritual in their daily lives, no prayers or reading of scripture, but in fact many of the qualities that Jesus had strongly condemned: pride, judgment, greed, and lack of concern for the needy. Though she and John had seldom discussed religion, she knew he was from a deeply religious family.

By the middle of January the bulge in Grace's belly was clearly showing, and consequently she was confined to the farm. The dresses she'd brought with her no longer fit, and she was desperate for maternity clothes but had no way to shop for them. After some hesitation, she wrote a long letter to her friend Doris, explaining that she and John had secretly become engaged before the Marines shipped out and that she was now expecting a baby, describing her anguish at not knowing if John was dead or alive and her lonely confinement at her uncle's farm. Was it possible, Grace wrote, that Doris could come see her on a weekend and bring along some maternity dresses that Grace would be happy to pay for? After addressing the envelope, she entrusted it, along with a letter to her mother, to Uncle Dick, who assured her he would see to it they were mailed.

At the end of another in a long, long succession of boring, tiresome days, Grace stretched out on her bed, kicked off her shoes, and lightly traced her fingers over her abdomen. She then knelt at her bedside, closed her eyes, and silently prayed, imploring God to spare John's life and bring him safely back to her so that together they could raise their baby, a child she sincerely pledged would be raised in the Christian faith. Uttering "Amen," she wearily rose and went to the bathroom to brush her teeth and change into her nightgown.

CHAPTER FOURTEEN

SITTING ON THE BACK STEPS OF THE FARMHOUSE, GRACE clasped her arms around her knees and studied the charcoal clouds billowing over the distant blue hilltops. After a moment she could just make out a rumble of thunder, a rarity on the North Island. It was by far her favorite time of year; bright sunshine with the afternoon temperatures rising into the seventies, the meadows verdant and blanketed with wildflowers, sheltered from the brisk winds of Wellington in the interior farmland. And thankfully she had a Saturday afternoon all to herself, as Uncle Dick and Aunt Martha had taken the car for a day trip into the city. And yet as she forlornly watched the gathering storm clouds, she wondered, for the hundredth time, why a loving God would have destined a young man as fine as John Reynolds to die on a tiny speck of land no one had ever heard of, far out in the middle of the vast ocean. And, for the hundredth time, she reproached herself; in the first place, it was not for her to know the mind of God, and in the second, there was the possibility, the very remote possibility, that John was alive, possibly clinging to life in some American hospital. Squeezing her eyes shut, she lifted a prayer that it might be so.

Grace opened her eyes at the sound of the border collie's sharp bark and the throaty exhaust of an approaching automobile. By the time she scooped up her shoes and walked into the house she could hear a car door slamming shut and footsteps on the front porch. There was a knock at the door, and as the Williams seldom had visitors, she cautiously opened it a crack. "Hello, Grace," said Doris Campbell with a bright smile. "I wasn't sure I'd found the right place." She was holding a box under her arm.

"Oh, my gosh, Doris! You have no idea how happy I am to see you."

Doris strode into the front hall and placed the box on a table. "And I've got a surprise," she said with a smile.

"You mean these?" said Grace as she lifted the lid and quickly examined several maternity dresses.

"No, I mean Andrew Cadbury, who's come along with me. He's outside getting acquainted with your collie."

After a few moments Cadbury, who was wearing his Royal Navy uniform with his hat under his arm, trooped up the steps and came inside. "Hello, Grace," he said, extending his hand. "What a pleasure to see you again." He was tall and of medium build, with light brown hair and an attractive though not especially handsome face and an easy smile.

Taking his hand, Grace smiled and said, "You've no idea how desperate I've been for company. And we're in luck, as my aunt and uncle are in Wellington for the day." She led her guests into the parlor and sat next to Doris on the sofa, while Andrew remained standing.

"Grace," said Doris with a pained expression, "I was so terribly sorry when I learned what happened. John seemed such a fine man, and now this."

"Yes," said Grace with a nod. "I suppose we were fools not to have run off and married while we had the chance. And now I'm guilty of the unpardonable sin of having a baby without a husband."

"Do you know for certain," said Andrew, "that John was killed at Tarawa?"

Grace shook her head. "I haven't heard a word. Not a letter or telegram, from John or any of his mates. The only plausible explanation is that he was killed. And yet . . ."

"Yes," said Doris gently, "I suppose it's best not to give up hope."

"Frankly," said Andrew, "I'm not so sure. From all that I've heard and read, Tarawa was truly a terrible battle for the Marines. It was a great American victory, of course, but so many Marines paid for their heroism with their lives." Grace looked up into Andrew's eyes and burst into tears.

"I'm so sorry," he said, walking up to her and placing his hands on her shaking shoulders. "I shouldn't have . . ."

"No," said Grace with a sniffle. "What you said is true. I'm afraid I'm a bit of a wreck and rather easily go to pieces."

"I've got an idea," said Doris with a smile. "We brought along some cold beer—just in case—and as you're free of your, ah, chaperones . . ."

"My captors, you mean," said Grace as she wiped away her tears.

" . . . we might as well drink them."

"A splendid idea," said Andrew. "I'll fetch them."

Seated around a rickety wooden table in the yard behind the farmhouse, Grace, Doris, and Andrew enjoyed the cold beer in the warmth of the midsummer afternoon, as the thunderstorm had moved off to the north. "I've actually grown rather fond of your local lagers," said Andrew, "in particular, this Speight's." He studied the label on the brown bottle and then tipped back his head and had a long swallow. Running his hand across his mouth, he said, "What is it they call your beers here?"

"New Zealand draughts," said Doris with a smile. She took a sip and added, "Don't ask me why."

"I assume you're on leave from your ship?" said Grace, who looked far more comfortable, having changed into one of the shapeless maternity dresses Doris had brought her.

"Shore leave virtually every weekend," said Andrew, "as we've been assigned patrol duty for the port of Wellington and Cook Strait."

"Lucky you," said Grace.

"Indeed. With the lovely weather I've had lots of time to enjoy the city and surrounding area. It's no wonder so many of our countrymen have fallen in love with your country and emigrated here."

Grace took a sip of beer, pleased with the taste and the sensation of warm sun on her face. It was the first time she'd felt anything like pleasure in many weeks. "How long will your patrol duty last?" she asked.

"Hard to say," said Andrew. His coat was draped over the back of a chair and shirt sleeves rolled up. "At the moment, the Yanks are doing virtually all of the fighting in the Pacific, and our fleet, apart from a few ships like mine assigned to patrol the home waters in Australia and New Zealand, has retreated to the Indian Ocean. But that could change, and we'd likely be given some assignment in an offensive operation."

Aware that Andrew seemed to be paying more attention to Grace than to her, Doris said, "Well, that would be a pity."

Andrew glanced at his watch and said, "This has been wonderful, Grace, but I'm afraid we should be off. I've got just enough petrol to get us back to town."

"Will you come again?" said Grace, looking from Andrew to Doris. "You've no idea how wretched it is for me here."

"Aren't you at least allowed to go into the nearest village?" said Doris.

"No. I'm not allowed to drive the car, and it's too far to walk. I'm stuck here like an indentured servant, doing all manner of housework and farming chores for my aunt and uncle."

"How dreadful," said Andrew. "They should be ashamed of themselves."

"How long will you . . . I mean, when is the baby expected?" said Doris.

"On the fifteenth of June," said Grace with a sigh. "A long time off."

"Well, of course I'll be back for a visit," said Andrew, smiling encouragingly at Grace. "Provided I have shore leave and save up on my petrol ration."

Seated across from him, Doris studied the way he looked at Grace. Doris pushed back from the table and said, "Take care of yourself, Grace. You'll get through this. And there's still the possibility you could hear from John. I'll be praying."

"Thanks." Grace rose a bit awkwardly and followed Andrew and Doris around the side of the house to the car. With a wave they were off, bumping along the lane in a cloud of dust. Shielding her eyes from the sun, Grace watched until the sedan was a mere speck in the distance. When she walked into the parlor she saw that Andrew had forgotten his white officer's hat with the Royal Navy insignia. With an inward smile, she thought, *well, of course he'll have to return for it.*

Starting her sixth month of pregnancy, Grace tired easily and could barely see her own feet when she looked down. And she was beginning to feel the baby move and kick, a remarkable, wonderful sensation. She was almost finished with the morning's chores, having milked the cows and run the milk through the separator. She latched the wire door to the henhouse behind her and began gathering up the still-warm eggs, carrying them in her apron. The smell of the chickens' feces always nauseated her. Though she was over the morning sickness, there were certain sights and odors that invariably turned her stomach, including the henhouse and the look and smell of the bluish skim milk that poured from the separator. She was only permitted to drink the skim milk, which she found she could choke down if it was chilled, while her aunt and uncle enjoyed the cream and half-and-half. Trying to avoid inhaling the odors, she cradled a dozen brown eggs in her apron and hurried out into the fresh air. As it was late February, she'd noticed the first hint of fall in the crisp air when she'd gone out to the dairy barn at sunup. Taking care not to drop the eggs, she went inside to the kitchen, where she found Uncle Dick at the table, drinking tea and spreading marmalade on a slice of toast. "Good morning," said Grace as she transferred the eggs to a basket on the countertop.

"Morning," said Dick. Her hands on her hips, Grace arched her back with a sigh. "Have a seat," he said, nodding at the chair opposite him, "and take a load off your feet."

Grace sat, folding her arms across her belly. Glancing at her uncle's newspaper, she said, "Anything of interest in the paper today?"

"Not really," said Dick after taking a bite of toast. "Mostly news about the big battle the Russians have fought with the Germans at a place called Stalingrad. Nothing much about the war with the Japs. I reckon the Yanks are gearing up for their next big push."

"Yes, I suppose," said Grace absently.

Noticing her engagement ring, Dick said, "If your parents receive a letter from this chap, are you sure they'll send it along?"

"This chap? Oh, John, you mean." Dick nodded. "My fiancé. Yes, I made my mother swear she'd immediately forward any mail or telegrams."

"You know, Grace," said Dick, pushing his teacup aside and resting his elbows on the table, "it's been three months now since the Americans fought that battle of, ah, what's the name?"

"Tarawa."

"Yes, Tarawa. And as you haven't heard anything from this chap . . ."

"John, Uncle Dick. His name's John Reynolds."

"I think it's time for you to face up to facts," said Dick. "That he was killed in the battle."

"But I just don't *know*. He could have been badly wounded and recuperating in hospital somewhere." Suddenly Grace felt her eyes well with tears.

Dick shook his head with a frown. "It's high time you got on with your life. The sad truth is that there are tens of thousands of girls just like you who've lost their husbands or boyfriends in this terrible war. And it's a long way from being over." Grace nodded glumly. "Now go look for your aunt," said Dick. "She needs your help with the wash."

For days her uncle's words echoed in Grace's mind, when she was doing her chores first thing in the morning and at unexpected moments throughout the day; she had to "face up to facts" and accept that he was killed. Imperceptibly, the tiny flame of hope she'd kept alive in her heart for so many months began to gutter and die. If John was still alive he would have found some way to contact her. No, John was gone; she'd never see him again. The acceptance of his death brought with it an unexpected realization. So long as she'd clung to the hope of seeing him again she'd given little thought to the baby. The baby was all she had left of the connection to John, but, she bitterly reflected, sitting on the back steps in the gathering dusk after supper, she'd undoubtedly lose the baby too. For a time she'd allowed herself to fantasize over raising the baby. But that was all it was, a fantasy. In reality she'd be forced, not just by her mother and father, but by the powerful mores of the day, to give up the child for adoption. It was unthinkable that a respectable young woman would raise her child born out of wedlock. Besides, she had no money, and her father wouldn't support her. In the anguish of her grief, the thought of losing the baby was almost more than she could stand.

The weekends brought Grace the only respite from the drudgery of her life on the farm. After finishing her chores and housework by noontime on Saturday, she was free to do as she pleased until Monday morning, though not to leave the premises, not even to accompany her aunt and uncle to church on Sunday. For the most part she kept to her room, reading for hours, taking long naps, or strolling around the property when the weather was nice, watching the ewes with their lambs in the pasture. It was mid-afternoon on Saturday, and Grace was in her room, curled up on the bed with a book, when she heard the sound of a car door and a man's voice. Closing the book, she strained to overhear the voices at the front door. "Grace?" said Aunt Martha a bit too loudly, as she was hard of hearing. After a moment there was a tap on the bedroom door, and her aunt peered inside. "Grace," she said, "there's a man here to see you. A British naval officer."

"Oh, my," said Grace. She swung her legs over the side of the bed and awkwardly stood up. "I'll just be a minute," she added. "Could you offer him some tea?" When Grace entered the parlor, her hair brushed and wearing a touch of makeup, Lieutenant Andrew Cadbury, wearing his Royal Navy uniform with his legs casually crossed, was seated in an easy chair opposite Uncle Dick. "Don't get up," said Grace, but the lieutenant rose anyway and offered Grace his hand. "You've come back for your hat," said Grace with a smile.

"Oh, I had a spare," said Andrew. "I thought I'd pop in for a visit."

"I've just been telling the lieutenant about my own grandfather's service as a rating in the Royal Navy," said Uncle Dick. "Back in the days of sailing ships."

"As you've driven all the way out from Wellington," said Grace, "I hope you'll stay awhile."

"I was hoping I could persuade you to come along for a spin around the countryside," said Cadbury. "As it's the weekend, and the weather's lovely."

Before her uncle could voice an objection, Grace said, "I'd be delighted!" She went back to her room and returned after a moment wearing a pale blue cardigan over her plaid maternity dress.

"Now, Grace," said Mr. Williams sharply, "Don't be too long . . ."

"Goodbye, Uncle," said Grace with a puckish smile as Andrew held open the door. She eagerly climbed into the car, a tiny Morris sedan of indeterminate age. As Andrew started the engine and released the handbrake, Grace put her arm on the car seat and turned to look at him. "This is such an unexpected treat," she said as they started down the dirt lane. "I haven't been off the property in ages."

"I thought it might do you good," he said with an easy smile. The wind ruffled his light brown hair.

"I'm surprised you didn't bring Doris along."

"Oh, I imagine Doris had things to do in town." Glancing up and down the paved two-lane, he turned to Grace and said, "Which way?"

"Well," said Grace, "I certainly don't want to go into town where my aunt and uncle shop and attend church. Do you think we might go as far as Masterton? It's about ten miles to the north."

"Of course." Andrew turned to the right and accelerated down the highway. "I left with a full tank of petrol and ought to be able to make it back to Wellington."

"Wonderful," said Grace, raising her voice over the wind noise. "My brother and I used to go into Masterton to see the movies when we stayed at the farm in the summer, and I'm sure there's a soda fountain. I've been craving a chocolate milkshake." By the time they were seated in a booth at the soda fountain, which was in fact directly opposite the cinema on the main thoroughfare, Andrew Cadbury had succinctly related his life story: his upbringing in an affluent family in Birmingham, where his father was the proprietor of a machine tool company that supplied parts to the aircraft industry; education in a public school and the University of Leeds; and enlistment in the Navy with the outbreak of the war. After ordering their milkshakes, Grace rested her elbows on the table and smiled at Andrew. She felt entirely relaxed surrounded by strangers, who no doubt assumed that the mother-to-be was married to the young naval officer. "What will you do when the war's over?" said Grace.

"Well, it was always assumed that I'd take my rightful place in the family business," said Andrew, "as I'm the only son. But after all I've seen and learned since going overseas, I'm not so sure. I might, for instance, decide to stay in New Zealand and see if I could make a place for myself."

"I'm sure you'd have no difficulty," said Grace, though inwardly she was keenly aware how little opportunity there was for an ambitious young man.

Andrew waited until the waitress served their milkshakes and then quietly said, "I've been meaning to ask you, Grace, about your plans." She sipped her shake through a straw and gave him a puzzled look. "For after the baby's born," he explained.

Lowering her voice, Grace said, "Nothing's been said, but I'm certain my parents will insist I put the baby up for adoption."

"That would be a shame." He reached across the table and gave her hand a gentle squeeze. "To lose one's fiancé, and then be forced to give up the child." Thankfully, no one was seated nearby at the mid-afternoon hour.

Grace nodded and said, "I try not to think about it." Brightening, she said, "Tell me about your adventures in the Navy. It's marvelous having someone to talk to after being cooped up for so long."

A natural raconteur, Andrew delighted Grace with amusing stories of his experiences at sea and in various exotic ports in the Pacific until long after their glasses were empty. With a glance at his watch, he said, "I had better get you home before that uncle of yours sends a constable for us."

"I'm sure you're right," said Grace, "though I'd give anything not to go back." It suddenly occurred to her how reluctant she was to part with Andrew's company. Arriving at the farmhouse in the fading daylight, Andrew walked Grace up to the front porch. Observing her aunt and uncle in the parlor through the window, he leaned close to her and said, "Will I see you again next weekend?"

"I have to work till noon on Saturday."

"Then I'll be here at noon." He bent down to kiss her cheek before walking back to the Morris and starting the engine. She stood on the porch, watching the car's red taillights, and then turned to go inside.

Grace awoke with a start in the pitch-black room. She could hear the wind in the trees outside and rain on the bedroom window. The fragment of a dream was slipping from her consciousness; she'd been with John in Wellington, riding on the cable car and then in the park, only it wasn't John, it was . . . The fragment was gone. *God,* she thought miserably, *how long would he haunt her dreams?* She reached over and switched on a lamp. Tossing off the covers, she stood up and walked over to take her robe from the hook on the back of the door. After listening for a moment to the rain, she sat at the small desk, took a sheet of stationery and her fountain pen from the center drawer, and carefully arranged them before her. She stared at the blank page and then unscrewed the cap from the pen and wrote:

My dearest John,

There is so much I want to tell you, and so much I want to ask you, but I don't know where you are. Have you gone away to Heaven, where there's no war and no pain, or are you still in this world? So I will simply try.

I'm going to have your baby. You'd laugh if you could see me now, as I'm big as a house. But I'm strong and healthy and it's going to be a beautiful baby.

My parents sent me away to live with my aunt and uncle on a farm outside Wellington because they're too ashamed for me to be seen by their friends and neighbors. I've been lonelier here than you could possibly imagine and missing you so much my heart is broken. Once the baby is born, in another two months, I'll be able to go home. Oh if only it was to be with you.

I've been reading the Bible, sweetheart, and what with everything else, I think it's changed me. I have this sense of assurance about God I never had before, and it's allowed me to believe, deep in my heart, that someday we'll be together again, though not in this world.

If you're watching over me John, don't pity me, but pray for me, if angels can pray for people on earth, to give me the strength to do what's right for our baby. And to do what I must do to go on with my life. I love you more than anyone could know.

Grace

She gently blew on the ink and then carefully put the sheet in the desk drawer. Resting her face on her arm on the desk, she wept.

CHAPTER FIFTEEN

IT WAS TRAVIS HENDERSON'S FIRST VISIT TO HONOLULU, AND he was astonished by the vast numbers of sailors, Marines, soldiers, and nurses crowding the sidewalks, restaurants, and lunch counters, making it impossible to find a seat on the bus that lurched from stop to stop. Hanging onto a stanchion, he peered out the grimy windows at the residential neighborhood on a hillside overlooking the city and Pearl Harbor, with neatly manicured lawns, bright tropical vegetation and tall palms, houses as different as he could imagine from the simple abodes back home in a small Texas town. When the bus came to a stop at the top of the hill, Henderson joined the queue of uniformed men and women jostling to get off. The bus stop was directly across the street from the Aiea Heights Naval Hospital, a modern four-story building with a wide expanse of St. Augustine lawn and a long, circular driveway. Just completed in the fall of 1942, the hospital was enormous, with 1,650 beds for wounded and ailing sailors and Marines. As he joined the throng crossing the busy intersection, Henderson was glad to be wearing his khaki service uniform for a change, with its red divisional patch on the shoulder and newly awarded ribbons on his chest, and especially relieved to have two days of leave after months of training at Camp Tarawa, the sprawling encampment the Second Division had erected on the Kona Coast of the

Big Island, where the exhausted survivors of Tarawa had been sent after arriving at the port of Hilo in December. Straightening the front of his jacket and his cap, he fell in with a group of navy nurses walking toward the hospital's main entrance.

The large lobby was crowded with doctors, nurses, and uniformed personnel. Henderson took a pack of Lucky Strikes from his pocket, slapped the end on the heel of his hand, and extracted a cigarette. After lighting it, he made his way to the information desk, manned by three young WAVEs in navy-blue dresses and brimmed white hats. When his turn came, he slipped off his cap, folded it in his belt, and said, "I'm here to visit Lieutenant John Reynolds, with the First Battalion, Sixth Marines."

Consulting a thick notebook, she repeated "Reynolds" and after a few moments said, "You'll find him in Room 3027 on the west wing, third floor. His visits are restricted to ten minutes, Lieutenant."

"Thank you, ma'am," said Travis. He took a final drag on his cigarette, crushed it out in a nearby ashtray, and walked to the nearest bank of elevators. He rode up to the third floor and followed a sign for the west wing, walking down a long, brightly lit corridor. Along the way he passed numerous wounded men, some missing limbs, in wheelchairs or on crutches, navy doctors in their white coats and dozens of nurses in starched white dresses and white caps and hose. Reaching a nursing station, where a sign on the wall indicated rooms 3000 – 3040, he walked up to a nurse at the desk and said, "I'm here to see Lieutenant Reynolds, in Room 3027. Can I go in?"

"Yes," she replied with a nod, "but I should caution you, Lieutenant Reynolds has suffered multiple serious injuries. Visits are restricted to ten minutes."

"Yes, ma'am." The door to room 3027 was slightly ajar. Peering in, Henderson could see two beds, both occupied and screened off by partitions. With some trepidation, he quietly entered and glanced behind the partition to his right. He immediately recognized John Reynolds, who was asleep, lying on his back with a peaceful look on his face. His left arm, which was bandaged and taped in a splint, was suspended from a stainless steel triangle. "John?" said Henderson quietly. "It's me, Travis." When there was no response, he walked over to the bedside, leaned close to Reynolds and gently placed a hand on his shoulder. "John," he said into Reynolds's ear. "Wake up." Reynolds's eyes remained closed, and his breathing was deep and regular. Travis pulled up a chair and sat at the bedside. "So that's it," he said, as much to himself as to John. "What rotten luck." Studying Reynolds's face, he noticed a small pink scar at his hairline. Otherwise, he looked perfectly fine, apart from his wounded arm, as if he were merely soundly sleeping. Henderson noticed two medals in their boxes on the small bedside table: a Purple Heart, Reynolds's second, and a Bronze Star.

"John," said Travis softly, his voice breaking, "there's some things I need to tell you. I guess you can't hear me, but I've got to tell you anyway. First of all, Spook didn't make it. His guys held off the Japs all night, but when I found him in the morning, he was gone. Shot in the chest." Travis paused and studied Reynolds's face, hoping for some flicker of comprehension. "Old White didn't make it either," said Travis. "I mean, we knew he wouldn't, but it was still tough.

"But the boys did a helluva job, John. Those guys made the Marine Corps proud. By the time the sun came up, just about every damn one of those Japs was dead. That was it. We won the battle." *Please John*, Travis said to himself, *do something to show you can hear me*. He sat there for another five minutes, watching his friend peacefully sleeping, then rose from the chair and let himself out. When he walked up to the nursing station a doctor was speaking with another nurse, who was holding a clipboard. "Excuse me," said Travis when the doctor glanced over at him. "Can I ask a question about one of your patients?"

"Certainly."

"It's about my friend, John Reynolds, in room 3027."

"Were you with him when he was wounded?"

"He was my company XO on Tarawa, but I didn't see it happen. Other than his arm, what are his injuries?"

"He has what's called a traumatic brain injury. We removed a small fragment of shrapnel which penetrated the skull and frontal cortex," explained the doctor. "But most of the damage was done by blunt force trauma, in all likelihood a larger piece of shrapnel that struck his helmet. It left him in a deep coma. And he'll never regain the full use of his arm."

"What are the chances," said Travis, "that he'll wake up?"

"It's impossible to say," said the doctor. "But the longer he remains in this condition, the less likely he'll ever regain consciousness. And even if he does, there's a significant risk of permanent brain damage."

"Is there anything you can do for him?"

"Pray," replied the doctor with a frown.

Travis lit another cigarette as he exited the hospital into the warm Honolulu sunshine. He knew John Reynolds had been badly wounded but nothing had prepared him for seeing his best friend unconscious or the doctor's stark assessment of his chances of recovering. Taking a deep drag, he debated taking a bus into town and checking out the cheap dives and cathouses on Hotel Street he'd heard so much about. After a while he crushed out the butt under his shoe and decided instead to head down to Pearl Harbor to the officers club at Camp Catlin. Thirty minutes later he was seated alone at one of the club's tables with a glass of cold beer. The place was packed with naval officers and Marines at the late afternoon hour. After taking a large swallow Travis stared out into the distance, tuning out the music blaring from a radio behind the bar. An image of Spook Beck came to mind, making some wisecrack at a meeting of the battalion's officers, followed by an image of his lifeless body as they rolled him onto a poncho. And now John Reynolds, probably the finest man he'd ever known and a true gentleman, in a coma with a useless arm. His two best friends, gone, just like that. And that poor s.o.b. Arnold Schulz, mowed down in front of their lines. Travis drank most of his beer in one long swallow and then fished in his pocket for another cigarette. Why in the name of God did Spook, who loved his wife, have to die, and John, who was planning to get married, end up in a coma, while he, who had nobody to go home to, came through the battle with hardly a scratch?

After his third beer, Travis pushed back from the table and made his way to the men's room. When he returned after a few minutes, he was surprised to discover his table occupied by two navy officers, both lieutenant commanders with three gold stripes on their sleeves. "Hey, this is my table," he said as he walked up. "Didn't you notice the empty glasses?"

One of the men looked up at Travis over his shoulder and said, "Listen, Lieutenant, why don't you shove off?"

"I don't think so," said Travis. "I think y'all had better find somewhere else to sit."

"Oh, you Marines think you're so tough," said the officer as he rose from his chair. He was shorter than Henderson and not in nearly as good shape. Presuming the young lieutenant would defer to his senior rank, the man repeated, "Now shove off." Travis smiled faintly and then suddenly threw a powerful punch, landing squarely on the man's jaw and knocking him to the floor. As the officer staggered to his feet, rubbing his jaw, an MP appeared out of nowhere and grabbed Travis by the arm.

"Let go of me, sailor," said Travis, jerking his arm away. He smiled at the two officers and said, "Maybe next time you fellows will show a little more respect." He turned and started walking toward the bar.

Grace was at the dining table with her hands folded on her large belly, meeting the sullen gaze of her Aunt Martha. As it was only six weeks until the baby's due date, the two had had another unpleasant argument over where Grace would go to have the child, with Grace unsuccessfully pleading that she should be allowed to return to the hospital in Wellington; and her aunt adamantly insisting she'd be fine at the much smaller hospital in Masterton. Adding to the tension was Grace's earlier declaration that, given the advanced stage of her pregnancy, she was no longer willing to perform her assigned chores. Aunt Martha had angrily threatened to send Grace home, until a moment later she'd realized that was precisely what Grace was hoping for. "I suppose your friend the British officer will be calling again?" she said frostily.

"Yes, I'm expecting him any minute." For six consecutive weeks, Andrew Cadbury had made the drive out from Wellington to spend Saturday afternoon with Grace. Though his visits were the only respite she had from the loneliness and ennui of her confinement, she couldn't imagine why he would squander his meager petrol ration to make the weekly excursions. Though she found him attractive and very pleasant company, he couldn't possibly have any interest in her, especially in her present condition. She concluded that he'd simply taken pity on her, as indeed there was much to pity.

With a glance out the window, she could see Andrew parking the tiny sedan. "In fact," she said, "here he is." Knowing it was futile to attempt to impose her will on her niece, Mrs. Williams merely rose from the table and disappeared into the kitchen. Grace went to the front door and stepped out on the porch. A sharp breeze was blowing down from the hillside, and Grace wrapped her sweater tightly around herself. Andrew, who was wearing his navy overcoat, walked up to the porch with a smile and said, "Hello, Grace my dear. You're looking well, but awfully large."

"Yes," she said with a rueful look. "I sometimes feel as though I'm following myself around the house. And I keep bumping into things."

"It's cold out here," said Andrew. "We should get you inside."

"I want to get away from here," said Grace quietly. "I've had another ugly row with my aunt."

"Fine," said Andrew. "Get your coat and scarf and I'll take you wherever you please."

As they drove along the blacktop, with seldom another car in sight, Grace considered that there was really no place it would please her to go, apart from the one place she was forbidden to go, namely, home. "Where to?" said Andrew, giving her a sidelong glance.

"I don't know," said Grace absently. "I wish there were some quiet place we could go to talk."

"Well," he said as he shifted the gear-knob, "let me see what I can turn up." After another mile or so he spotted a country lane and impulsively turned off the two-lane. "Let's see where this takes us," he said with a smile. The unpaved road curved past enclosures filled with sheep and began winding up the hillside. As the road grew steeper and narrower, he down-shifted and concentrated on staying in the well-worn tire tracks. Finally, after climbing for several minutes there was a break in the trees along the roadside and a gentle curve that formed an overlook. "Here we are," said Andrew as he pulled over and came to a stop.

"Oh, my," said Grace. Spread before them was a panoramic vista of the whole of the valley in varying shades of light and shadow. "What a beautiful spot."

Andrew switched off the engine and set the hand-brake. "And we have it all to ourselves," he said, placing his arm on the seatback behind Grace and leaning over to her side to peer out the window. Far below they could see a farmer on a tractor plowing his field and several horses running in an adjoining pasture. Leaning back in his seat, he looked at her thoughtfully and said, "It won't be long before the baby comes."

"Six weeks," said Grace. "More or less."

"And then what will you do?"

"Go home, I suppose. And try to start my life over."

"It seems such a shame."

Grace nodded, staring into her lap. She raised her eyes to look out at the beautiful landscape. Turning to Andrew, she said, "Why have you taken such an interest in me?"

"Isn't it obvious?" Again, he placed his arm on the seatback.

"No," said Grace with a small shake of her head. "In fact I find it quite peculiar that you would choose to spend your free time with me. After all, a dashing British officer like you with all the girls of Wellington at your disposal, now that the Yanks have gone . . ."

"At my disposal?" Andrew uttered a soft laugh and then his expression turned serious. Gazing into her eyes, he said, "I guess you really don't know."

"Know what?"

"How much I care for you." He leaned over, kissed her lightly on the cheek and took her hand. She responded with a questioning look. "I'm mad about you, Grace," said Andrew. "I have been almost from the first time I met you, that night at Doris's with John Reynolds."

"But I thought," said Grace, "that you simply felt sorry for me. That you were trying to cheer me up."

"Of course I was." He gave her hand a gentle squeeze. "But it's much more than that." He leaned over and kissed her again, this time on the lips.

Grace closed her eyes. When she reopened them, he was leaning back in his seat, looking at her affectionately. "But why me? Especially in my condition."

"Because you're sweet and funny and intelligent. I've marveled at the strength of your character with all you've been through. Yes, I may have pitied you, but you don't pity yourself."

"This is all so sudden," said Grace. "What I mean is that, even though we've been together for weeks now, I had no idea how you felt about me, and I have to let it sink in . . ."

"Grace." He reached over, gently lifted her chin with his fingertips, and stared into her hazel eyes. "I wanted you to know. And now that you do, I'm hoping you might feel the same way about me." She nodded. "Now, I've brought along a thermos of tea," said Andrew in a businesslike way. "Let's pour a cup and do a bit of exploring."

In her condition, Grace was easily tired, and after a short walk up the lane they returned to the car. Despite her long coat, she was shivering as she climbed in, as the wind had picked up and she was certain the temperature was falling. "Well," said Andrew as he reached for the starter button, "I'm afraid I should get you back to the farm. I have to report to the ship by six, as I've been assigned duty for the balance of the weekend." Grace nodded but remained silent as he turned the car around and started down the narrow track.

After a few minutes she looked over at him. "What you said earlier," she began. He gave her a brief, encouraging look. "About your feelings for me. Well, to be honest, it's taken me aback."

Reaching the paved two-lane, Andrew waited for a lorry with sheep penned in the back to go past before turning and stepping on the accelerator. "How so?" he said with another quick glance at her.

"I'm still in love with John," said Grace. "I still think of him as my fiancé. It doesn't matter that he's . . ." With a trembling lower lip, she said, in a voice just loud enough to be heard over the rushing wind, "That he's dead."

"I understand, Grace," said Andrew, "and I wouldn't expect you to feel any other way. But what I hope—what I believe—is that in time you might come to care for me in the same way I care for you." She nodded, staring ahead down the arrow-straight roadway. After another five minutes Andrew slowed and turned onto the dirt track that led to the farmhouse. As they approached they could see that the lights were on in the front parlor. After parking and switching off the engine, Andrew turned to Grace and said, "Before I walk you to the door, there's something else I want to tell you." She responded with a questioning look. "I've been thinking about this a lot, Grace. In fact, it's all I've been able to think about for weeks. You see, I've come into an inheritance . . ."

"Your father?"

"No, Father's fine. It's my Uncle Harry, who I learned passed away very suddenly, and as he had no children of his own, left me and my sister each a bequest of 50,000 pounds."

"Oh my, you're rich."

"Not rich, but well enough off to start my own life after the war. As I see it, it changes everything. I won't have to return home to work in the family business, as everyone, myself included, always assumed."

"You're thinking of staying here?"

Andrew nodded and said, "Yes, and I'm also thinking what a terrible pity it would be for you to put the baby up for adoption . . ."

"I haven't any choice."

"True. Unless, that is . . . you were married."

"Married?" said Grace. She stared at him with wide open eyes. "Surely, Andrew, you're not implying that you'd consider . . ."

"I'm not implying anything, Grace." He shot a nervous look toward the house, fearing her aunt or uncle might appear at any moment. "I'm merely stating a fact. That if you and I were married you wouldn't have to give up the baby."

"But Andrew . . ."

"Please, Grace, let me finish. I'm not asking you to marry me. I know you're not prepared to consider that. But I *am* asking you to think through it." Hearing the sound of the door, they both looked up to see Uncle Dick standing on the porch.

"Grace?" he called out.

"Please, Grace," said Andrew. "Think about it and pray about it. But there isn't much time." He climbed out and walked around to open her door. Helping her out, he leaned down to kiss her cheek and whispered, "Goodbye. I love you."

CHAPTER SIXTEEN

HAVING SECURED A SEAT ON THE OVERCROWDED BUS, TRAVIS Henderson peered out at the distinctive architecture of the Hawaiian houses, with verandahs or "lanais" that wrapped around the side and front, and enjoyed the pleasant breeze that poured through the half-open window. Though the sun was almost constant, it never felt hot. Someday, he vowed, when the lousy war was over, he'd come back to Hawaii for an honest-to-goodness vacation. As the bus reached the top of the hill, the massive structure of the Navy hospital came into view, and the mere sight of it made Travis feel queasy.

Finagling an overnight leave to Honolulu had taken a lot of doing. Everyone at Camp Tarawa on the Big Island, which was a beehive of activity, knew that it was only a matter of weeks, if not days, before the division packed up and shipped out for the next big action: a landing on a heavily fortified island somewhere in the vast Pacific. The only questions were when and where, somewhere far to the west to be sure, advancing inexorably closer to the Japanese home islands. Travis had managed to trade a favor from Colonel David Shoup, who was credited with saving the day at Tarawa and now was the division's chief of staff, since Travis had risked his neck, at Shoup's request, to go along as an observer in the Fourth Marine Division's landing on Kwajalein Atoll.

And Shoup, who'd been awarded the Congressional Medal of Honor for his remarkable valor at Tarawa, was determined that the division incorporate the lessons they'd learned from that near catastrophe in its next amphibious assault.

The bus came to a stop with a squeal of brakes, and Travis squeezed past a burly sergeant into the aisle to exit. Standing for a moment in the bright sunshine, he gazed at the large, modern hospital, wondering how many men from his battalion might end up there after this next big battle. The light changed, and he crossed the busy intersection, joining a large number of sailors, nurses, and WAVEs heading for the building's main entrance. After confirming that John Reynolds had not been moved, he took the elevator to the third floor and found his way to the nursing station nearest Reynolds's room. Explaining whom he was there to see, he was instructed to wait in one of the chairs against the wall, as the orderlies were bathing and changing him. As he sat there smoking a Lucky, Travis absently studied the tips of his finely polished shoes, trying to take his mind off his visit, as the prospect of seeing his friend lying helplessly in a coma filled him with dread.

"All, right, Lieutenant," said the nurse at the station, "you can go in now, but no smoking's allowed in the room."

After stubbing out his cigarette Travis straightened the front of his jacket and walked to the room. Two nurses were quietly speaking to the man who shared it with Reynolds, partially obscured by a partition. Travis slipped behind the other partition and stood at the foot of the bed. As on his previous visit, John was lying on his back under the covers with his eyes closed, but several days' growth of beard shadowed his face. The sling that had suspended his injured arm was gone. Staring at his unconscious friend, whose cheeks were sunken from the loss of weight, Travis felt almost sick to his stomach, and for some reason hesitant to try to communicate. And so he stood there, silently watching John Reynolds for a full five minutes and then quietly returned to the brightly lit corridor. After checking his wristwatch, he walked up to the nurses' station and said, "I guess there hasn't been any change in his condition?"

A nurse raised her eyes to meet his and said, "No. And frankly, at this stage, we don't expect any."

"Okay," said Travis. "Well, I'll be back after lunch to look in on him."

He briefly considered and then dismissed the idea of heading down to the Officers Club at Pearl, remembering his encounter with the two navy officers, which could easily have landed him in the brig. Instead, he strolled along the sidewalk away from the hospital, passing through a typical residential neighborhood, until he reached a small commercial area, with a drugstore, dry cleaner, and a diner with a sign that advertised "Mabel's—Soup and Sandwiches." Stepping inside, he spotted a vacant booth in the corner and decided to take it. Three attractive WAVEs in the adjoining booth were engaged in a lively conversation. Under normal circumstances Travis would have been unable to resist the temptation to flirt with them, as he'd finally gotten over Bonnie and was always on the lookout for cute American girls. He chose to sit with his back to them and glumly studied the coffee-stained menu. "Iced tea?" asked a waitress, wearing a bright yellow uniform and white apron, who appeared at his table with a pitcher.

"Sure," said Travis and she poured him a glass. "I'll have a ham and Swiss sandwich and some french fries."

"Comin' right up."

As he stirred a generous amount of sugar into his tea, the girls behind him erupted in laughter. What had started out as a bad mood was growing worse by the minute. The whole idea of the trip to Honolulu to visit Reynolds had probably been a mistake. He hadn't really expected to see any change in John's condition, but the fact that he was still unconscious, and in such degrading conditions, with navy orderlies having to wash and dress him, was deeply depressing. The waitress reappeared and lowered a plate to his placemat. "There we are," she said. "Ham and cheese on toast."

"I didn't say toast," said Travis as he looked up at her.

"Well, sonny," she said with a smirk, "it's toast you got."

Swell, thought Travis as he reached for the salt and pepper. He took a bite of his sandwich, which was largely tasteless, and then tried a few cold French fries. Catsup would help, but he didn't care to have another conversation with that bitch of a waitress. He couldn't get the image of John Reynolds's face out of his mind. Why couldn't they at least give him a shave every day? Did people in a coma have dreams, or was it like . . . well, like being dead? Forcing himself to finish half of the sandwich and a few more fries, he took a long swallow of tea and got up from the booth. Standing in line behind the WAVEs at the cash register, he debated heading down to the Officers Club for a beer or two and then returning to the pier to catch the boat back to the Big Island. When his turn came he handed the slip of paper the waitress had left on the table to the cashier and reached into his pocket for a dollar and two quarters. Slipping on his cap as he walked out into the sunshine, he decided instead to make the short walk back to the hospital to tell John Reynolds goodbye, as it might, he considered morosely, be his last chance.

Standing at the foot of the bed, Travis watched the way John's chest rose and fell slightly with each breath and then studied the expression of tranquility on his face. The patient in the other bed had been wheeled out for some excursion or procedure, and so Travis found himself alone in the room with John for the first time. He picked up the chair in the corner and positioned it next to the bed so that he could talk to Reynolds without having to raise his voice. "Well, old pal," he began, leaning close to Reynolds's face, "I'm gonna have to tell you goodbye. The scuttlebutt is the division's packing up any day now and shipping out for the next big fight." He paused to study Reynolds's features. "So I don't know when I'll be back," he continued in the same low voice. Reynolds's uninjured right arm was lying at his side on top of the covers, and Travis decided to take his hand. "You need to wake up, John," he said in a fierce whisper, squeezing Reynolds's hand as he spoke. To Travis's surprise, he felt gentle pressure from Reynolds's fingers. "Johnny," he said in a louder voice. "Johnny, can you hear me?" He gave Reynolds's hand another squeeze, and again he felt the pressure, slightly stronger. "Dammit, John," said Travis, "if you can hear me, open your eyes, goddammit!" As he stared at Reynolds, his left eye opened by the tiniest fraction, and then the right, and then both eyes fluttered open. "John!" exclaimed Travis. "By God, you woke up!"

Reynolds stared at Travis, blinked, and then in a barely audible voice said, "Where am I?"

"Hey, it's me, Travis, and you're in the hospital," said Travis. "In Hawaii. Hang on a sec. I gotta get the nurse." Travis half walked, half ran, to the nursing station, causing the two nurses at the counter to drop their clipboards with alarmed expressions. "He woke up!" said Travis breathlessly. "John Reynolds woke up!"

It was early on a Friday evening in late May, and Aunt Martha was at the stove in the kitchen, stirring a pot of soup with a wooden spoon while Uncle Dick was working on some mechanical problem in what he referred to as the barn, though it was really nothing more than a large shed with a corrugated tin roof where he kept the car and the tractor and his tools. Grace walked into the kitchen, holding one hand on her enormous belly, and said, "Would it be all right if I used the telephone?"

"The telephone?" said Mrs. Williams, turning to look at Grace. "What on earth for?"

"I need to call home."

"Well, all right. But don't be too long."

Grace returned to the sitting room and walked over to a small table where the only telephone in the house was located. Glancing out the window, she saw that it was already dark and could feel a cold draft coming under the sill. She lifted the receiver and dialed the number. After a few rings her mother answered. "Hello, Mother? It's Grace."

"Is there something wrong?" In the eight months Grace had spent at the farm, she'd only called home once or twice, and her parents had rarely come out for a visit.

"No, nothing's wrong. I just wanted to tell you that I . . . well, that I'm coming home tomorrow. And bringing someone with me." Grace was conscious of some movement from the kitchen, certain that her aunt was listening.

"Why, Grace," said Mrs. Lucas, "that won't do. In your condition."

"Mother, I need to talk to you. And to Dad. It's important."

"Well, we can't have the neighbors seeing you . . ."

"I'll come after dark, Mother. It gets dark early now. You don't have to worry . . ."

"Grace, what's this all about?"

"I'd prefer to discuss it in person," said Grace calmly. "And it's important that Dad's there. I can be there by six."

"Well, I never," said Mrs. Lucas. "And what's this about someone coming with you?"

"He's driving me, Mother. His name is Andrew Cadbury, and he's an officer in the Royal Navy."

"The British Royal Navy?"

"Yes, he's English. Goodbye, Mother. I'll see you tomorrow evening."

When she hung up and turned around, Aunt Martha was standing in the doorway.

"Is everything all right, dear?" she asked.

"Yes," said Grace with a nod. "I've no doubt you overheard."

"What is it you need to discuss with your parents?" said Mrs. Williams. She was nervously drying off a drinking glass with a dishtowel.

Grace looked her in the eye and said, "Andrew's asked me to marry him."

During the entire fifty-minute drive into Wellington hardly a word was spoken between Grace and Andrew. The atmosphere was as pregnant with anticipation of the events looming over them as Grace was pregnant with her child. It was entirely dark when they arrived at the Lucas bungalow, and a light rain was falling, visible in the cones of light from the headlamps as Andrew turned into the drive. He briefly gave Grace a smile of encouragement and then went around to open her door and help her out. Grace's father answered the door after the first knock, obviously in a hurry to get them inside, where the drapes were drawn over the living room windows. Andrew, who was wearing his uniform and overcoat, slipped off his hat and offered his hand to Mr. Lucas. "Hello, sir," he said. "I'm Andrew Cadbury."

"Pleasure," said Mr. Lucas, giving Andrew a quick handshake. "Hello, Grace, dear," he added, his gaze shifting from her face to her abdomen.

At that moment, Grace's mother, who was wearing jewelry and a dress of the type she'd wear to church, strode into the room. With a slight smile, she said, "Hello, Grace. And this must be Mr. . . ."

"Lieutenant Andrew Cadbury," said Grace. Without waiting for the others, she sank into an armchair.

"Let me take your coat, Lieutenant," said Mrs. Lucas, who seemed anxious to have something to do. Andrew shrugged off the heavy wool coat and handed it to Mrs. Lucas, who disappeared into the other room, and then accepted Grace's father's invitation to sit in the other armchair. When his wife returned they both sat on the sofa, gazing at Grace with expectant expressions.

Briefly looking around the familiar room, Grace said, "It's been such a long time since I've been home. I can't tell you how ready I am to end my exile."

Ignoring the remark, Mr. Lucas turned to Andrew and said, "I understand you're serving in the Royal Navy?"

"That's right," said Andrew. "On the HMS *Tenacious*, one of the destroyers assigned to patrol Cook Strait and the Wellington harbor. Quiet duty."

"Andrew is an acquaintance of Doris Campbell," said Grace. "We met at a dinner party at Doris's beach house last September."

"And as I've had shore leave virtually every weekend," said Andrew, leaning forward to rest his elbows on his knees, "I've been out to visit Grace quite often."

"I see," said Mr. Lucas. "I think it would be best to end this small talk and get straight to the point of your insistence on seeing us, Grace."

In the past Grace would have responded meekly to her father's scolding, but the harsh reality of the last eight months had changed her. "In due course," she said, "but first I would like Andrew to tell you something about himself." This elicited a puzzled expression from Mr. Lucas, who'd assumed that Andrew was merely providing Grace with transportation into town.

"I'm from Birmingham," said Andrew, "where my father is the owner of a very successful business, a supplier of parts to the aviation industry. As you might imagine, business has been booming ever since the outbreak of the war. I enlisted in the Navy following my graduation from university, and it was my intention, and my father's expectation, that I would return to the family business at the end of the war."

"Well," said Grace's father, "that's very nice, but I . . ."

"However, I've changed my plans," said Andrew, looking from Mr. Lucas to his wife, who was listening attentively. "I've come into an inheritance, and I've decided to remain in New Zealand after the war, and go into business for myself."

"Get to the point, young man," said Mr. Lucas.

"The point is, I love Grace very much. And I've asked her to marry me."

"Oh, my," said Mrs. Lucas, raising a hand to her mouth.

"What?" said Mr. Lucas. "Marry Grace, in her condition?"

"I was in love with John Reynolds," said Grace in a strong voice. "We were engaged, and I'm having his baby. But John was killed. And just when I thought I couldn't be more miserable, and was faced with having to give up my baby, Andrew came into my life." She turned to look at him with a sweet smile. "He's been terribly good to me and is willing to make an enormous sacrifice and raise the baby as his own."

"Oh, my," repeated Mrs. Lucas. "I think I could use something to drink." Her husband wordlessly rose from the sofa and walked to the kitchen, where he kept a bottle of Scotch in the pantry. Returning after a few minutes, he handed his wife a glass of whiskey with several lumps of ice and kept one for himself. After taking a swallow, he looked at Andrew and said, "You'd be willing to do this? To raise Grace's baby as if it were your own child?"

"As I said, Mr. Lucas, I love Grace very much. And I believe she will love me, though naturally she has to get over losing John. If she'll marry me, the baby will be mine and Grace's, as far as the world is concerned. No one, except, of course, for you and my own parents, will ever have to know."

"Grace?" said her father.

Grace pressed her lips together and tears welled in her eyes. "It's the finest thing any man could do," she said, "and of course I'll marry Andrew. I'll keep my baby, and we'll make Wellington our home." Putting her drink aside, Mrs. Lucas stood and walked over to embrace her daughter.

Andrew too rose and looked Mr. Lucas in the eye. "With your blessing, sir," he said.

Mr. Lucas stood up and reached out to give Andrew a warm handshake. "Why don't I fix you a drink, Andrew," he said, "and we can toast the engagement."

"It won't be much of an engagement," said Grace, wiping away her tears. "We're getting married tomorrow."

Having spent the night in her old room, Grace remained out of sight of any curious neighbors until, in mid-afternoon, she dressed for her wedding. As she examined herself in her mother's full-length mirror, looking utterly ridiculous in a pale pink maternity dress she could barely fit into, she was struck by a wave of sadness. Marriage to Andrew meant the death of the tiny fragment of hope she'd kept alive, of being reunited with John Reynolds, and in its place, she considered as she lightly ran a hand over her abdomen, she felt an irrational pang of guilt, as if she'd betrayed him. Returning to her bathroom, she applied a final touch of makeup and perfume and went to the living room to wait. Promptly at 3:30 p.m. the tiny Morris appeared in the drive, and Andrew hurried to the front porch, his face obscured by an umbrella. "We'll see you at the church," said Grace to her mother as she stepped out the door and hurried with Andrew to the car.

Andrew had persuaded the priest at the small Anglican church where he and several of his fellow officers occasionally attended services to officiate at the wedding, which necessitated an interview in the priest's office before the service could begin. During the short drive to the church, Andrew glanced at Grace and said, "Are you sure you're all right?"

"Oh, yes," said Grace. "I'm fine."

"I know this is difficult for you," said Andrew, "feeling as you do about John, but over time . . ."

"Don't think about it," said Grace. "Everything will be fine." Staring into the road ahead as the wipers slapped the windshield, Andrew thought *yes, yes it will. John was the past, but I'm the future.*

Following a brief but exceptionally awkward conversation with the priest, to whom Grace had explained that, no, Andrew was not the father; the father had been killed in the war, so that in the eyes of the church her marriage to Andrew was permissible. "Yes," the priest had said after a moment's reflection, "it's permissible and"—turning to Andrew—"a very honorable thing, young man."

Grace stood at the steps below the altar of the small church, which smelled pleasantly of lemon oil and candles, holding Andrew's hand and looking up at the priest in his vestments, who gazed out at the small gathering, consisting of Grace's parents, Uncle Dick and Aunt Martha, Doris Campbell and two of Grace's close friends from schooldays, and three young officers from Andrew's ship, who like Andrew were wearing their best uniforms. The priest proceeded to conduct the Anglican service, and vows were exchanged, though without rings as there hadn't been time to purchase them. Closing his prayer book, the priest gazed out at the audience and then turned to Grace and Andrew and said, "I now pronounce you man and wife. Whom God hath joined together let no man put asunder."

Gazing into Grace's hazel eyes, Andrew bent down and lightly kissed her lips.

CHAPTER SEVENTEEN

JOHN REYNOLDS STOOD AT THE DOOR TO THE DOCTOR'S OFFICE on the fourth floor of the hospital. After a moment, he knocked and let himself in. The doctor, whose name was M. E. Williston, according to the small plaque by the door, was seated at his desk in shirtsleeves, puffing on a briar pipe. Unlike the other doctors Reynolds had encountered in the hospital, he was wearing civilian clothes, without the usual white frock coat. "Come in, Lieutenant," said the doctor, "and have a seat." The overhead light reflected on the lenses of his wire-rimmed glasses, and the papers on his desk stirred in the breeze from the partially open windows. Reynolds chose one of the metal armchairs facing the desk. His left arm hung limp at his side. Dr. Williston leafed through a manila folder. He looked up and said, "So you suffered a traumatic brain injury which left you in a prolonged coma and now with amnesia? Complete memory loss." Reynolds merely nodded. "I'm probably not the right doctor to help you," said Williston, taking another puff on his pipe, "as I'm a psychiatrist. It seems the Navy was unable to spare a neurologist, so they've assigned your case to me." In truth the doctor was relieved to have Reynolds as a patient, as most of his other cases were men suffering from extreme combat fatigue. "But that's all right," he added with a small smile, "as amnesia is often accompanied by depression, which is an area I may be able to help."

ALWAYS FAITHFUL

"I can't even remember my name, Doctor," said Reynolds. "Or where I'm from . . ."

"You're John Reynolds," said Williston, "from . . ."

"Yeah, I know. The nurse told me."

"Another Marine was visiting you when you regained consciousness. Did you recognize him?"

"No, sir. I have no idea who he is."

"Apparently an officer in your company," said Williston. "Let's see. Able Company, First Battalion, Sixth Marines. You were wounded at Tarawa."

"If you say so."

"By all accounts, it was a terrible battle, with heavy American losses. But a great victory for the Marines. Do you remember anything leading up to it?" Reynolds shook his head, staring at the pale green linoleum floor. "Your division was in New Zealand, according to this report. After Guadalcanal, where apparently you were also wounded. Does that ring a bell?"

Reynolds raised his eyes and looked at the doctor. "No," he said sadly. "I can't remember a damn thing."

"Well, the good news," said Williston, "is that you don't appear to have any brain damage. Apart from your arm, you've made a complete recovery. And while we honestly don't understand much about amnesia, in most cases it's temporary. Your memory of past events gradually comes back, maybe triggered by one thing or another."

"I sure hope so," said Reynolds.

"For now, I'm going to prescribe some medication that will help you sleep. And I'd like to see you three days a week to help you work through the depression. You can make an appointment with my nurse."

"Fine," said Reynolds. He rose from his chair.

"One other thing," said the doctor. He reached behind his desk for a cardboard shoebox. Handing it to Reynolds, he said, "These were some personal effects they sent when you arrived here, and some letters from home. They may help you start to remember things."

"Thanks," said Reynolds, holding the box under his good arm. He turned to go.

Though he had no recollection of the past—nothing, a blank slate— Reynolds could remember with perfect clarity everything from the moment he'd regained consciousness. The experience deeply unnerved him.

Who was he? Why should he answer to John rather than George or Bill? What did his mother look like? He was stuck in the hospital, sharing a room with a badly injured Navy officer, though the only treatment Reynolds was receiving was physical therapy for his shattered arm and the sessions with Dr. Williston, which were aimed at helping him deal with his depression and had nothing to do with restoring his memory. After a week of therapy, he'd discovered a rooftop terrace with chaise-lounges and potted plants where he could relax in the pleasantly warm sunshine and gaze out on the large complex of buildings and ships at anchor at Pearl Harbor in the distance. Following lunch one day in the cafeteria, where he'd chosen to eat alone as he had nothing to talk about with the other men, he retrieved the shoebox with his personal belongings and letters and a newspaper from his room, took the elevator to the top floor, and made his way up the stairs to the terrace. Several doctors were leaning against the railing smoking cigarettes; a number of injured men wearing blue robes and pajamas were sitting in wheelchairs; and a few other men like himself, dressed in uniform, were stretched out on the chaise-lounges. Reynolds found an unoccupied chaise, and placing the box beside him, gazed up at the cottony clouds in the deep blue sky. The air was perfumed with an exotic fragrance . . . the sweet bouquet of frangipani blossoms.

After reading a long article in the Honolulu newspaper about the fierce battle his old division was fighting for the Japanese-held island of Saipan, he put the paper aside, took the lid from the box, and reached for the first anguished letter from his mother. Each time he read it he felt like he was reading a letter from someone else's mother to someone else. Unfolding the pages—it was written in blue-black ink in neat cursive, not on stationery but rather the kind of inexpensive paper you'd find in a five-and-dime—he reread the first several sentences. The writer, who'd signed the letter "your loving Mother" and addressed it to "My dearest son," was distraught over the news, presumably received by telegram, that her son had been wounded in action. The letter didn't say where or how this had happened, but it was dated December 8, 1943, or about two weeks after the battle for Tarawa had ended, according to the newspaper accounts Reynolds had been able to find. The letter mentioned the son's father, who is described as "well, but sick with worry," and his grandparents, who are "visiting family in Cherokee County." If the letter really was from his mother, she must be beside herself with worry for her son's fate—his own fate?—as over five months had now passed since it was mailed.

With an audible sigh, Reynolds folded the letter back in the envelope. That was when he noticed the return address on the back. He'd been so anxious to study the letter, looking for clues in its words, that he hadn't bothered to look at the return address: 2411 Milford, Houston, Texas. As he searched through the meager contents of the box a word suddenly registered in his mind, as unexpected as a leaf floating in through an open window: the word "Harris." Harris County. Was there such a place? Besides his dog tags, a Hamilton wristwatch, pocketknife, and a handful of other letters from his mother and father, there was a curious object: a slip of paper carefully folded in a piece of waxed paper, tied with a string. All of these things, apart from the letters, must have been on him when he was wounded and evacuated, first to a hospital ship and ultimately to Honolulu. He carefully untied the string and, for at least the tenth time, read the note, printed in pencil in a man's handwriting: "Mrs. Sally Beck, 401 Davenport St., Portland, Oregon." Reynolds shook his head. Why in the world would he have been carrying this into battle? If he was who the letters said he was, someone from the city of Houston, Texas, why would he be carrying the name and address of a married woman in Portland, Oregon? Carefully refolding and tying the note in the waxed paper, he put the lid on the box and leaned back on the chaise. He closed his eyes and, with the warm sun on his face, quickly fell asleep.

When he awoke, he realized he'd been dreaming about the first moments he came out of the coma. The man standing over him had identified himself as Travis, a name that meant nothing to him. But hadn't he mentioned two other names? Two other guys he'd said didn't make it? Or had Reynolds simply dreamed it? He could swear the Marine had said something about two other men, and the names were on the tip of his tongue. *Dang it,* he thought. *What were they?* And then, like a voice whispering in his ear, it came to him: Spook. And Old White. If it was only a dream, he thought as he rose from the chaise, his injured arm aching, it was a mighty strange dream.

Returning to his ward on the third floor, on an impulse he stopped at the nursing station. "Feeling better, today?" said the nurse at her desk. Blond with bright blue eyes, she was one of the few pretty nurses on the ward.

"I suppose so," said Reynolds. "A little. Can I ask you a question?"

"Of course."

"Is there another patient on this ward from Texas?"

"I wouldn't know."

"The navy man in room 3012," said another nurse standing nearby, "the one with the broken arm, might be from Texas. I'm from Oklahoma, and I can pick out that Texas accent. Just like yours," she said to Reynolds with a smile.

"Thanks," said Reynolds. "I'd like to ask him a question."

Reynolds stood outside the door of room 3012, which was slightly ajar. Peering in, he could see a man in one of the beds with his arm in a cast, reading a magazine. The other bed was unoccupied. He tapped on the door and said, "Excuse me."

"What is it?"

Reynolds walked in and said, "Sorry to interrupt. Just had a quick question."

"Sure," said the man, who, according to the nurse was a navy lieutenant, j.g., who'd broken his arm in some mishap aboard ship. "And you are?"

Reynolds had to think for a moment. "I'm, ah, John Reynolds. My room's just down the hall."

"Bill Ferguson. What's the question?"

"The nurse thought you might be from Texas."

"That's right. From Fort Worth." He gave Reynolds a curious look.

"Well, you might think this is screwy, but do you know if there's a county in Texas called Harris?"

"Sure there is," said Ferguson. "That's where Houston is." He gave Reynolds a curious look and said, "Why do you ask?"

"To be honest," said Reynolds, "I got a knock on the head and it's messed up my memory. I'm tryin' to get it back, and they told me I'm from Houston, Texas."

"Well," said Ferguson, "it's always good to meet another man from the Lone Star State. You in the Second Marine Division?"

"Yep, apparently."

"The poor bastards who got sent to Tarawa."

"Right. Well, nice to meet you, Bill. Good luck with the arm."

Reynolds sat on his bed, thankful to be separated from the other patient by the cloth screen. Something about seeing "Houston, Texas" on the back of the envelope had triggered his memory of Harris County. And from somewhere in his subconscious the names "Spook" and "Old White" had come to mind. Apart from that, he only had the strange scrap of paper with the name "Sally Beck." Well, he'd written to his parents, explaining his situation and asking for their help in getting his memory back. Who knows, he considered with the tiniest ray of hope, one small clue might lead to another.

The maternity ward at Wellington Hospital was full to overflowing nine months after the twenty thousand men of the Second Marine Division had been in their final weeks of training before sailing for Tarawa. A few months earlier it seemed that the city was in the midst of a baby shortage. Most of the young mothers in the ward had, like Grace, been married or engaged to Marines, and some of their babies were destined never to see their fathers. Grace shared a room with three other mothers, all strangers, whose babies had been born within days or hours of each other. As is usually the case with a first delivery, Grace's labor had been long and painful, and unattended by her husband, who was at sea. Grace's mother had stayed at her bedside throughout the ordeal, up to the point that she'd gone under the general anesthesia. But she'd given birth to a perfectly healthy baby girl, weighing seven pounds ten ounces, whose birth certificate bore the name "Katherine Dalton Cadbury." Grace and Andrew had chosen to name the baby, if a girl, for his mother, in part to assuage Andrew's guilt for not having involved his parents in the decision to marry Grace, and to whom his intention to emigrate to New Zealand remained undisclosed.

Grace awoke from a light nap with the arrival of the nurses carrying the four newborns, as it was far more efficient for the babies to be nursed at the same time. The timing of their feeding, however, did not necessarily coincide with the onset of the babies' hunger, and several of them were squalling with gusto when the nurses delivered them into their mothers' waiting arms. Little Kate, as Grace was already calling her, was well behaved, glancing around at the other women and babies with an expression of wonder. When Grace opened her nightgown, the baby began to suckle greedily, a pleasant sensation that Grace was certain cemented a bond between mother and child. It was Friday afternoon, the third day since Kate had been born, and with any luck they'd be permitted to go home in the morning. For now, "home" was her parents' house until Andrew could arrange to let a flat somewhere in the vicinity of the naval base. Grace smiled at the sound her tiny baby made as she nursed, the quietest sort of slurping noise. She was thankful that nursing came easily for her, as one of the young mothers had already given up in frustration and was feeding her baby with a bottle.

As it was Friday, Andrew's ship should be returning to port, and he'd make straightaway for the hospital to meet for the first time the child he would raise as his own daughter. Grace tried to imagine how she would feel if there were no Andrew, and she was faced with giving up her baby for adoption. The thought made her shudder. She was exceptionally fortunate to have met Andrew and for Andrew to have fallen in love with her. Though a year earlier she would have considered the idea ridiculous, she now deeply believed that it was the work of a loving God, who, having taken John from her, had given her Andrew in a kind of providential dispensation. And who, she considered with a contented smile, had also given her the amazing gift of Kate.

Grace awoke at the sound of voices in the corridor. With a sleepy yawn, she glanced at the luminous dials of her watch: ten past nine. The room was dark and the other young mothers were sleeping, one of them softly snoring. Light from the corridor streamed in with the opening of the door. Andrew was standing in the doorway, fingering his hatband. In the darkness he recognized Grace. Walking quickly to her bedside, he bent down and kissed her. "Hello, sweetheart," he whispered.

"It's a girl," said Grace quietly. "A beautiful baby girl named Kate."

They shared a tiny flat, on the ground floor of a two-story fourplex in a quiet neighborhood, with a small living room, a kitchen not much larger than a broom closet, and a single bedroom and bath. Another married officer from the naval base, a New Zealander, occupied one of the upstairs units, and the two couples often played bridge after dinner on weekends. It was midwinter, but in Wellington's mild climate nighttime lows were seldom below 40°, and the temperature warmed into the fifties most afternoons. The house was located on a streetcar line that Andrew and his fellow officer could take to within a block of the main gate of the base. Weekdays they were at sea, returning to port on Friday evenings. Grace would pack up the baby's things and spend the time with her parents. Somewhat to her surprise, both her mother and father had quickly grown fond of Kate, holding her in their laps in the living room, talking nonsense, or taking her on strolls in the pram in the neighborhood. It struck Grace that they'd willingly accepted the fiction that Andrew was the baby's father, as perhaps it made their explanations to friends and neighbors more convincing. But all that mattered to Grace was that she and Andrew were together, with her parents' blessing, and that her precious baby was healthy and happy.

Kate was especially happy with Andrew, the stepfather everyone assumed was her real father. Grace took care to return home with the baby on Friday afternoons, to have a decent dinner and a bottle of wine waiting when Andrew arrived at the door. He naturally treasured the weekends: time for him to play with the baby and take her on walks, and time to share with Grace, including the beginnings of physical intimacy that eventually led to lovemaking when the baby was sound asleep, though they decided to take precautions to avoid another pregnancy, at least for the duration of the war. Because their courtship—she wasn't aware it was a courtship until later—had been of such short duration, Grace was only now getting to know Andrew, his family story, likes and dislikes, what he'd studied at the university, and most importantly his deeply held convictions. Fortuitously, they discovered that they were well-matched, having both come from middle-class backgrounds, without pretensions, but valuing education, with an appreciation for good books and classical music, and a common Christian faith, though she had been raised a Scots Presbyterian and he was an Anglican. Grace admired the fact that Andrew had decided to strike out on his own in business when the war was over, though a good-paying position in the family-owned company was his for the asking. For his part, Andrew was more in love with Grace with each passing week and felt as devoted to the baby as if she were his own daughter.

At unexpected moments, almost always when Andrew was away at sea and she was thinking about him, or watching her beautiful little girl, Grace felt light-hearted, vaguely aware of a sensation of well-being. When she had finally accepted the fact of John's death, in the depths of her grief she'd wondered if she would ever feel happy again. And so, in these moments, she was immensely relieved to discover that she genuinely could, and thanked God for it.

One Monday morning in late July, once the baby was down for her morning nap, Grace carefully removed the framed photograph she kept out of sight in one of the dresser drawers, the one the studio photographer in Wellington had taken of John in his olive green uniform with his arm around her waist, both of them smiling happily. Staring at his image, a wave of sadness swept over her that was more than she could bear, and she sank on the sofa in the living room, clutching the photo, in a spate of tears. After a while she put the photo aside and went to the kitchen to light the burner under the teakettle. Waiting for the water to boil, she tried to imagine John's home in Texas. She remembered the name of the city, Houston, and the name of the beachfront town he described with such affection—Galveston. Perhaps someday, she reflected as the kettle whistled, when Kate was a little girl and the war over, they'd travel to America and find John's home and family. Kate could meet her paternal grandparents, and Grace could learn something about the circumstances of John's death.

By the end of the week, which had been too cold and rainy to take the baby outdoors, Grace had sunk into despondency and fear for Andrew's safety. On Friday evening, she forced herself to tidy up the flat and, after nursing and bathing the baby and putting her to bed, prepared a simple supper to share with Andrew. Although he usually arrived home by seven, it was past eight when she heard the key tumble the lock. Switching off the radio, she went to the door to give him a welcoming embrace. After kissing Grace on the cheek, Andrew briefly looked her in her eyes and said, "Hello, darling. Sorry to be late." Grace could sense something was wrong as she took his hat and helped him out of his heavy coat.

"Are you ready for supper?" she asked as she hung his coat in the hall closet. "It's warming in the oven."

"Not just yet," he said. "Do we still have that bottle of Scotch?" He walked quietly into the bedroom to look in on the sleeping baby. When he returned, Grace was holding a bottle of Bell's and a glass with several ice cubes.

"There you are," she said, handing them to him.

"Thanks." He unscrewed the cap and poured an inch of whiskey. He took a swallow and then sighed audibly. "I'm afraid I've got some news," he said with a careworn expression that turned down the corners of his mouth. "Why don't we sit?" Grace sat close to him on the small sofa, leaning forward to rest her arms on her knees. "I suppose I shouldn't have expected this patrol duty to last," he began, "but I did."

"What do you mean?"

"When we returned to port this evening we learned we have orders." Grace hung her head, staring at her hands. "It appears the fleet has departed the Indian Ocean and is sailing for the Southwest Pacific. To resume offensive operations in the area of Malaya and Dutch New Guinea. Our orders are to join the fleet in the South China Sea. We sail first thing Monday."

She raised her eyes and gave him an anguished look. "Oh, Andrew," she said. "How long will you be gone?"

"There's no telling. Quite possibly until the end of the war."

CHAPTER EIGHTEEN

IT STARTED WITH A DREAM. JOHN REYNOLDS AWOKE FROM A nightmare so terrifyingly real that his convulsions shook the bed and a strangled cry escaped his lips that brought a nurse running to see what was the matter. Sweating and his heart racing, Reynolds said, "It's okay," as the nurse switched on the bedside lamp. "It was just a bad dream." Only fragments remained; crashing explosions, bright headlights on an onrushing tank; firing his rifle at crouching forms in the darkness; and trying to call out, but no sound came from his lips . . . Reynolds swung his legs over the side of the bed, sat up, and rubbed his eyes. He must have been dreaming about Tarawa. Somewhere he'd read that his battalion had held off a Jap banzai attack on the last night of the battle. The vivid dream had not only been terrifying, but it left him feeling a strange, almost nauseating, unease. Squeezing shut his eyes, he tried to remember the scene . . . the explosions, the brilliant lights, men screaming . . . Old White, he thought suddenly! They'd left Old White, the Gunny sergeant from his old platoon, out there to die! Reynolds muffled a sob. He remembered now, and it made him feel sick.

Reynolds sat facing Dr. Williston at his regular appointment. "So you were having a dream," said Williston, "about the battle, and in it you could see this sergeant . . ."

"No, I didn't see him, but I think I heard him screaming . . . And when I woke up I remembered that we'd left him out in front of our lines to die. And the guy who came to see me in the hospital . . ."

"The man named Travis . . ."

"Right. He said that Old White didn't make it. That's what the men called the gunny."

"And you feel like it was your fault?" suggested Williston.

"It *was* my fault," said Reynolds with a nod. "I gave the order."

Williston had heard countless similar stories and was well aware that guilt was one of the most common and debilitating effects of the ordeals of combat. "Have you remembered the circumstances?" he said. "Don't be so hard on yourself."

Reynolds nodded glumly and said, "Well, at least my memory's starting to come back."

"What else do you remember from the dream?" Williston expelled a bluish cloud of pleasant-smelling pipe smoke.

"Nothing," said Reynolds with a shake of his head. "You know how it is with dreams. They fade away as soon as you wake up."

"Well, John," said Dr. Williston with a smile, "That's enough for today. Why don't you get some rest and see what else comes back to you?"

Lying on his bed with his shoes off, Reynolds dozed. It was a shallow, dreamless sleep that lasted only a quarter hour, but when he woke up he was thinking about that night on Tarawa. A filmy memory of the afternoon or evening before the big Japanese attack came to mind; something deeply disturbing had happened, but what was it? It seemed like his commanding officer—what was his name? Jones, that was it. Bill Jones had ordered him to do something he hadn't wanted to do, something dangerous. Jones was worried about Baker Company, that was it, and he ordered Reynolds to go check with . . . All at once he remembered, and the sudden recollection triggered a wave of guilt far more powerful than the memory of leaving Old White out to die all alone. Arnold Schulz had taken over command of Baker Company when Captain Krueger was shot. When Reynolds finally found him in the gathering darkness Schulz was scared to death, with eyes as wide as saucers. Scared and threatening to pull the company back. Reynolds stood up and began to pace. Memories of that night suddenly flooded over him. Schulz was terrified, and who wouldn't have been? But

Reynolds had berated him and, worse, cursed him, taken the Lord's name in vain. He could remember the scene as clearly as if had happened yesterday. He took a deep breath and slowly exhaled. Now he remembered telling Jones, when he managed to raise him on the radio, that Schulz was planning to pull the company back. Jones was furious and demanded to know if Schulz was capable of performing his duty.

Reynolds slumped on his bed and rubbed his eyes in his hands. No, he told Jones. Not *I'm not sure*, or *possibly*, but *no*. And so Jones relieved Schulz of command, the most shameful thing any officer could endure, and it was all his fault. And then another image suddenly flashed into his mind: a lone Marine walking straight toward an oncoming tank in the glare of its headlights, firing his rifle from the hip . . . Arnold Schulz, in effect, committing suicide . . . Reynolds groaned.

Later, alone in the cafeteria with a cup of black coffee, his thoughts returned to Arnold Schulz and all his big talk about killing Japs, and who, at the critical moment, was paralyzed by fear. But if Jones had given him a direct order to hold the position when he spoke to him on the radio, Reynolds imagined Schulz would have obeyed it. But thanks to his own blunt assessment, Jones had relieved him. But how did he know that? Reynolds wondered as he sipped his coffee. If Jones hadn't told him, someone else must have. As Reynolds stared across the nearly empty room another memory, unbidden, flashed into his mind. He was making his way back in the dark, terrified of being shot by his own men, when he ran into someone who told him that Jones had relieved Schulz. He could visualize the man's face, but who was he? Then it hit him . . . it was Spook . . . his best friend. *Oh my God*, thought Reynolds, the Marine who'd come to see him in the hospital had said . . . Spook didn't make it.

Returning to his room, Reynolds undressed for bed, slipped under the covers, and switched off the light. Listening to the snoring from the other bed, he concentrated on the events of that terrible night. It was all coming back now. On his way back to his company's position he ran into Spook, who told him Jones had relieved Schulz and ordered Spook to gather up a bunch of people and plug the gap between Baker and Able Companies. He'd complained about having to defend themselves with the inferior carbines, which he'd called "popguns." It was the last time he saw Spook. Good old Spook. Reynolds bitterly choked back tears. Why did Spook have to die, while he survived? He couldn't help feeling that somehow all of it was his fault, Old White and Schulz and Spook. He closed his eyes, and after a long time fell asleep.

When he awoke at first light his mind was blank. Then suddenly the terrible memories came back to him. He kicked off the covers and pain- fully swung his crippled arm onto his lap. As he debated getting up to go to the bathroom he remembered the note folded in the waxed paper. He quickly found it in the shoebox on the bedside table. When he looked at the name—Sally Beck—he knew she had to be Spook's wife. But why had he been carrying it? Reynolds closed his eyes in concentration. He dimly remembered a conversation with Spook on board ship . . . What was its name? The *Feland.* They were up on deck. Spook had given him the note and made him promise to contact his wife if something hap- pened to him. If he "bought the farm." Had he made Spook promise to do something in return? Write to Reynolds's parents? For the life of him he couldn't remember.

That evening, after supper, Reynolds found a spot on the terrace overlooking Pearl Harbor where he could watch the sunset. The sky was streaked with pink and orange, and the rooftop air was just right; warm with a slight cooling breeze scented with frangipani. His memory was slowly and erratically coming back to him, like watching a movie in re- verse: the terrible fighting on Tarawa, landing on the island in rubber boats, the furious naval bombardment, episodic memories of the time on board the ship, as far back as their practice landing at Éfaté, but no far- ther. He knew the division had sailed from New Zealand and had spent the previous nine months outside the city of Wellington. But he could summon no memory of it, beyond a vague, troubled sensation when he tried to remember their actual departure.

The following day, the realization that six months had gone by since Spook was killed, and Reynolds's failure to honor his promise, cast him even deeper into despair. He finally summoned the courage to write a brief letter of condolence to Sally, assuring her that Spook was one of the battalion's finest officers and Reynolds's best friend and that his death had not been in vain.

Within days of regaining consciousness, Reynolds had written an awkward letter to his parents, awkward because he had no recollection of them and felt he was writing to strangers. He was certain they'd received the usual telegram informing them that he'd been wounded in action and assumed they'd learned he was recovering in the hospital. In his letter, he'd simply explained the nature of the injury to his brain, that it had left him in a coma for over five months, and that though he was now conscious, he'd lost all memory of the past. He'd briefly mentioned his ruined left arm and closed by asking them to pray for his recovery and to write with any information that might help him to remember things that had occurred prior to the battle. The day following Reynolds's recovery of his memories of Tarawa and the events leading up to it he received a letter from home, written in a woman's neat cursive and signed "your loving Mother." He sat in his room by the window with a view of the lush green hills and carefully read her letter. After expressing her "joy" and "heart-felt thanks to God" that he'd awakened from the coma, she wrote: "Your father and I are deeply saddened to learn of the loss of your memory and of the severity of the injury to your arm. We will pray with all our hearts that you will recover, as you've had a good life that should leave you with many happy memories." Putting the letter aside, Reynolds gazed out the window, wishing that he could remember his mother and father and that she'd provided him with some concrete details that might help him to remember the past. And then, almost miraculously, an image of his mother's face, and then of his father's, suddenly came to mind, which filled him with inexpressible joy. He read his mother's closing words: "We trust you'll be returning home soon," and, almost as an afterthought, "and hope that the news of your injuries was passed along to the friends you made in Auckland, the McDonalds, and of course to that dear girl Grace you seemed so hopeful for us to meet."

Reynolds stared at the words, his mind spinning. The McDonalds in Auckland . . . Had he been in Auckland? He reached for his thigh and massaged a tender spot. He'd wondered about the scar when he'd taken his first shower after waking up. Auckland, yes, the navy hospital in Auckland, in the . . . what was it called? The Domain. The McDonalds, the wonderful couple, Malcolm and Bell, who'd taken him into their home. And "that dear girl Grace" . . . His heart was pounding. Grace, Grace, he repeated to himself with his eyes shut until, all at once, he could see her beautiful face. Oh, my God, Grace. Burying his face in his good arm, resting on the windowsill, Reynolds wept.

That night after supper, while the ambulatory men on his ward were watching a movie, Reynolds stretched out on his bed with several sheets of Red Cross stationery resting on his drawn-up knees. He took his fountain pen from his shirt pocket and wrote:

Aiea Heights Naval Hospital
Honolulu, Hawaii
July 22, 1944

My dearest, darling Grace,

I can only imagine the agony you've suffered for so many months without a single word from me, undoubtedly assuming the worst, that I had been killed on Tarawa, the terrible battle our division fought last November, which I'm sure was widely reported. I very nearly was killed by an exploding shell but thankfully my life was spared. I suffered what the doctors call a traumatic brain injury, which left me in a deep coma that lasted over five months. And when I woke up, over six weeks ago, I had amnesia and couldn't remember anything. So that explains why you haven't heard from me before now.

Before we landed on Tarawa I made a deal with Spook that if anything happened to me he'd let you know. But sadly, Spook was killed.

Miraculously, over the past several days, my memory has started coming back, though there are lots of little things I can't get straight and some gaps. But otherwise my brain seems to be working just fine. I took a lot of shrapnel to my left arm and I'm afraid it'll never work right again, so that's the end of my career as a combat Marine.

Grace, darling, I feel like I've come back from the dead. My heart is literally bursting with joy. One way or another, I'm going to find a way to get back to New Zealand, as soon as humanly possible, and we'll have that wedding we've been dreaming about. I long for the day I'll hold you in my arms again.

With so much love,
John

After folding the letter in an envelope, Reynolds addressed it to Grace at her home in Wellington—an address he amazingly could now remember—and wrote his return address in the upper left corner.

With her son Charlie serving in the Second New Zealand Division in North Africa, Vera Lucas nervously anticipated each day's delivery of mail, which usually arrived punctually around 3:00 p.m., but dreaded seeing a messenger boy from New Zealand Post & Telegraph, as parents were always notified by cable when their sons had been wounded or killed in action. Walking from her kitchen to the living room, she glanced out the window to observe the postman walking up with his mailbag slung over his shoulder. After listening for the clank of the mailbox lid, she went to the front porch and retrieved the bundle of mail. Putting aside the usual bills, fliers, and magazines, she took the small stack of letters and settled on the sofa. Her heart fluttered at the sight of a British Army envelope, with an exotic stamp, that had traveled half way around the globe. Saving it for last, she sorted the other mail. The last was addressed to Miss Grace Lucas, which she considered odd until she looked at the return address. "Oh, dear God," she said aloud as a spasm of fear tingled her spine.

Mrs. Lucas took John Reynolds's letter to the kitchen, thinking at first she might try to steam it open over the teakettle. With a shake of her head, she carefully opened it with a paring knife and then sat at the breakfast table to read it. When she was finished, her pulse was racing, and she felt sick at her stomach. Carefully refolding the pages in the envelope, she decided to hide it in her dresser until she could discuss it with Tom. Surely Tom would know what to do.

Tom Lucas arrived home at six o'clock in an especially peevish mood, as he'd spent most of the afternoon at the offices of a government bureaucrat arguing over the fee Lucas had charged in an arbitration proceeding. In the end, he'd agreed to reduce his fee, which was modest to begin with, and consequently he was eager to pour his usual Scotch and had no patience for small talk. Seated in his favorite armchair with his drink and the evening paper, he glanced up at Vera with annoyance when she entered the room, wringing her hands. "Tom," she said. "There's something we need to discuss."

"Some other time, dear. Let me have a moment's peace."

"I'm sorry, dear, but this is dreadfully important." The worry on her face furrowed her brow and curled her mouth into a frown.

"Dreadfully important? Certainly it's not Charlie . . ."

"No," said Mrs. Lucas. "It's about Grace. A letter came today from . . . well, from John Reynolds, the American she . . ."

"John Reynolds? Do you mean to say, he's alive?" He noticed she was clutching an envelope, which she wordlessly handed to him. Donning his reading glasses, he extracted the letter and quickly read it. "Oh, for the love of God," he muttered. "This can't be."

"What shall we do?" said Mrs. Lucas, wringing her hands again.

"We mustn't, under any circumstances, tell Grace about this." He shoved the pages back into the envelope as if they were unsafe to handle.

"But, Tom, how can we? I mean, it's her letter . . ."

Tossing back his drink, he said, "It's not just about Grace, goddammit!"

"Please, Tom, don't . . ."

"It's that fine young man Andrew, who's promised to raise the child as his own, and to make their home here, in New Zealand. And what about the baby, Vera? What about our dear little Kate?"

"But she's John's child," Mrs. Lucas protested.

"So what," said Tom, the veins in his neck bulging. "He's the one who got Grace pregnant, for God's sake, without marrying her and then, with the rest of those damnable Marines, sailed off to sea."

"But Tom, he and Grace were engaged."

"Destroy that letter, Vera. Burn it." She nodded, her lower lip trembling. "And if another shows up, have the postman return it. Is that understood?" He handed her the envelope. She walked sadly to the bedroom while he went to the kitchen to pour another drink. Standing before the mirror over the dresser, she looked at her reflection and then at John Reynolds's neat handwriting before concealing his letter in the drawer with her nightgowns.

John Reynolds stood in the corridor outside Dr. Williston's office and raised his hand to knock. Wearing his summer khakis with a number of ribbons—the Purple Heart, Bronze Star, Presidential Unit Citation, and Asiatic Pacific Campaign—above the left breast pocket, he appeared to be a perfectly healthy and handsome Marine officer. After knocking, he let himself in. "Come in, John," said Williston. "I suppose you've come to say goodbye."

"That's right," said Reynolds as he slipped off his cap, "and to thank you for all you've done."

"You were a pleasure to work with," said Williston as he returned to his chair. "Please, have a seat." Reynolds sat, resting his left arm on his lap. "You're headed back to the States, I presume?" said the doctor. "Back to civilian life?"

"No, sir," said Reynolds. "I'm planning to stay here at Pearl."

"But why? You're rated fully disabled."

"I figured I could still make a contribution. So I applied for a position at CINCPAC, and I just learned I've got it, thanks to Colonel Shoup's recommendation."

"Well, I suppose I should say congratulations, John, but after all you've been through no one could blame you for heading home."

"Well, there's something I've got to take care of first," said Reynolds. "You know how bad I felt about my best friend being killed?" Williston nodded. "Well, you helped me to understand that my living was a blessing."

"Are you still struggling with guilt for the deaths of those two other men?"

Reynolds nodded and said, "Yes, I suppose so. Especially the one I was responsible for being relieved of command."

"Well," said Williston, "from everything you told me, the man was about to disobey orders and could have endangered the lives of the entire battalion. And it certainly wasn't your fault that the man chose to be killed by the Japanese."

"Yeah, I know," said Reynolds. "Logically, that is. But . . . well, it's not just what happened that night." Reynolds slowly exhaled and stared at the floor.

"Tell me about it."

"Well, this guy . . ."

"Schulz."

"Right. He didn't fit in with the other officers. He was a lot older and was transferred to the battalion after Guadalcanal. And he was a mustang, you know, a former NCO who hadn't gone to college and had a chip on his shoulder. And looking back, I'm afraid I was awful hard on him."

"And then," said Williston, "after what happened to him during the battle you not only feel guilty but ashamed. Am I right?" Reynolds nodded with a frown. "Well, John," said the doctor, "that's just one of the lessons life teaches us. I'm afraid you'll have to live with it."

Reynolds said, "Yes, sir, I'm afraid so." He rose from his chair, reached across the desk to shake the doctor's hand, and said, "Thanks again for everything."

Upon his discharge from the hospital Reynolds managed to secure a room in the Bachelor Officer's Quarters at the foot of Makalapa Hill, where all the top brass resided. Getting a room was a lucky break, considering the thousands of officers passing through Pearl Harbor each month. He took the Navy bus each morning to the nearby Makalapa Support Facilities in the sprawling CINCPAC complex at Pearl Harbor—which oversaw the entire Pacific theater under the command of Fleet Admiral Chester Nimitz. Reynolds reported to a Marine colonel in the Logistics Group. To the other men he appeared to be a typical staff officer, except for the fact that his left arm almost always hung limply at his side and he had a chestful of combat ribbons on his uniform. Returning to the BOQ at the end of each day, Reynolds anxiously waited for a letter from Grace. But by mid-August none had arrived. He reasoned that his letter might have taken weeks to make it to Wellington, with an equally long span for hers to travel to Hawaii. He nevertheless decided to take the precaution of sending a telegram, addressed to the Lucas residence, merely stating: AM ALIVE AND WELL STOP HAVE WRITTEN AND ANXIOUS FOR YOUR RESPONSE STOP MUCH LOVE JOHN FULL STOP. But after a week no response had come.

During his lunch break, Reynolds sat at his desk in the office he shared with two other officers, holding a pencil over several sheets of military-issue stationery. He gazed for a moment out the window at the bright green coconut palms, and then wrote:

Makalapa Support Facilities
Pearl Harbor, Hawaii
August 28, 1944

Dearest Grace,

I admit I've been mighty worried since I haven't received
an answer to the letter I mailed over a month ago, or my
telegram. So much time had passed without hearing from me,
and as you undoubtedly feared the worst, it wouldn't surprise
me if you've met someone else. Or is it possible your family
has moved, and my letter was sent to the wrong address? In
either case I darn sure have to be certain you know I'm alive
and well and love you as much as ever. I should probably just
stop worrying and expect that our letters will cross somewhere
over the Pacific.

Well, since my last letter my memory has completely
come back, and while that's generally a good thing, there
were some terrible things that happened on Tarawa I'd just
as soon not remember. Several of our best men were killed
and many more wounded. And now our division has fought
two more big battles, at Saipan and Tinian, and whipped the
Japs in both of them. It's just a matter of time now until they
surrender.

As far as me, I skipped the chance to be sent home and was
able to get a staff job at Pearl Harbor, and though the work's dull,
it keeps me involved in the war effort. And more importantly, in
the Pacific where I hope to be able to hop on a plane before long
to take me to New Zealand.

I pray you're doing well, darling, and am desperate to hear
from you.

With much love,
John

Reynolds glanced at his watch, hastily addressed the envelope, and hurried down to the base post office.

Over a month had passed since Grace's second tearful farewell on
Aotea Quay, holding the baby on her hip as the Royal Navy destroyer

steamed from Wellington harbor, and her life had become increasingly solitary. Three months old, Kate slept through the night now, and took long naps each morning and afternoon, leaving Grace with many hours to occupy herself with reading—newspapers, books, and her Bible—housework, especially the laundry that came with caring for a baby, and listening to the radio after putting the baby to bed. None of her acquaintances had babies; few of them were married; and old friends like Doris almost never invited her to social gatherings. And though she continued to take the baby to visit her parents, something subtle had changed since Andrew had gone away, an inexplicable tension not only between her mother and herself but also between her mother and father. Her father seemed interested only in the baby, balancing her on his knees and making faces, seldom engaging in conversation with Grace. As a consequence, Grace spent more and more time alone with the baby in the tiny flat, worrying about Andrew and, occasionally, dreaming about John. She kept their photographs in frames on the dresser: John in his Marine uniform with his arm around her waist, and Andrew in a studio portrait wearing his Royal Navy uniform. Staring at the photographs at odd times during the day, she conceded that she was still in love with John; she supposed she always would be, and as well as strong affection for Andrew, she felt enormously grateful to him.

Grace had received two letters from Andrew, the first mailed from Darwin on the north coast of Australia, and the second from Rangoon in Burma. In both he'd described his life at sea as boring and without peril and filled most of the letters with charming sentiment and inquiries about the baby, as he wasn't at liberty to write anything specific about their location or the nature of their mission. Given the enormous distances and the extended length of the sea voyages, she didn't expect more letters from him any time soon.

Unbeknownst to Grace her mother had intercepted two more communications from John Reynolds. The first, a telegram, had terrified her, since somehow she hadn't imagined that he might send one to Grace, and she immediately destroyed it. The second, a letter, she'd resisted the temptation to open and read. After hiding it with the first one in her dresser, she fell to her knees at her bedside and prayed for forgiveness. The following day, however, she accosted the postman, and with a small gratuity persuaded him to have the letter returned to its sender stamped undeliverable.

The days were growing longer and the afternoon temperatures warmer, and soon it would be spring and Grace could spend more time out of doors, taking walks in the park or the Botanic Gardens. Her one source of relief from her loneliness and isolation was her baby girl, a beautiful child with a sunny disposition who would light up with a smile that touched Grace's heart and reminded her of John when Grace leaned close. Holding the baby in her arms in the rocking chair, looking into her intelligent, delicate eyes, Grace realized that as long as she had Kate she would always have something of John, and she would forever be grateful to Andrew for making that possible.

CHAPTER NINETEEN

WITH EACH PASSING DAY JOHN REYNOLDS SANK DEEPER INTO despair. Having lost all memories of the time in New Zealand before the division sailed for Tarawa, he was now tormented by them, recollections of all the happy moments with Grace, on the sidewalks of Wellington, at their favorite drugstore counter drinking milkshakes, candlelit dinners at Bolton's, riding the cable car up to Kelburn, and necking on a park bench; vivid memories that crowded his waking hours and intruded on his dreams. Over two months had passed since he'd first written to her, and there was still no response. The likely explanation, he sadly conceded, was that, having received no word from him for over six months, she assumed he'd been killed and moved on in her life. In all likelihood, her parents had moved too, and his letters had simply found their way to the dead letter department. And, he was forced to admit, Grace had probably found someone else. But not knowing was slowly driving him crazy.

After finishing work in the offices of the Logistics Group, Reynolds often accompanied several of the other men to one of Pearl's officers clubs, a sprawling affair with long bars at both ends and dozens of tables under the building's exposed rafters and ceiling fans. Unable to shake his despondency, he succumbed to the temptation to drown his sorrows, in his case in an ocean of beer. After consuming four or five of them, dulling the pain, he'd order a sandwich or bowl of soup before catching the bus for the short ride back to the BOQ. One sultry evening, listening to the dance music on the radio in the background with a couple of acquaintances, midway through his third beer, Reynolds noticed the familiar face of a Marine standing at the bar. "I'll be right back," he said as he stood up. "Got to say hello to an old buddy." Approaching him from behind, Reynolds blurted out, "Travis!"

Travis Henderson spun around and gaped at Reynolds. "Johnny?" he said after a moment. "Do you remember me?"

"You're damned right I do," said Reynolds with a smile, giving Travis a firm handshake. "It all came back to me."

"Well, thank God. That was the scariest thing I've ever seen." Travis glanced at Reynolds's left arm, noticing the way he was holding it at his side.

"Well, grab your beer," said Reynolds, "and come over to the table. We've got a lot of catchin' up to do."

Finding a smaller table, as the other men had left, Reynolds waited for Travis to light a cigarette and then said, "What brings you to Pearl?"

Expelling a cloud of smoke, Travis said, "I'm just passin' through." Tapping his breast pocket, he added, "I've got my ticket home."

"Lucky dog," said Reynolds. He tipped back his beer and took a swallow.

"After we got done with Saipan and Tinian," said Travis, "the guys like us who came out in '42 had enough points to rotate back to the States."

"How bad was it?"

"Pretty bad, especially Saipan, but nowhere near as bad as Tarawa, and the coordination between the Marines and that army division was just awful. But the landings on Tinian were a thing of beauty. Completely faked out the Japs."

"Tell me about Tarawa. All I remember is jumping into a foxhole and firing another guy's M-1 until I was hit."

"Well, the Japs just kept on comin'," said Travis, "all night long. Wave after wave, with those damn little tanks. Some of our people got killed runnin' out and tossin' grenades in the turrets. And in a lot of places the fightin' was hand-to-hand. It was kinda their last stand, if you know what I mean. When it was all over, and the sun came up, it was, well . . ." He paused to take a deep drag on his cigarette before crushing it out in an ashtray. "It was unbelievable. Every damn one of those Japs was dead, and a whole lot of Marines were killed and wounded too. That's when I went lookin' for you and Spook. First I found Arnold Schulz, who apparently was killed when he charged one of their tanks . . ."

"Yeah, I watched him," said Reynolds. He took another pull on his beer. "Poor bastard just cracked up."

"And then I found Spook," said Travis. "Shot through the chest. His guys did a terrific job. And when I found you . . ." Travis's voice broke. He took a sip of beer and started over. "When I found you, I thought you were a goner, too. And out there in front of your foxhole I counted somethin' like thirty dead Japs."

"Well," said Reynolds, "that was a night you'll remember for the rest of your life and it's just as well I don't. I'm glad you're headed home, Trav. Are you okay about, you know, your girl?"

"Oh, hell, yes," said Travis. "I can't wait to get back to Brady. I'm plannin' to find some pretty little lady to marry and have a bunch of kids."

"I'd be headed home too," said Reynolds, "but there's one thing I've still got to take care of."

"What's that?"

"You remember Grace?"

"Sure, that cute gal in Wellington?"

"Well, I've been tryin' to get in touch with her, but so far . . ." He let the sentence die with a frown.

"Well, don't give up on her, Johnny. She was crazy about you." With a glance at his watch, Travis said, "I'd better get moving. Got to catch a flight out first thing in the mornin'."

Reynolds stood up and warmly shook Travis's hand. "Safe travels," he said. "And Semper Fi. I'll look you up as soon as I make it home."

Overcome with worry about Grace, Reynolds decided to turn to the one source of advice that had helped him his entire life: his father. He wrote him a long letter, explaining how much he and Grace were in love and confessing that they were secretly engaged, with the intention of having a wedding in New Zealand as soon as it was feasible and then returning to make their home in Houston. After asking his father for forgiveness, he described the mystifying silence that had followed his attempts to contact her, ending with a plea for his father's wise counsel. A week after his chance encounter with Travis Henderson, Reynolds arrived in the lobby of the BOQ on a Saturday morning just as the mail delivery truck pulled up. Joining the officers crowding around the sailor with his sack of letters, he listened as the names were called and then stiffened as the young man called out: "Lieutenant John Reynolds!" As he reached out to accept the envelope, the sailor said, "Came all the way from New Zealand."

His heart pounding, Reynolds decided not to look at the envelope until he was back in the privacy of his room. Slumping on his bed, he lowered his eyes to an airmail envelope. It was addressed to Grace in his own hand and stamped with the words: "Return to Sender—Undeliverable." He fell back on the pillow, covering his face with his good arm.

After another week had passed, standing in the same lobby among the same crowd of Navy and Marine officers, Reynolds again heard his named called. Taking a deep breath and squaring his shoulders, he stepped forward to take the letter from the sailor's outstretched hand. This time he immediately looked at it. With a sigh of relief he recognized the familiar handwriting and postmark. Returning to his room, he took off his shoes and stretched out on the bed. Dated September 6, 1944, the letter from his father began simply with: "Dear John, how I grieve for the hardships you've had to bear." The letter continued:

> Wounded not once, but twice, and this last time almost mortally, and then to awake from an extended coma with a complete loss of your memory. Only to regain it to reach out to the woman you love and intend to marry and receive no response, nothing.

A devout Christian, Mr. Reynolds used the opportunity to ask the eternal question, why we must suffer? And then provide the answer that John Reynolds expected, that God had sent his own son to walk among us and to suffer, as we suffer; that our hope in times of suffering is to turn our face to our compassionate, empathetic Savior. But then with a typical economy of language, he provided a father's practical advice to his only son:

From everything you wrote me, you and Grace were deeply in love. She is no doubt aware of the terrible battle your division fought at Tarawa, indeed we all were, and with no word from you for so many months it seems almost certain that she assumed you'd been killed. And there would have been no way for her to obtain any information from the American authorities.

I am therefore convinced, John, that her lack of response to your letters is due to the fact that she is ignorant of them, for whatever reason. I believe, therefore, that for both of your sakes you should contrive to return at once to New Zealand and try to find her. If you're still in love with her, and she will have you, you should marry her and God willing bring her home, where I'm sure your mother and I will soon become very attached to her.

You have served your country with great distinction and honorably done your duty to the Marine Corps. With the war entering its final phase, and you no longer able to serve in combat, I can't imagine why your commanding officer wouldn't grant you leave to travel to New Zealand and find the woman you love.

Reynolds quickly finished his father's letter, with the usual news from home, and put it aside with the single determined thought: first thing Monday morning he would request a thirty-day leave and find a seat on one of the hundreds of military flights that departed Pearl each day for destinations in the South Pacific.

Reynolds sat across the desk from the adjutant to Colonel Byron Howard, the commander of the Logistics Group. With five full Marine divisions now deployed in the Pacific theater, an additional three army divisions under Admiral Nimitz's direct command, and the largest naval fleet in history, Logistics was an enormous operation, occupying an entire building in the Pearl Harbor complex and employing hundreds of Navy and Marine officers and enlisted men. The adjutant answered his intercom and then turned to Reynolds and said, "You can go in now, sir." Reynolds had dressed in a freshly pressed uniform and shined his shoes to a high gloss. He entered the spacious corner office, which commanded a view of a palm tree-lined parade ground.

"Sit down, Lieutenant," said the colonel. A World War I veteran, Howard had fought at Belleau Wood in France with the Sixth Marines, which entitled him to wear a green fourragère on his left shoulder. "What can I do for you, son?" he asked impatiently.

"I appreciate your willingness to see me, sir," said Reynolds as he slipped off his cap and sat before the desk. "I'm here to request a thirty-day leave."

"To go home?"

"No, sir. To go back to New Zealand." As soon as he said it, Reynolds realized how inappropriate the request must sound.

"Why New Zealand?"

"Well, sir . . ." Reynolds started to apologize but changed his mind. "To see a young lady, sir," he said, "to whom I'm engaged."

"Can't that wait till the war's over?"

"The thing is, sir, I was left in a coma for almost six months after I was wounded, and then I had amnesia, so I'm afraid she—my fiancée—may not realize I'm still alive, and I turned down the chance to be sent home, so I . . ."

Colonel Howard raised his hand, silencing Reynolds. He briefly studied the ribbons on Reynolds's chest, the Purple Heart, Bronze Star, and Presidential Citation Unit for the men who'd fought at Tarawa. And the fourragère, worn only by the men of the Sixth Marines. "You've done your duty, Reynolds, and frankly I've got more people requesting staff assignments than I know what to do with. So go find that girl in New Zealand and let her know you're okay. Tell my adjutant to write up some orders giving you priority on a flight to Espiritu Santo. You can figure out how to get from there to Auckland."

"Aye, aye, sir," said Reynolds with a smile as he rose from his chair. He snapped to attention and gave the colonel a smart salute.

Within days Reynolds was on board an Army Air Corps C-47 ferrying men and supplies to the newly constructed airfield and base on Tarawa. Because the distance from Honolulu, some 2,100 miles, was at the outer limit of the C-47's range, there were only a handful of passengers on board and less than half the plane's cargo capacity. Reynolds gazed out the Plexiglas window as the plane made its takeoff roll and ascended through cottony clouds to its cruising altitude. Many hours later, he was awakened by a change in the pitch of the engines and a mild jolt as they flew through a cumulus cloud. Peering out, he could see a tapered sliver of land, shaped like a hook, and a large turquoise lagoon enclosed by a reef. As the plane slowly descended Reynolds stared with intense curiosity at the blasted remains of Japanese pillboxes and fortifications and the stumps of thousands of palm trees shredded in the battle. Somewhere on that godforsaken stretch of sand and coral was the place where he'd fallen and Spook had perished. Leveling off, the plane touched down on a new runway constructed by the Seabees following the battle and taxied past freshly painted Quonset huts and a squadron of Navy Hellcat fighters. After an hour's respite, Reynolds boarded another C-47, fully loaded with supplies and a few other passengers, for the second leg of the journey, the 1,400 mile flight to Espiritu Santo in the Santa Cruz islands, where he'd spent several days en route to Auckland after being wounded on Guadalcanal. Reynolds slept for most of the long flight, and it was dark when he awoke to see the long line of landing lights on the airfield runway.

The once modest naval base had been transformed into a sprawling logistical center supplying vast quantities of munitions, rations, medical supplies, and equipment to both the Army command under General MacArthur and the combined Marine and Army forces commanded by Admiral Nimitz. As the island-hopping campaign had moved to the north and west toward the Japanese home islands, the use of New Zealand as a base for American forces had become obsolete, and consequently Reynolds discovered that there were very few flights. The occasional merchant ship, however, made the run from Auckland, and after several frustrating days Reynolds persuaded a New Zealand skipper to take him along as a passenger on the return voyage.

Standing at the railing in his fleece-lined jeep-driver's coat, which had arrived at the Navy hospital with his footlocker, Reynolds gazed out over the deep blue ocean in the strong sunshine, just able to discern the hundreds of small islands at the entrance to Auckland harbor. After four days at sea his heart fluttered in anticipation of the next day's journey south on the train.

After checking into a hotel across from the train station, Reynolds looked up the number and placed a call to the McDonald residence. It was Bell who answered, delighted to hear John's voice and insisting he come for dinner. On his way over, Reynolds instructed the taxi driver to take him past St. Andrew's Church and then to the Domain, where he caught a glimpse of the navy hospital. Everything looked exactly the same, though it seemed that far more than eighteen months had passed since he'd departed from Auckland. The McDonalds welcomed him with their usual warmth and hospitality, eager to hear the story of the terrible fighting at Tarawa, John's wounds and miraculous recovery, and especially his engagement to Grace Lucas. "And you're on your way to see her in the morning?" said Bell.

"Yes, ma'am."

"She must be thrilled that you were able to arrange leave and come to see her," said Malcolm.

"Well, she's . . ." Reynolds hesitated.

"What is it, John?" said Bell.

"Well, the truth is, she doesn't know I'm coming."

Malcolm exchanged a troubled look with Bell. "Don't you think you should call her, son? To let her know?"

Reynolds nodded, fighting back the irrational fear that if he placed a call to the Lucas's number he'd find it had been disconnected or that she'd moved away. Or worse, was involved with someone else. "I suppose so," he said with audible sigh.

"You can use the telephone on the table," said Malcolm. "We'll give you some privacy."

Once the McDonalds had left the room and closed the door, Reynolds walked over to the telephone, hesitated, and then lifted the receiver and dialed the operator. "A long distance call to Wellington," he said, and then gave her the number, which he knew by heart.

Grace Lucas, who was visiting her parents with the baby, was walking past the telephone in the hallway when it rang. She lifted the receiver and said, "Hullo?"

"Is this the Lucas residence?" said Reynolds, his heart pounding.

"Yes. May I help you?"

"Is Grace in?"

"Speaking. And who . . ."

"Grace? Is it you, Grace?"

"Yes, but . . ."

"Grace, it's John!"

"John?"

"John Reynolds."

"But that can't be . . ." She slumped against the wall and sank to the floor, in the process dropping the receiver. *Oh dear God*, she thought, her heart racing.

"Grace?" said Reynolds. "Grace, are you still there?"

Her breaths coming in gasps, she noticed the receiver dangling on its cord. It seemed to be slowly spinning, and she could just make out a man's voice.

"Grace, what's wrong?" said Mrs. Lucas, who was standing at the end of the hall. "Have you fallen?"

Grace gave her a bewildered look and then shook her head. She heard the man's voice again on the phone. "Give me a minute, Mother." Mrs. Lucas reluctantly walked into the living room. Grace reached for the receiver and said, "Sorry. Who did you say this is?"

"It's John. I know it must be a shock . . ."

"John," repeated Grace softly. "John Reynolds? But that's impossible."

"If you'd let me explain."

"I . . . I'm sorry," she murmured. Surely, she thought, it's some kind of sick joke. "Could you call me back? In about five minutes?"

"Okay."

Grace struggled to get to her feet and then hung up the phone. Rubbing her brow, she thought, this can't be happening. "Grace!" called her mother from the other room. "Are you all right?"

"Just give me a few minutes," said Grace weakly. She walked to the small guest bathroom, bent over the basin, and splashed water on her face. As she dried it with a hand towel, she thought *this isn't real* and then heard the phone ringing. Fearing her mother would answer it, she dashed to the hall and grabbed the receiver. Out of breath, she said, "Hullo?"

"Listen Grace," said Reynolds calmly, "I'm at the McDonalds' house in Auckland. I just got here today."

The McDonalds . . . Auckland . . . Oh my God, it might really be John. "But I thought you'd been killed?" she managed to say. "Hold on, please." Her mother was standing at the end of the hall. "You have to give me privacy, Mother," she said, cupping her hand over the phone. "Please."

Reynolds could hear Grace breathing, short, ragged gasps. "I tried to let you know I was okay," he said, "but you never answered my letters. Or my telegram."

Letters, telegram, thought Grace, massaging her forehead. "Where did you send them?"

"To your house, in Wellington."

Grace felt a sharp stab of fear, some terrible foreboding. "I've got to sort some things out," she said. "Is there a number where I can call you?"

"Sure." The McDonalds' number was at the center of the rotary dial, and he gave it to her.

"I'll call you," she said, making a mental note. "In a bit." She hung up and walked slowly into the kitchen where she jotted the phone number on a slip of paper. Turning to go into the living room, her mother was in the doorway.

"Who was that?" said Vera Lucas.

"John Reynolds."

CHAPTER TWENTY

HER FACE AS WHITE AS A SHEET, VERA LUCAS TOOK SEVERAL steps backward and then hurried into the living room where her husband Tom was sitting with his newspaper and the baby on a blanket at his feet. Grace walked slowly into the room as if in a trance.

"The person who called," said Mrs. Lucas in a shaky voice, "was claiming to be John Reynolds?"

"What!" said Tom, tossing his paper aside.

"He was calling from the McDonalds' home in Auckland," said Grace. "The family who were so kind to him when he was recuperating in hospital."

"But that's impossible," said Mrs. Lucas.

"He wrote to tell me he was all right," said Grace. "He mailed the letters here. And he sent a telegram." Mrs. Lucas stared at her like a cornered animal. "You knew, didn't you?" said Grace. "You knew he was alive and didn't tell me!" Grace burst into tears.

"That's ridiculous," said Tom Lucas. "Don't use that tone of voice with your mother . . ."

Brushing away her tears, Grace said, "When did John's letters arrive?"

"There aren't any letters," said her father calmly. Mrs. Lucas looked nervously from her husband to Grace.

With a sudden clarity of mind, Grace said, "John Reynolds is alive and well, and he's probably arriving here tomorrow or the next day. I'll let you explain to him, Father, what you did with the letters he mailed here." Tom Lucas stared at her sullenly.

"It's my fault," said Mrs. Lucas in an almost inaudible voice.

"Shut up, Vera!"

"I kept one of John's letters," said Mrs. Lucas in a stronger voice.

"You did what?" said her husband, his face suddenly pale.

"Yes, I kept it!" Vera said, turning to face him. "What we did was wrong! Oh, my God, look what we've done." After a full fifteen seconds of silence, Mrs. Lucas walked quickly from the room. When she returned, Grace was holding and rocking the baby. Her mother hesitantly handed Grace an envelope.

After glancing at the postmark, Grace said, "I'm taking the baby and going to my flat." After starting for the hallway, she spun around and said, "But what about the other letter? And the telegram?"

For a moment it looked like Mrs. Lucas would be sick at her stomach, and then she stifled a sob and said. "I threw away the telegram. And told the postman to return the letter marked undeliverable."

"I just can't believe it," said Grace.

"Your father told me to do it."

"Yes, I goddam told her to do it! We all thought this Marine—who got you pregnant—had been killed! And then you married Andrew, and had the baby . . ."

Grace sadly shook her head and walked from the room.

After putting the baby to sleep, Grace went to the kitchen and was relieved to find the bottle of Scotch Andrew had left in the pantry. She poured a glass, added water and ice, and sat in the chair in the living room by the telephone. After taking a sip of her drink, she took the slip of paper from her pocket and dialed the long-distance operator. "I'd like to place a call to a number in Auckland. It's Victoria-2-6-8-4-7."

After Reynolds's call to Grace, the McDonalds had immediately sensed his deep unease. Having told no one, apart from the one letter to his father, about the agony of his unanswered letters to Grace, John unburdened himself on Malcolm and Bell McDonald. After listening to the tale, Malcolm said, "When you were here in Auckland, recovering from your wound, we thought what a fine young man, proudly serving your country. Had we known, even half, of the terrible things you were going to go through . . ."

"Yes, but you made it, John," said Bell, leaning forward. "And here you are in New Zealand, and now you've spoken to the girl you love."

"Yes," said Reynolds. "And intend to marry."

The telephone in the adjoining study rang, and Malcolm McDonald, rising from his chair, said, "I'll get it." Lifting the receiver, he said, "McDonald residence."

"Is John Reynolds in? It's Grace Lucas."

"Just one moment." Returning to the living room Malcolm said, "It's Grace."

Reynolds hurried to the study, closing the door behind him, and lifted the receiver. "Grace?"

"I'm so sorry, John," said Grace, "but your call was such a shock. I thought I was going to faint."

"I understand."

"There's so much I need to explain, but not over the phone. Can you come here?"

"Of course. That's why I came all the way from Hawaii."

"But first I need to read your letter," said Grace.

"My letter? I don't understand."

"The first letter you wrote. My mother saved it but never told me about it. She threw away the telegram and had the other letter sent back."

"Oh my God, Grace! When did you find out about this?"

"Tonight, after you called."

"I can't believe she'd do such a thing."

"She blamed it on my dad. I'm so, so sorry. Can you come in the morning?"

"I've got a ticket on the express train. It gets into Wellington around six."

"Take a taxi to my flat," said Grace. "It's a fourplex at 421 Hawker Street, and I'm in unit number one. Oh, John, I have so much to explain. And be prepared for some shocks."

"I love you, Grace, and can't wait to hold you in my arms."

"I love you too, John. Goodbye." After hanging up, she freshened her drink and sat down to read John's letter. As she read it the second time, the tears streamed down her cheeks. She could barely comprehend the hardships and losses he'd endured and then, when he'd finally recovered from his wounds and amnesia, to receive no reply to his letters. It must have broken his heart. Driving home from her parents she'd felt nothing but anger and resentment but now, in the quiet of her flat, now that at last she knew what had happened to John, that during all those months she'd desperately prayed he was somehow alive he was lying in a hospital bed in a coma, she was overwhelmed with sadness. Not just for John, but for herself, and for Andrew. But the months of desperate loneliness at the farm had changed her in a fundamental way. Brushing away her tears with the sleeve of her blouse, she dropped to her knees and, resting her arms on the cushions of the sofa and bowing her head, thanked God for the miracle of John's deliverance, for the extraordinary blessings she'd received, for John's life and return, for Kate, and for Andrew. And she prayed, dear God, grant us the wisdom to know what is right and the courage to do it.

After dressing in his olive drab uniform, Reynolds boarded a second-class compartment of the Scenic Daylight train to Wellington, which departed from Auckland punctually at 8:30 a.m. Seated by the window, Reynolds listened to the rhythmic *clack* of the rails and gazed out on the dipping telegraph wires and the beautiful North Island countryside. He'd lain awake most of the night struggling to understand why Grace's parents would possibly have done something so cruel. Surely Mrs. Lucas had read his letter, and not to have told Grace he was alive? Why? There had to be an explanation, but for the life of him he couldn't think of what it might be. The train was half empty and arrived at the Wellington station a few minutes past six. Within twenty minutes he exited the taxi in front of a two-story brick apartment building in a quiet residential neighborhood. Carrying his suitcase in his good hand, he walked up to the entrance, let the suitcase drop, and knocked on the door with a numeral "1."

Within seconds the door swung open, and Grace, looking radiant and holding a baby on her hip, stood facing him. Slipping off his cap, he wordlessly put his arm around her and kissed her. "Oh, John," she murmured. "I can't believe it's really you. It's truly a dream come true."

"Let me look at you," he said, pulling away. "You look even prettier than I remembered. And who's this little thing?"

"This is Kate, John. And she's your daughter."

"My daughter . . ." He looked at Kate, who seemed to be studying him. "Can that be?"

Grace crowded in close, with one arm around John's waist and the other holding the baby. "Yes," she said with a sniffle as the tears streamed down her cheeks. "Yes, it's true. Oh, John, I have so much to tell you." She'd placed a vase with fresh flowers on the coffee table in the living room and sat on the sofa with the baby in her lap.

John sat beside her and immediately noticed the gold wedding band on her left hand. Giving her a searching look, he said, "You're married?"

Grace nodded, her lips trembling, and then said, "I . . . well, I was sure you were . . ." Her voice broke, and she fought back a sob.

"Let me get you a glass of water." Reynolds returned from the small kitchen after a moment and handed her a glass.

After taking several swallows, she said, "That's better. You see, I'd finally given up hope on ever seeing you again, and Andrew Cadbury—do you remember Andrew?"

"Sure, the officer in the Royal Navy."

"Well, he'd been driving out on weekends to visit me. His ship had shore leave, and he had a car."

"Where was this?"

"On my uncle Dick's and aunt Martha's farm about an hour outside of Wellington. My parents sent me there till I could have the baby."

"When did you find out," said Reynolds, "well, you were having a baby?"

"We didn't have any news for about three weeks after you shipped out. I did get the letter you wrote me from the ship—such a sweet letter. And then the newspapers were filled with stories about Tarawa and the terrible Marine losses. I was literally sick with worry. It was right about the time I suspected something and went to see the doctor and found out." Reynolds nodded. "My parents were mortified, and they insisted I move out to this farm. I was so lonely and unhappy. I kept hoping and praying I'd hear from you. When Andrew drove out to visit I assumed it was just to cheer me up. There wasn't anything romantic about it. And then, when it was getting close to my due date, he shocked me when he told me he wanted to marry me and raise the baby as if she were his own.

"By then, I'd given up hope on you. I knew my parents would make me give the baby up. So I told Andrew yes."

"Were you in love with him?"

"No, I swear it. And he understood that."

"But obviously he was in love with you." Grace nodded. "Oh my God," said Reynolds, "I could never have imagined."

"Not too long after the baby came," Grace continued, "Andrew got orders that his ship was joining the British fleet off the coast of Malaysia. So now you know my story. When I read your letter last night, I was shocked by what you'd gone through. It must have been terrible . . ."

"Tarawa was a close thing for the Marines," said Reynolds. "They sent our battalion in when things were looking pretty desperate. Our men did a helluva job."

Giving him a troubled look, Grace said, "Tell me how you were injured."

"The Japs attacked our position at night. Wave after wave of them, with tanks. I don't remember much, just jumping in a foxhole and firing the weapon of a . . . another Marine. I must have been hit by an artillery or tank round. The shrapnel tore up my left arm and struck me in the head. My helmet saved my life."

"How dreadful."

"I was in a coma for something like six months, and when I woke up, I'd lost my memory. My friend Travis told me that when it was all over, the Jap attackers were all dead, and that was pretty much the end of the battle."

"Losing your memory must have been awful."

"I had no idea who I was and got really down in the dumps. But then, gradually, it started coming back. That's when I wrote to you. Why did they do it, Grace? Hide the truth from you?"

"I'll never understand it, and I don't think I can ever forgive them. It was after Andrew and I were married and the baby had come when your first letter arrived. Andrew had decided to make his home in New Zealand when the war's over . . ."

"So your parents figured, Grace is married to this nice English fellow, she can keep her baby, and they'll make their home here. Fine and dandy, till I came along."

"Something like that."

"Well, it's hardly your fault, or Andrew's."

"No." Grace reached over to take John's hand. "I stayed up most of the night thinking through this. Let me put the baby to bed, and then I'll tell you what I've made up my mind to do."

When Grace returned to the living room, John had fixed a drink from the bottle he found on the kitchen counter, and she could tell from his red-rimmed eyes he'd been crying. "I'm so sorry about all this," she said as she stood beside him. He nodded and sipped his drink. "The truth is, I don't want to be married to Andrew . . ."

"You shouldn't say that."

"I want to be married to you, John. I never stopped loving you. I want to go home with you to Texas and raise our beautiful little girl."

"But how is that possible?"

"I don't know. But in my heart of hearts I'm certain Andrew would never have asked me to marry him if he'd known you were still alive. Before going to bed last night I wrote him a letter explaining everything. I didn't ask him to, well, consider ending the marriage but only to think and pray about what we should do. You're free to read it."

"No. That's between you and Andrew. But I think it's the right thing to do."

"I'm sending it today. I don't know how long it will take to reach him, or for him to write back."

"Weeks, possibly months," said Reynolds. "Well, I'd like to stay for several days to be with you and the baby before heading back to Hawaii."

"I hate for you to leave."

"We'll both be waiting for Andrew's decision. I think it's best if I'm back at Pearl Harbor."

About three weeks after John Reynolds left, returning to Hawaii by the same route he'd come, Grace received a telegram from Andrew. With the baby taking a nap in the bedroom, she brewed a cup of tea and then sat in the living room to read it. "My dear Grace," he began, "how happy I am for you and how sad, heartbroken." Holding the yellow sheets in a trembling hand, she read:

WHAT A MIRACLE THAT JOHN SURVIVED AND CAME
BACK FOR YOU AND WHAT A TRAGEDY THAT YOUR
PARENTS CONCEALED THE TRUTH FROM US STOP I'VE
BEEN GRANTED A LEAVE AND FLY TO WELLINGTON
FROM MELBOURNE SOON STOP UPON MY RETURN
WE SHALL DECIDE WHAT IS BEST STOP YOUR LOVING
HUSBAND ANDREW FULL STOP

Having left Kate with her parents, with whom she'd managed some degree of reconciliation, Grace was waiting for Andrew in the terminal
when he de-planed from the DC-3, looking tanned and handsome in his
Royal Navy uniform. They kissed and embraced, and then Grace said,
"I've left Kate with my mother. I think we should talk at the flat."

Seated in the living room with cups of tea, Grace began to make small
talk about the baby and the approaching end to the war when Andrew
interrupted her. "Sorry, dear," he said, "but when I got over the shock of
your letter—and it was the shock of my life—I went through the stages
of what I suppose was grief. The first stage was anger, truly bitter anger
at your mother and father for what they'd done to John, and you, and
to me. And then came sadness. I couldn't bear the thought of losing you
and the baby . . ."

"Oh, Andrew, I'm so sorry. I can't stand you having to . . ."

"And then, finally, acceptance," said Andrew. "Had we known John
was alive and intended to return for you, of course we would never have
considered marriage. It was a marriage, Grace darling, based entirely
on false premises. Shakespeare himself couldn't have written a greater
tragedy."

Grace nodded, brushing tears from the corners of her eyes. Looking
up at Andrew, she said, "But what shall we do?"

"I've given this a great deal of thought," said Andrew. "We must have
the marriage annulled."

"Annulled?" said Grace. "As though it never happened?"

Andrew nodded. "I'd like to spend a few days with you and the baby, of
course. And then it can be arranged in a quiet proceeding at the courthouse."

"Oh Andrew, I'm so, so sorry. I doubt I'll ever know anyone even half
as fine and decent as you."

"Of course, I love you Grace. But I married you believing John was dead, so that you could keep your baby."

The day following the annulment proceeding, attended only by Andrew, Grace, and a solicitor, John Reynolds received a telegram from Grace informing him that the marriage to Andrew had been dissolved and that at her father's expense she would be traveling with Kate to Honolulu as soon as possible, where at last they would be married.

John and Grace Reynolds were seated in a second-class compartment, with fifteen-month-old Kate between them, on the Sunset Limited, which departed from the Southern Pacific Station in San Francisco on a sunny October morning. It was a three-day journey to Houston in a Pullman car, after sailing from Honolulu on a passenger ship of the Matson line. With Kate asleep on her lap, Grace gazed out the window at the gently rolling farmland of central Texas, live oaks and Spanish oaks, green pastures with grazing cattle, and fields filled with the stalks of harvested corn and sorghum. "It's not at all what I expected," she said, turning to John. "I thought Texas was all cactus and wide open spaces with rugged mountains in the distance."

"Well, West Texas is, but we were sleeping when we passed through it last night." After a while the terrain grew flatter and wide expanses of cotton appeared, the white bolls looking like snow on the dark green fields. "I imagine they'll be picking all that cotton any day now. And a little farther along we'll pass through the rice fields and then we'll be there."

"John," said Grace. "How does it make you feel?"

Gazing out the window, Reynolds, who was wearing his khaki uniform, said, "It's been almost three and a half years since I left home. Looking out on this familiar country, well, it's like a dream come true. Almost as special as the dream of coming back to you, sweetie." Arriving at Union Station in downtown Houston, Grace and John peered anxiously out on the platform, observing several redcaps standing beside luggage carts, a number of young men in uniform with their wives or sweethearts, and finally a middle-aged couple, nervously searching the windows of the dark green carriages. "There they are!" said Reynolds, pointing at the couple. "Mom and Dad! Why don't you take the baby and I'll see to the luggage." The carriage traveled slowly past them and then came to a halt with a hiss of escaping steam. At the foot of the steps down from the train Tom Reynolds, in his best navy-blue suit, stood beside his wife Mary, who wore a polka-dot dress, gloves, and pillbox hat. Holding Kate, who was still sleepy from her nap, Grace carefully climbed down onto the platform.

Mr. Reynolds stepped forward, smiled, and said, "You must be Grace. I'm Tom, John's dad, and this is my wife Mary."

Mrs. Reynolds leaned over to give Grace a kiss and said, "Hello, dear. Welcome to Houston. Oh, and hello little Kate. I'm your grandmommy." She suddenly burst into tears. As the baby carefully studied her grandmother, John bounded down the steps, dropped two suitcases on the platform, and said, "Mom! Dad! I can't believe I'm finally home!"

Tom Reynolds waited for Mary to embrace her son and then warmly shook his hand and said, "Home at last, John. Thank the Lord."

John let go of his father's hand and wrapped him in a hug. "Yes, Dad," said Reynolds. "At last. And I see you've met Grace and baby Kate." Grace beamed at her in-laws.

"Well, son," said the elder Reynolds, "let's get you kids home. Your mother's killed the fatted calf and we'll have a proper celebration. My car's parked just outside the station." Each man hefted a suitcase, and with the baby on Grace's hip and John's mother beside her, the reunited Reynolds family began walking toward the station.

EPILOGUE

GRACE REYNOLDS, HER HAIR ENTIRELY WHITE AT AGE SEVENTY-four, was in the entry hall at their suburban Houston home sorting the day's mail. "Remember," she said to her husband John, now retired from his law practice, "that Kate and her boys are coming to dinner."

"Wonderful," said John as he walked past her.

Grace studied the postmark on an envelope, addressed in neat cursive to "Mrs. Grace L. Reynolds." Taking the letter to her sewing room, she sat and slit it open, removing a hand-written note attached to a newspaper clipping. "Grace," read the note, "I hope you're well and will visit us one of these days. I thought you should see this. Your old friend, Doris." Grace unfolded the newspaper clipping, an obituary. "Andrew W. Cadbury," it read, "of Christ Church peacefully passed away on May 15, 1994 following a brief illness. Andrew served with distinction as a lieutenant in the British Royal Navy in the war and afterward settled in Christ Church, where he was a leading member of the business community. He is survived by his wife of 48 years, Eileen, his daughter Grace, her husband Louis, and three grandchildren . . ."

His daughter Grace, she reflected, wiping away a tear.

ABOUT THE AUTHOR

JOHN C. KERR, a native of Houston, has lived in San Antonio for forty years with his wife Susan. *Always Faithful* is his sixth novel. He is also the author of two works of history. He is a graduate of Stanford University and the University of Texas Law School.

CPSIA information can be obtained
at www.ICGtesting.com
Printed in the USA
LVHW042343160422
716126LV00005B/19

9 780875 658032